The

Tolwyn moved wi........................,
wincing at the noise Bryc............ behind her. The dwarves
moved well, and Mara and Djil were ghosts behind
them. But Tom had feet of stone. Ah well, not much to be
done about it.

She found the stairs Kurst had taken, started up them
one slow step at a time. There were side passages almost
immediately, and he could have taken any one. Trying
to find him appeared hopeless, but the offshoot passages
were small and smelled musty with age. It did not seem
likely he had gone that way.

She bent low over the next stair, staring at it through
the gloom. Was that a footprint, marked with claws at
the tips of the toes? It was hard to tell if she was
imagining it or not, but it looked like his tracks, and they
were moving up. She followed, hunching over every
step, still seeing faint prints. Were they really there? She
sighed and continued.

It was foolish to have let him leave the group — he
was their only guide! Even if he was trustworthy, if he
was killed they would have to stumble around in the
dark, just like they were doing now.

She did not notice the writing on the archway through
which she passed, or the way the letters glowed and the
corridor shifted.

Seconds later her subconscious realized that
something was wrong: silence followed her. The rustle
of the dwarves, the scrunch of Bryce's shoes — the
sounds were gone. She whirled, sword ready.

And she found herself alone. Alone in the Gaunt
Man's keep.

Torg
The Possibility Wars

They have come from other cosms, other realities, raiders joined together to accomplish one goal — to steal the awesome energy of Earth's possibilities!

This spectacular epic of adventure, magic, and high-technology is set on a reality-torn Earth — an Earth warped into *someplace else*. Don't miss any of the volumes in the Possibility Wars saga!

Book One
Storm Knights
by Bill Slavicsek and C.J. Tramontana

Book Two
The Dark Realm
by Douglas Kaufman

Book Three
The Nightmare Dream
by Jonatha Ariadne Caspian

The Possibility Wars™
created by Greg Gorden and Bill Slavicsek

Book Two
The Dark Realm
by Douglas Kaufman

Cover Art by Daniel Horne

Interior Art by Bob Dvorak, Francis Mao,
Jeff Menges, Alan Jude Summa and Valerie Valusek

Graphic Design by Bernadette G. Cahill
and Stephen Crane

Series Edited by Bill Slavicsek

Additional Editing by Jennifer A. Williams

THE DARK REALM
Book Two of the Possibility Wars
A West End Games Book/July 1990

First Printing: July, 1990.
Printed in the United States of America.

0   9   8   7   6   5   4   3   2   1

Library of Congress Catalog Card Number: 90-70245
ISBN: 0-87431-302-3

West End Games
RD3 Box 2345
Honesdale, PA 18431

*To all those people we promised
to dedicate our first novels to.*

*And to our art department, Steve Crane,
Cathy Hunter, Sharon Wyckoff, Jackie Evans,
Bernadette Cahill and Rori Baldari,
and the numerous illustrators
who worked on the Torg project.
They're Rembrandts all!*

Prologue: The Battle for the Heart

My dreams are made of this; swirling mists of blue sky and splashes of crimson blood. And then there is the darkness, waiting to reclaim me as its own. My dreams leave me sorely afraid.

— Tolwyn of House Tancred

The dream took hold of Tolwyn's sleeping mind. Again.

The demon dragon called Carredon pushed its way into the small chamber, scraping its crowded scales across the stone walls. It was a fragment of Tolwyn's memories come to life.

It was the creature that had killed her.

And now it was here to kill her again.

Behind her, the small blue and red stone sang its fear and terror into her mind, pleading for her to help it. But Tolwyn could not even help herself. She saw the beast's huge dagger-like claws, and she remembered the pain those claws had brought her a lifetime ago. She saw its armored hide and recalled how blade and spear and arrow had bounced away without harming the creature.

And for the first time in her memory, Tolwyn was afraid.

"Remember me, Tolwyn of House Tancred?" the dragon asked. Its voice was hollow, like a bottomless pit. "I killed you once. I have come to kill you again."

Tolwyn shrank back at these words, curling up against the far wall. She did not want to die again. She did not want to return to the dark place.

She was barely aware of Rick Alder, she barely heard the explosion of his pistol as he directed three shots at the Carredon. One shot hit its mark, and dark fluid ran from the dragon's left eye.

"The stormer draws blood!" the dragon bellowed. "Now the Carredon has a turn!"

She watched without response, curled up in her own fear, as the dragon's taloned paw flashed opened and three clawed nails pierced Alder's body and lifted him from the floor.

His pain must have been excruciating, but Alder forced his body to turn in her direction. "It can be hurt, Tolwyn," he gasped, forcing his vocal chords to work. "It can be hurt."

The Carredon flexed his claws, and Alder slid off them, landing in a puddle of his own fluids. Before the dragon could do anything else, Kurst exploded into the chamber. But the hunter stopped, unsure of what action to take against the killing machine.

"You, the one called Decker," the dragon intoned, ignoring Kurst's intrusion. The Carredon waved the claws still covered with Alder's blood as it spoke. "No unnecessary deaths need occur. My master is impressed with you, stormer. I bring you an offer from the Gaunt Man, High Lord of Orrorsh and Torg of the cosmverse."

Decker stepped forward, but stayed beyond the Carredon's reach. "What is this offer?"

The dragon seemed to smile. "The Gaunt Man has the power to grant your greatest wish."

"And how does this High Lord know what I wish for?"

"Because he has looked into your heart."

Taken aback, Decker was still able to respond. "What did he see, dragon?"

"He saw your love for this country, and he saw your sorrow at its wounds from Baruk Kaah's invaders. He has authorized me to offer you this."

The Carredon clacked its claws together and an image appeared within the chamber for all to see. It was the image of a black stone, as dark as night and shapeless. It radiated power, not unlike the blue stone the group had come to find.

"With this object of power, you could become the High Lord of this world and join the Gaunt Man as an equal being. Instead of destroying this world, you could save it. You could impose the laws and doctrines you hold so dear not only in this country, but in every country. You can be president, and then you would have the power to reshape this world into the image that burns so fiercely in your heart. And more, with the power of reality, you could bring back the woman named Vicky."

Decker lowered his head for a moment, then looked into the Carredon's remaining eye. "That's a very tempting offer. But if I were to impose my will onto this country, then it wouldn't be America. It would be something less, no matter how strong it was. It would be a sham."

The Carredon was losing patience. "What is your answer, stormer?"

"My answer? Go to hell!" Decker raised his pistol, a Beretta, and fired at the dragon's other eye.

Tolwyn feared for Decker, but the congressman was not swayed by the offer. Instead he fired shot after shot into the beast until the sound in the enclosed area was deafening. And then his pistol clicked, indicating that it was empty.

Mara took up the battle then, firing blasts of high-intensity light from her laser pistol. These caused burn marks to appear across the dragon's chest, and it roared in anger. It prepared to launch itself at the girl, but she resumed firing.

"She will run out of energy soon," Kurst said. "Pray to your god, Bryce. I do not think we will defeat the Carredon."

"You speak as though you know the creature," Tolwyn heard Father Bryce say.

"I do."

Then Kurst's body began to shift, flowing from flesh to fur. He grew to over six feet tall, and widened as his body grew muscle. His features elongated, stretched, and formed into a muzzle full of sharp teeth. As Tolwyn watched, Kurst had become a man-shaped wolf of gigantic size. The wolf charged toward the Carredon.

With a mighty leap, the wolf was upon the dragon, raking it with his powerful claws. The wolf slashed at the burns Mara's laser made, adding to the beast's injuries. Deep cuts sliced across the dragon's scales, staggering it. But it was stronger than Kurst. The wolf was no match for the terrible engine of destruction. It grasped the giant wolf in one powerful claw and dug its talons into his flesh.

"You should never have challenged me, Kurst," the Carredon boomed. "I am not some stormer for you to dispatch, and my claws can harm you." The Carredon squeezed its talons together to prove its point, and the life began to slip out of Kurst, splattering the ground with bright drops of red.

Decker, his gun reloaded, resumed firing at the monster. He picked up on the wolf's strategy and aimed for the wounds already inflicted upon the creature. The wolf was dropped when the bullets hit, forgotten in the haze of pain that Decker brought to the dragon.

"Never have I been so wounded, stormer!" the Carredon screamed. "But the pain I feel is nothing compared to the pain I will bring you."

The congressman stood his ground, firing bullet after bullet until his clip emptied. And still the Carredon advanced. It raised its talons high into the air, prepared to bring them down on Decker. But Mara leaped between them, releasing her own metallic claws from their recessed housing in her fingers and driving them deep into the dragon's chest. In pain-driven rage, it struck out blindly and caught Mara with the back of its paw. That saved her from being decapitated, but it still sent her flying across the chamber. She landed in a heap and was still.

"Go ahead, monster," Decker declared. "Go ahead and strike me down."

"No, Decker," the Carredon said. "The rage has left me, and I have a more lasting pain to inflict upon you."

The Carredon raised one talon and brought it to rest upon a scale near its shoulder. It carved a symbol into the scale, scratching it through the top layer of its metallic hide.

Tolwyn saw Kurst, again in man form, try to rise. But his wounds were too great and he fell to the chamber floor. But he read the rune that the Carredon carved. "Never life."

Then the beast moved to a second scale. It repeated the carving ritual, forming another rune upon its own body.

"Never death," Kurst read weakly.

The Carredon gripped the scales and tore them from its flesh, ripping away meat with the pieces of armor. It spoke words that Tolwyn did not understand, and it blew upon the twin scales, pointing them toward Decker. With the words of magic completed and the breath to move them, the scales flew from the monster's claws. They spun in the air, forming into pointed staves of metal each about a foot long. The carved runes could be clearly seen upon the shaft of each staff, glowing brightly with magical energy.

Faster than either Bryce or Decker could move, the staves struck the congressman, burying themselves in his chest. Decker screamed in agony as lambent energy played across his body, flowed into the jutting staves, and shot out into the darkness beyond the chamber. Decker collapsed, but the energy continued to dance along the metal rods formed from the Carredon's own body.

"Now, priest," the monster laughed, "perhaps I'll let you watch as I flay the skin from Tolwyn's bones."

"No, spawn of hell, I'll not let you hurt her!" Father Bryce screamed across the chamber.

The Carredon chuckled, and the sound was frightening. "And what will you do to stop me, stormer?"

As the dragon and Bryce glared at each other, Tolwyn stood up. The fear was still with her, but she was fighting it, pushing it away.

"I am tired of hearing the word 'stormer', Carredon," she said. Her voice began weak, but grew in strength as she spoke. "Would you like me to call you worm?"

"But that is what you are, Tolwyn," the Carredon said. "You are worms. You are stormers."

"We are storm knights!" she shouted, drawing her saber from its sheath.

"You are dead, little woman. Look around you. Your companions have fallen, like that last time we battled so many centuries ago. History repeats itself, and I see that you have failed to learn from it."

"I have learned enough, worm!"

Tolwyn launched herself at the dragon, slashing away with the saber. Her intensity drove the dragon backwards, but it would soon realize she was unable to truly hurt it. Then it would strike back. The last time she fought the Carredon she had her sword and armor, and even those magical items were not enough to stay the dragon's claws. Now all she had was a dress saber and the images of her friends falling: Rick Alder, whom young Coyote called a cop; Kurst, a shapeshifter from the cosm of Orrorsh; Dr. Hachi Mara-Two, a young woman who was a scientific prodigy come to save this cosm from the horrors that almost destroyed her own; Andrew Jackson Decker, a congressman. Only Father Christopher Bryce, the priest, remained standing, and he would fall quickly once she had spent herself.

"Enough of these games, Tolwyn!" the Carredon yelled. It swung back at her, driving her away step by step with mighty swipes of its claws. "Lay down your weapon and I will make this death quick."

"Like you have done for Decker?" she said, referring to the glowing rune staves jutting from his chest. But while it looked as though Decker should be dead, his chest continued to rise and fall with breath. "Never shall I simply surrender, monster!"

She fought on, intensifying her attack. She used every move she could think of, every half-remembered skill that her body could call upon, searching for an opening. But no matter her skill and daring, she knew she could only last as long as her strength held out.

And the strength of the Carredon was far greater.

Behind her, Christopher Bryce stood before the stone that Decker called the Heart of Coyote and listened to its song. There were no words to the song, and he could not hum the melody, but he knew it as a song nonetheless. It was a song of life, like the song of nature you could hear in a breeze, in the babble of a running brook, in a peaceful forest. But this song, while akin to those others, was louder, more intense. It sang of possibilities, for that was what life was. As long as there was life, there were endless possibilities.

And suddenly the stone filled his mind with one possible outcome to the battle that raged behind him. He reached out and grasped the stone.

Tolwyn was covered with cuts and scratches. Blood ran down her body, mingling with her perspiration. None were serious yet, but the total effect was painful. She blocked out the pain and continued to hack and stab at the Carredon, slicing deep cuts into its armor but unable to get to the soft flesh beneath.

Then Tolwyn slipped on a splash of blood, hitting the chamber floor hard.

The Carredon rose over her, victory shining in its evil eyes. "And now this ends, Tolwyn," it sneered.

"Yes, demon, it does!" yelled a powerful voice from elsewhere in the chamber.

The Carredon looked up to see Bryce. The priest held the blue and red stone firmly in his hands, pointing it at the dragon.

"Please, God," Father Bryce called out, "make the image I was shown come true!"

A beam of pure light burst from the stone and struck the Carredon in the chest. The energy danced across the dragon's armor, bathing the creature in lightning. The Carredon screamed in pain, but the energy seemed unable to penetrate the beast's scales. However, a portion of the light had been deflected by the armor. It bounced clear and wrapped itself around Tolwyn's saber, drawn to it like lightning to the highest tree.

As the dragon writhed in the pain caused by the light, Tolwyn watched as her saber blade glowed with the same power. She did not know what it meant, or why she wasn't being assaulted by the lightning as well. But she knew an opening when she saw one. The Carredon had dropped its defensive stance and forgotten about her as it vainly tried to brush away the crackling light.

With all the strength she had remaining, Tolwyn aimed her glowing blade at the Carredon's shoulder, at the spot where the creature had removed two of its own scales. She screamed a war cry that rocked the chamber. Then she drove the blade home.

The beast screamed in agony as the energy exploded into fire within its body. The fire burned with an intensity that was too much for the dragon, boiling its blood and searing its soft flesh. As it crumbled to the chamber floor, Tolwyn raised her sword and prepared to continue hacking and slicing until the dragon was totally destroyed.

A voice from behind her stayed her hand, however, compelling her to turn around.

"That's enough, luv," said the small black man standing where Christopher had been. He was old and lean and wiry, with a mound of white hair that jiggled as he spoke. "This battle is over, and you did good. But there are other battles to fight, and I need to be with you and the other blokes when they occur."

Confused, Tolwyn lowered her sword and asked, "Who are you?"

The black man smiled, revealing a missing tooth and a tongue with a hole in it. "Come to me, Tolwyn. You know the way. West. And down. West and down …"

The dream ended and Tolwyn awoke. But even in the darkened room, she could hear the black man's voice echo in her mind. There was another journey to make, and perhaps the rest of her memories would be found at the end of this next trail.

Hunting Time

Keep me from the hunting time, when darkness swirls and the moon is full.
— Ayslish prayer

Better to take your own life than let the huntsman take it for you.
— Ayslish proverb

1

Kurst had been standing at Decker's bedside throughout the night, trying to find understanding in the swirling energy slowly draining from the congressman's body. Here he was, in an alien cosm, sent to do what he had done countless times before. But this time everything was different. This time he had gone against the Gaunt Man.

He examined Andrew Jackson Decker again, but there was no change. He was still lying in the same position, with the same tubes running into and out of his body. His eyes were still closed, although Kurst could see rapid movement beneath the lids. And the rune staves were still in place, sucking away life and possibility energy to feed the Gaunt Man's machine half a world away.

The staves had been fashioned from the scales of the Carredon, the runes carved by the great dragon's own talons. They were the runes of never life and never death, for that was the condition they left their host in. As far as the hunter knew, there was no way to remove the staves without killing the host — but to leave them in place was to condemn the host to an even worse fate. For the sixth time this night, Kurst contemplated murdering the congressman. And for the sixth time, he held his claws in check.

The Gaunt Man, leader of the invasion of Earth, had sent Kurst to find the stormers named Mara and Tolwyn. He was to bring them back to Orrorsh realm, in what was once Indonesia. The two women were in the company of other stormers — Decker, the priest Bryce, Rick Alder and his edeinos partner Tal Tu, and the two youths Coyote and Rat. They were in search of a stone, and Kurst had decided to accompany them on that search. It sounded as though they knew the location of an eternity shard, and to bring such a powerful artifact back with the women would be a definite bonus for his master. But then the Gaunt Man changed the rules.

Without informing Kurst, the Gaunt Man sent others after the group. An Earther named Malcolm Kane led a band of hunters into the Grand Canyon, but their mission was very different from Kurst's. They were to kill the group. Obviously, they had not succeeded, and Kane and his companions were dead. At least, they assumed Kane was dead. His body fell into the raging river at the bottom of the canyon and was whisked from sight.

But those were not the only hunters the Gaunt Man had sent. He also sent the Carredon.

The great dragon had come to kill the stormers, and Kurst had fought beside them although he knew that nothing could stop the monster. But something did stop it — Tolwyn and the eternity shard called the Heart of Coyote.

Alder was dead now, and Decker was as near to death as one could be and still be called alive. Kurst had gone against the obvious orders of the Gaunt Man, and he did not know what that meant. He told himself it was because of the words that Thratchen had said. The demon from Tharkold had said that the Gaunt Man was only reacting to a few minor setbacks when he ordered the stormers' deaths. He would be better served, Thratchen had said, if we kept them alive for study. And Kurst said he would do what he could. But was it because he believed the demon, or was it because of some inner purpose of his own that he had yet to understand? The confusion ate at him like the Gaunt Man and the other High Lords ate at this world.

Now they were at the medical facility of a military base called Twentynine Palms, in the portion of America called California. It was where the army copter had taken them when they left the Grand Canyon.

The door to the room opened and Kurst's senses were filled with the odor of flowers and sunshine. It was the nurse, Julie Boot, making her rounds. She did not say a word to Kurst. She simply checked the machines attached to Decker and dabbed at his forehead with a cool sponge. She kept her eyes down, trying not to meet Kurst's gaze. I frighten her, he thought. Tonight, that thought bothered him.

The nurse cleared her throat, but her voice was still a whisper when it emerged from her lips. "Why have you been sitting here all night?" she asked.

"I have been watching Decker," Kurst replied, his own voice low and deep.

"Why?"

"He is ... my friend," Kurst said, and he could almost believe it was true.

Then the door opened again, and the smell of thought, learning, and renewed faith assaulted the hunter's senses. Father Christopher Bryce was standing in the doorway.

"Have you been here all night, Mr. Kurst?" the priest asked cautiously. They still did not trust Kurst.

"I have," Kurst replied, looking into the nurse's eyes, keeping his back to Bryce.

"You really should have slept. You're still not a hundred percent yourself."

"Have you come for a reason, Father Bryce?"

"Yes. Yes I have," the priest stammered, taken aback by Kurst's lack of comradery. "Tolwyn has asked us to gather in the rec area. She wants to talk to us."

"Of course." But Kurst did not move from Decker's side until Bryce shut the door and was well on his way.

Then he turned away, leaving Decker to his own troubled dreams and the ministrations of Nurse Boot.

2

It was most definitely *not* a day like any other in Cheyenne, Wyoming.

For one thing, it was hotter than hell — far hotter than Mark Hope could remember. Hot ash sifted down out of the mud-gray sky like pepper from God's shaker, hissing as it fell and turning the city a dirty shade of black. Heat rippled up from the streets, belly-dancing into the sky.

It was also quiet, except for the hissing of the ash and a low rumbling coming from somewhere to the northeast, rolling through the air like angry thunder. There were few cars on the road, and fewer animals in yards to bark or call out to the day. Machinery was silent in factories and on construction sites. People weren't out today — a day that was already thirty-five hours old — for fear of the growing heat. Night, which last showed itself thirty-five eternal hours ago, had been a long period of darkness and record-setting cold. Now, beneath the ash covering that offered some protection, the two-day sun was baking the city into oblivion. The only people still moving about the city were looters, a few loyal policemen, the stubborn who tried to keep their businesses going, and Mark Hope.

Out on Route 30, Mark urged a little more speed out of the once-shiny Chevy truck, and prayed that the air-conditioning wouldn't quit before he reached his family. His wife, daughter, and parents were waiting for Mark to arrive so they could head north, to the rumored safe lands in Canada. Sure, the President had called for Americans to unite against the invasion. Mark had heard the speech over the radio. But as far as Mark was concerned, flight to Canada was a time-honored tradition for his family. His Uncle Josh, a draft dodger from the Vietnam days, would welcome them to his home in Yellowknife without political comment. They hadn't heard from Josh in a while, but it was a destination, a goal in these troubled times.

Mark thought about recent events, and tears threatened to explode from his eyes. No, he told himself. Calm down. If he fell apart now, he'd never reach his family. And if he didn't arrive, they might not make it to safer climes. Still, images of the last few weeks flashed through his mind, and Mark was forced to examine them. First there were the mysterious reports concerning New York and the east coast. It was like a blackout as communications ceased. Then rumors of some kind of war started to make the rounds, igniting the first stages of panic. Then the refugees appeared, bringing with them tales of dinosaurs and lizard men called edeinos. When the rest of the country finally realized the United States had been attacked, the edeinos invaders appeared on the west coast. Then the planet itself started to slow down; days lasted longer and longer until the heat became unbearable, nights went on until it seemed dawn would never break and the cold would remain forever.

It was like the end of the world.

Mark slowed down through a winding curve, looking for a fuel sign and wondering if anyone still had working pumps, or if they had all been bled dry during the first few days of the panic when survivalists and cowardly hoarders had looted and taken what they claimed they needed without regard for the law. Mark himself had once been forced to take gas at gunpoint, from a garage owner who didn't want cash anymore. The owner claimed it was no good now that the government was gone. That was a dirty rotten lie, as anyone who listened to the radio knew, but Mark had paid him fair and square. He dropped the money right there on the ground where the man could take it as soon as Mark stopped pointing the shotgun at him. He winced at the memory.

Mark spotted a Sunoco sign and veered toward the exit. A particularly dense cloud of cinders was falling from the sky as the Chevy pulled off the highway, making the going slow and treacherous, but Mark thanked God that when the Earth slowed down the volcanoes had all gone off at once. He heard the report, how scientists claimed that such a series of eruptions was impossible, but then he thought about everything else that he had heard about over the last month. Nothing would ever seem impossible again.

He pulled the Chevy out of a skid. Driving on ash was similar to driving on snow, he thought. Once he cursed snow, but he was unwilling to curse the ash. Without the ash the volcanoes had sent into the sky to block out the sun, they'd all have roasted or frozen to death by now. As it was, who knew what was going to happen if the planet continued to slow? A reflex glance in the rear-view mirror showed a towering thunderhead moving in from the northeast. It was blacker than the gray-ash sky, moving across the expanse of gray with almost definite purpose. It was unnatural for a storm to move from east to west, but with the Earth turning so slowly, the storms had a tendency to move wherever they pleased. He almost hoped it would catch him with its cooling rain, and he slowed the truck a bit more. After all, caution was more prudent than speed as he traveled over the fallen ash.

Slow and cautious would not bring safety and cool

rain this time, though. This time it would bring death.

3

Within the tower of cloud and darkness that rumbled across the ash-gray sky, the Horn Master flew. He was an imposing specter, cloaked in swirling storm and raging thunder. Lightning crackled from his shoulders, an electric cape flaring in his wake. Monstrous in size, he rode atop a monstrous, foam-spattered stag. His muscled arms and naked chest were stained wet with crimson, and on his head he wore an antlered helmet that hid his face in shadow. But his eyes glared out of the shadow, two points of fire in the night.

Lightning flashed, illuminating the Horn Master as the bolt slashed across the sky. And for those brief seconds, the Horn Master's form changed.

In the light of the bolt, flesh became transparent and the specter was revealed. Gigantic skeleton arms held the reins of his mount, crimson running wet down white bone instead of knotted sinew. His powerful chest faded to expose rib cage, which housed chittering shadow forms that reached through the bone bars with long, sharp claws. His head was not helmeted. The lightning revealed a human skull with flaming eyes and antlers that rose in cruel curves. The stag itself became a black, misshapen thing that ran on four cloven-hooved appendages. Its shadow skin rippled and shifted constantly in the glare of the bolt, as though trying to retain some semblance of form before the shadows dispersed.

When the bolt expended itself, flesh flowed back into place and muscle re-formed. Horn Master and stag galloped on through the tower of cloud and darkness, the waiting storm riding fast beside them.

High above the city, the Horn Master pulled the stag to a halt. He looked down at the man-structures and laughed. The sound was like distant thunder. These tall huts of metal and wood had not slowed the Horn Master in any of the previous cities he had plundered — cities named Boston, Chicago, Lincoln. They would not slow him now.

He raised a bone horn to his lips and blew the long cry of a wild beast. It was time to gather the Wild Hunt! He sounded the horn a second time, and the storm itself took up the cry. The Horn Master sat atop his stag, his own anticipation building in time with the growing call.

As the noise built, pieces of storm dislodged to swirl about the Horn Master. At first they were bits of cloud and dark mist, but they took on shape as they swirled faster. Flittering night-black forms spouted wings and flowed until they became a flock of night-black ravens. Crawling shadows took on definition and became wolfhounds of enormous size. Cawing and baying joined the wild cry, and the city below shivered with fear and dread.

Still, the hunt was not complete, and the Horn Master blared his horn again. New forms emerged from the clouds, galloping shadows mounted by skeletal riders that became night-black horses and armored hunters as they rode forth. The horn blared a final time, and the slithering shades that flowed behind the riders added their cry to the cacophony as they formed into running squires and men-at-arms.

The Horn Master surveyed the crowd swirling about him; the mounted hunters, the squires, the ravens, and the wolfhounds. He saw beyond the flesh, and reveled in the shadows and bone and demon creatures that truly made up his troop. With a triumphant shout, the Horn

Master led the Wild Hunt down to plunder and destroy in a bone rattle of power and frenzy, riding the clouds of darkness like thunder in a storm.

4

Mark Hope hit the off ramp at a respectable twenty miles per hour, hoping to find an open gas station. The ash was still falling, a perpetual cloud that turned the long day into a pseudo twilight. But when he rounded the bend of the ramp, he saw more than ash in his headlight beams. Dark clouds of flying insects swarmed around a stream of animals that flowed across the road and rushed toward some unknown destination.

Or rushed *from* something.

He swerved his truck to avoid hitting the animals, an odd mix of dogs, cats and rodents turned into ash-covered replicas of themselves. He almost laughed at the sight, but he was too busy fighting to control the vehicle. He failed miserably as the wheels lost contact with the blacktop and spun freely in the blanket of ash. The truck skidded, spinning completely around, before he was able to regain control and stop the vehicle as the engine stalled. He took a deep breath to settle his racing heart, then looked through the insect-spattered windshield. He missed the animals, but the clouds of bugs were unavoidable.

The scene reminded Mark of an article he read in a magazine once, about animals fleeing en masse from an earthquake or forest fire. They stampeded blindly, in utter terror, just like the animals running past his truck.

He rested his forehead on the padded steering wheel and closed his eyes. Mark still had such a long drive ahead of him, and he was already feeling the effects of navigating through the ash blizzard. His nerves were frazzled, his eyes ached, and the tension in his shoulders knotted his muscles into a tight coil. God! He needed a warm bath and two aspirin!

Mark slowly rotated his head to work out some of the kinks, then reached for the ignition to restart the engine. His fingers found the cool metal of the key ring and lingered for a moment. He was about to turn the key when a loud noise from outside the truck caught his attention.

Crashing out of the brush on the side of the road were sword-wielding horsemen straight out of the Middle Ages. One of the riders locked eyes with Mark and directed his mount straight for the truck. The horseman wore furs and leathers over a tanned, muscled frame. A horned skull cap rested atop his long, grime-caked hair. The rider shouted harsh, guttural words that Mark did not understand and rode for the truck.

Mark turned the key, pumped the gas pedal, and waited for the familiar sound of the engine turning over. It sputtered, caught, and coughed, sending a rumble through the truck but not starting. He cursed, then turned the key again. This time the engine started, but Mark never got the opportunity to shift into gear. The heavy metal of the rider's sword smashed through the windshield and sliced into Mark Hope, cleaving his head from his torso.

The rider did not stop the inspect his work. Instead, a dark shape scampered out of the brush, through the broken glass, and reached into Mark's dying body with long, black claws. When the claws were pulled back, they held the glowing essence of Mark's soul. The dark shape protectively cupped the glow to its chest, then scampered back into the brush to add its spoils to that of the rest of the Hunt.

5

Captain Adam Burke scrambled his F-15 Eagle air-superiority fighter when the first distress call came out of Warren Air Force Base. Lowry, the closest base with aircraft, answered the call. Burke's squadron had only recently been assigned to Lowry from its original home at Holloman in New Mexico, and he had hoped they'd see some action. The war status had units moving and relocating all over the country, trying to anticipate where forces would be needed most. If the call had any basis, Burke thought, then his Eagle was going to get a workout. And that suited him just fine.

The swirling ash made visuals difficult, so Burke constantly scanned his instruments, knowing they were his senses in this storm of volcanic dust. The familiar chatter of his wingmen spilled through his radio, and Burke's chest swelled with confidence. They were fifty miles out of Cheyenne. Forty. Thirty. His instruments still hadn't picked up any in-air threats. Could Warren be wrong? He hoped not. Burke was definitely looking forward to blasting the pseudo-dinosaurs he had heard so much about.

"We're getting close, boys," Burke said over his radio. "Let's stay alert. The first one to bag a lizard gets the President's undying gratitude."

"I'd rather have a three-day pass," said Zahn, flying in the fighter on Burke's left wing.

"When this is over," Burke laughed, "I'll see what I can do."

6

The Horn Master led his terrifying band of spectral riders over the city, letting huntsmen dart to the ground to wreak havoc where they would. He noted that the squires were hard at work gathering the souls of those slain by the huntsmen. These souls would be added to the Hunt, eventually taking their places as hunters, or being transformed into shadow creatures to run with the pack or fly with the flock.

The furious host was in motion, and the Horn Master knew that his own lord would be pleased. He remembered the orders given him, orders that came down from Lord Uthorion (who still played his game of deceit in the body of Pella Ardinay, but to what end the Horn Master could not fathom). The Wild Hunt was to fly to the aid of Baruk Kaah, High Lord of the Living Land, and provide support until such time as Uthorion called the Hunt back. There was one clause, however, that burned brightly in the Horn Master's memories.

"If you find Tolwyn of House Tancred, kill her quickly and bring me her soul," the voice that whispered in the Horn Master's mind was Ardinay's, but the words were Uthorion's.

And through it all, whether aiding Baruk Kaah or hunting down the paladin, the Wild Hunt would get to do what it did best — cause untold destruction and gather souls to replenish the Hunt.

The night wings alighted on the Horn Master's shoulder, drawing him from his thoughts as he felt the tingling touch of their shadowy feathers. He regarded the raven-things momentarily, then shifted his gaze toward the horizon, toward where the danger they had come to warn him of originated. Blazing eyes glared from the dark hollows of his helmet, and the horn master listened to the approaching sound that rivaled the clamor of the Wild Hunt. Metal bats streaked toward him, his mind shouting the word Lord Uthorion gave him — "airplane." But to the Horn Master, "iron bat" made more sense. He raised his horn and blared an order, and immediately a wave of hunters rushed forward.

Yes, the Horn Master thought as he replaced the instrument, now the challenge begins.

7

Captain Burke placed his fighter on a course that would take it over the heart of the city. His instruments still showed the "all-clear," and he was beginning to think they had been scrambled for a wild goose chase.

"Anybody have anything to report?" he asked his wingmen.

"Negative," replied Zahn.

"Not a peep on the screens," answered Whit.

"Let's do a flyby and see what we see," Burke said.

"Hey, Captain," Whit came back excitedly, "take a look at your two o'clock. What do you make of that?"

It took Burke a moment to distinguish the rolling black storm cloud against the backdrop of ash, but when he did it was easy to track.

"Looks like one hell of a storm," Burke said over his radio. "But I can't get it to register on my scopes. Zahn?"

"Negatory, Captain," Zahn responded quickly. "According to the radar, it isn't there."

Now Burke was becoming concerned. Not nervous, mind you. Just concerned. Perhaps, he thought, our scopes are down. Or worse, maybe the enemy has a way to disable the radar. If that was the case, then the unidentified threat could be anywhere.

"Stay alert, people," Burke ordered. "If the radar is down, then we're going to have to rely on visuals."

"That's not going to be easy in this volcanic crap," Zahn said.

"Heads up!" Whit shouted.

Part of the storm broke off from the main host and moved toward the approaching F-15s. Not drifted, Burke told himself, but moving as if with purpose and intent. Lightning flashed, and for a moment the storm was filled with riders on horseback and packs of dogs. Then the flash was over and the dark cloud was closer.

"Evasive action!" Burke screamed into his radio. "Move it, people!"

Burke forced his fighter into a roll, not waiting to see if the others were following his orders. But a second later, he knew that Whit had hesitated by the chatter coming back through his headset.

"Captain, what's the problem?" Whit asked. "It's just a cloud for God's sake. Wait a minute. Will you look at that. Captain, there's a guy with a sword —"

Whit's voice was cut off and an explosion followed. Burke strained to see out his cockpit. He saw the bright flash of the exploding plane. And he saw that the cloud was turning, placing itself on an intercept course for him and Zahn.

"What do we do?" Zahn asked over the radio.

"Do? We do what we came to do," Burke replied. "We fight and destroy."

8

The Horn Master howled in delight as the iron bat fell from the air. What a masterful stroke the hunter had delivered! If this was challenge, then the High Lords would take this sphere without raising a sweat, the Horn Master thought. He watched a moment longer to make certain that the hunters were engaging the remaining iron bats — airplanes, he corrected — then ordered the rest of the hunt to descend.

9

Behind the drawn shades and bolted doors of Cheyenne, people became increasingly afraid. It wasn't the unnatural ash that coated the sky that caused this new fear. They had grown used to that in recent days. It wasn't the long day or the promise of a long night to come. That was a fear that had been with them and was almost familiar. The new fear was much more immediate — and much more intense.

It was a fear carried in on the storm winds, a fear that blew against the houses and shook them with a ferocity that inspired images of someone — or something — trying to get in. It was a communal fear, a deep-rooted fear from the depths of primal memory, a fear that shouted to run and hide.

Outside, people heard the storm rushing through the air. But other sounds echoed in the storm as well, a great clamor of shouts and horn-blowing and the baying of hounds. Any who peered through half-closed curtains or cracked doors saw the thundercloud move over Cheyenne like a giant. From its rolling mass came horselike beasts with riders of storm and death, and red-eyed hounds with tongues of fire, and a flight of black birds to laugh and taunt with sounds near enough to speech to make people shudder. The descent of the riders and hounds was like a lightning bolt, and it leveled the buildings all around the area of impact, leaving curls of flame and twisting pillars of smoke in their wake.

The Wild Hunt moved on, cutting a swath through the city, knocking down apartments and houses with hammer blows of great iron-shod hooves, and smashing winds from horns of power, and sometimes a bright spear would lick out of the clouds, leaving bits of broken flesh or metal where there had been humans hoping to resist. Those that emerged from their hiding places met the fate of the hunted and were brought down like deer, fleeing mindlessly from place to place.

And still the hunt moved on, slowly and methodically grinding the city to dust as it moved through. The hunters passed one another as they rode, and some had hair matted from effort, and others had red-stained beards where they had tasted the hearts of their prey, and still others carried shiny trinkets or trophies commemorating the hunt. They were spirit things, the dead; demons, some said. They were all these things and more. They were the Wild Hunt, and Uthorion had set them free upon this world.

10

Burke's F-15 screamed eastward on a fast vector toward the cloud that had destroyed Whit and was now moving to engage him and Zahn. From one kilometer out, Burke fired two Sparrow missiles into the swirling black cloud, assuming that his true target was hiding somewhere within the dark mass. The missiles calmly arced through the sky, into the fast-approaching cloud, and out the other side.

"No luck, Captain," Zahn noted.

"Switch to radar painting and try to get a reading," Burke ordered.

"Nothing doing there, either," Zahn came back, confirming what Burke's own instruments told him — or didn't tell him.

"Radio Warren and give them an update, then follow me into that thunderhead," Burke said as he circled wide to approach the cloud from a different angle.

Then the riders appeared.

They galloped out of the storm cloud in a burst of thunder, riding atop black spectral horses whose hooves sparked with lightning as they raced across the sky. The spectral horses had red eyes, red mouths, and spraying nostrils; the riders were demonic men of great size, with spears and swords and gleaming shields. On their heads they wore horned helms, and there was an aura of smoke and blood all about them. They rode toward the war planes with great cries of joy and battle-lust. Some were more skeletal than flesh, others were insubstantial, ghostlike. All were flying death.

Burke refused to believe his eyes. He knew the world had changed, had become very strange, but he wasn't aware that it had gone mad.

"Zahn, tell me what you see," Burke ordered.

There was a pause. Then Zahn spoke. "It can't be real. How can horses gallop through the sky? And why do those riders shift from real and solid looking to skeletal when the lightning flashes? What are they, Captain?"

Burke didn't answer. Instead, he put the fighter into a forward roll and fired its rotary cannon at the riders. They seemed not to notice, or at most to brush at their faces and shoulders, and to hunch a little lower in their saddles as they drove forward. Then Burke and Zahn engaged the demonic beings, frantically wheeling and attacking with cannon fire.

"It's no good," Burke shouted into his radio. "The cannons don't pack enough punch to get through their armor and shields. Pull up and let's put a little distance between us."

Burke's F-15 spun free of the pack of riders and shot skyward. He checked his scope for Zahn and saw that his wingman was flying in the other direction, toward the larger cloud that rested over the city far below. Burke positioned his craft so that he could get a visual. He saw the other fighter on the tail of one of the riders, chasing him into the tower of cloud and darkness.

"Zahn, pull out of there!" Burke screamed. "I gave you an order, mister!"

"I've got this bastard, Burke," Zahn shot back, his voice almost lost in the building static. "This is for Whit!"

But before Zahn could loose his missiles, two other riders exploded out of the cloud cover. They wielded large, gleaming swords that whistled over their heads as they charged forward. Then, like lightning, the twin blades struck, searing the wings from the F-15. The other rider, no longer fleeing, spun his mount and brought his own blade to bear upon Zahn's jet. Burke heard his wingman scream defiantly as his jet raced on a collision course with the rider.

"Eject! Zahn, ditch the Eagle! Now!" But Burke knew his command would go unheeded, just as he knew he had no hope of avenging his wingmen, no chance of taking out this enemy.

The rider dived beneath the oncoming fighter which, without wings, could not correct its own course. As he dropped out of the F-15's path, the rider slashed out with his sword. Zahn's Eagle exploded in a shower of fire, and Burke felt his stomach drop away.

"Damn you, monster!" Burke screamed, his fingers punching the triggers that released his Sidewinder missiles.

The two projectiles raced at the rider who had ended Zahn's life, but the demon stood his ground confidently and readied his throwing spear. With an evil grin, the rider tossed the shaft at Burke just as the twin missiles slammed into him and exploded. Burke grinned back as he saw the horse plummet. Then the spear smashed through the cockpit, skewering Burke before his own plane was consumed in a ball of flame.

11

The swirling melee ended as quickly as it had begun, and all that remained was the ash, the storm cloud, and the riders and their hounds.

The Horn Master surveyed his minions and saw that the battle-frenzy was overtaking them; eyes were glazed with a drunkenness born of killing; the hounds ran to and fro excitedly, baying and snapping at one another. The ravens, above them all, swirled frantically in a pillar of smoky feathers, faster and faster. The Horn Master had seen this before, on a thousand such hunts, and knew that now was the time to rein in, to call the Hunt to gather. He reached again for the horn, and winded a great double blast. "Return!" the great horn ordered. "Return!"

His very will boiled out in the horn call, and that will bent the desires of his minions, brought them to a halt, shaking their heads and letting the battle-lust melt away like snow in spring. The Horn Master sounded the call again, and they returned: the horses and hounds, the ravens and the squires. All moved slowly to gather about their leader, heeding his call and the crackling power of his desire as they returned to the tower of cloud and darkness.

As they drew closer, they shifted into their true forms. Horses and hounds became shadow-black creatures without definition, four-legged demons with glowing eyes and pointed fangs and claws. The birds were fragments of night, with night wings spread wide and night beaks serrated with sharp teeth. The squires were shadowy apparitions with featureless faces, transparent skin, and skeletal limbs. Finally, the hunters themselves were restless spirits of gigantic proportions, with long, misshapened limbs that seemed to constantly shift and reform.

When all were gathered, the Horn Master wheeled his mount and broke into a trot, leading the way southwest to where their presence had been requested by Baruk Kaah.

The Hunt followed sedately behind, the riders relaxed in ghostly saddles, the raven-things at rest atop convenient shoulders, and the hound-things idly gnawing bits of metal and flesh as they trotted beside their masters. Soon the Hunt was gone from sight, and Cheyenne was alone again. But a great swath of flattened, destroyed city was left in its wake, as if made by hurricane, tornado and tsunami all at once. All that remained was dancing flames, twisting columns of smoke, and hissing cinders that fell from the sky.

12

Tolwyn of House Tancred waited for her companions to arrive. She was in the rec room of the hospital at Twentynine Palms Marine Corps Base, somewhere in the area Christopher Bryce called Southern California. Much of her memory had returned during the recent confrontation with the Carredon, but there were still annoying gaps that refused to fill. She was Tolwyn of House Tancred, Captain of the Knight Protectors, paladin of the Lady of the Houses of Aysle, defender of Pella Ardinay. In a terrible battle against the dark forces of Angar Uthorion, Tolwyn and her knights fell against the power of the Carredon. How long ago that first meeting with the demon dragon was, she had no way to judge.

Time was measured differently on this world called Earth. But she had been dead, floating in an in-between place, waiting to be claimed by either the darkness or the light, when she suddenly found herself on this world, seemingly called back to life by Christopher's voice.

She examined her hand before her face, flexing away the stiffness. It was her hand! She recognized it! But others still called her Wendy Miller. Sometimes, when the other dreams ended, the dreams of Carredons and enigmatic black men, she dreamed of a woman with her face, staring at her. The woman, however, did not have Tolwyn's emerald eyes. Instead, she had eyes as brown as the bark on a tree. Tolwyn felt sorry for the woman — for Wendy.

She reached for the knapsack on the table and removed a wrapped object. She could hear its song, the song that called her to travel across this vast country to the place named Grand Canyon. Slowly she unwrapped it, and the brilliant blue light bathed her face in a warm glow. The stone was the same color as her crys flower, a swirling combination of blue and red, and it was shaped like a human heart. Was there a connection between the similar colors? Yes, she was certain, but what that connection was eluded her.

"Can you give me back the rest of my memories?" she whispered to the stone Decker called the Heart of Coyote. "What is it you want me to do?"

The song remained constant, neither rising in intensity or lowering. It continued to provide support through its presence, but it gave her no answers.

Then the companions entered the room. Father Christopher Bryce came first, wearing his usual black uniform and white collar. Dr. Hachi Mara-Two followed, wearing a black jumpsuit, but her face was clean of her usually mask-like makeup. Her wild mane of silver hair was held in check by the bandage over her right temple. She had suffered a concussion from the Carredon's blow, but was recovering well. Coyote was next, helping the edeinos Tal Tu into the room. Coyote had suffered no physical injuries on their trek, but he had lost some of his fire. Tal Tu, on the other hand, had been injured gravely. The doctors at the base were surprised that he was up and around at all, and they warned him that any exertion could open his wounds. Behind them was Rat, whose arm was still in a sling. He, too, had become withdrawn, and Christopher was doing his best to pull the boys out of their depression.

They all took seats, looking expectantly at Tolwyn. She, in turn, looked at them, and a pang of sorrow touched her when she noticed the empty chairs. Rick Alder would not be at this meeting. They had buried him in the military graveyard located on this base. And Decker would not be walking through the door, for he was in a state very similar to death. The door opened again, and Kurst moved into the room the way a stalking cat moves. Without a word, he found a seat and looked up to indicate that he was ready.

"Thank you all for coming," Tolwyn began, still holding the stone heart in her hand. "I have decided on my next course of action, and I wanted to inform you of that. Understand, I tell you this because I would expect the same from people I have served with and grown to care about. But the telling in no way obligates you to anything."

"We understand, Tolwyn," Mara said with a smile in her voice. "Now, are you going to tell us or not?"

Tolwyn smiled as well, then raised the stone heart for all to see. "This was the object of the first part of my quest. It is a thing of this world, and for some reason it has chosen me to help it. It is frightened, as I was frightened by the Carredon, but it has power that can be used against these invaders."

"We've seen its power," Bryce agreed. "What is your next step?"

Tolwyn hesitated, matching Christopher's gaze with her emerald stare. "I must take the heart west. West and down."

"West," Kurst whispered, "and down?"

"How do you know these things, Tolwyn? I'm not doubting you, but ..." Bryce asked, unsure of exactly where he wanted his questions to go.

"More dreams, Christopher," she said with a hollow smile. "First the heart called to me through my dreams and showed me where to go. And now a small black man does the same, showing me a knotted rope and speaking of battles to come."

"We are almost to the edge of this land mass," Mara joined in. "If we go much further west, we'll be in the ocean."

"No," Kurst said in his low, deep voice. The single word silenced the group, and all eyes turned toward the shapeshifter. He saw the hint of fear in Bryce's eyes, the caution in Mara's. Only Tolwyn's gaze was unreadable. They had fought together, no matter what form he took, and for the moment she was giving him the benefit of the doubt. Because of that, he addressed his words to her and her alone, although everyone could hear him.

"Go west and down and you will find a land mass and a group of islands," Kurst continued. "That is where Orrorsh realm is. That is where you will find the Gaunt Man. I do not know if your stone can stop him, but it could be possible to release Decker from the spells that bind him."

"Orrorsh," Tolwyn said, turning the word over in her mouth, tasting the decay of it. "That name is familiar to me." She paced the room, fighting to pull the memory from its hiding place. Finally, with more and more ease, the memory tugged free. "That is the place Uthorion came from!"

"Uthorion?" Bryce questioned.

"The monster that attacked my land and had me killed."

"I see," Bryce said.

"I am going to this place called Orrorsh, and there I shall find Uthorion and have my revenge!" Tolwyn swore before the group.

Kurst decided not to tell her that Uthorion was no longer in Orrorsh. In fact, he had never returned from the conquest of Aysle. He was a High Lord now, ruling Tolwyn's home cosm in a way that would greatly upset the paladin — if she were to find out about it. But if he kept her thinking Orrorsh was where she was to go, then she would be returning of her own accord, making things much easier for the hunter.

"I will go with you," Kurst said, still focused on Tolwyn's emerald eyes. "I must try to free Decker from the Gaunt Man's runes."

"Now wait a minute!" Bryce exclaimed. "I've been through one of these discussions once before and this has the same feel. I know where this is going and I have to say …"

"I am not asking you to come, Christopher," Tolwyn said soothingly. "You have helped me enough. But this world still needs help, and the heart sings out its plea in such a way that I cannot turn my back on it. It is the reason why I am alive again."

Bryce sighed mightily. "You're trying to make me feel guilty. That's not fair ..."

"I will go, too," Mara interrupted.

"Oh, of course, why didn't I see that coming! Isn't anyone here going to help me talk Tolwyn out of this?" Bryce looked around beseechingly, but Rat and Tal Tu remained silent. Coyote, however, had one thing to say.

"Sometimes you gotta do what you gotta do, Father. You know?"

Bryce let his shoulders slump. "I guess that leaves me only one thing to do. I'll go speak to the colonel about getting us transportation."

"Us?" Tolwyn asked innocently.

Bryce halted in the doorway and looked back over his shoulder. "Yes," he said, gazing fiercely into her emerald eyes. "I wouldn't miss the rest of your quest for the world."

13

In the new city of Thebes, Dr. Mobius, Pharaoh of the new Nile Empire on Earth, observed the construction of his palace. It was going to be a grand building, for the Royal Builder Muab was personally overseeing the work. Of course, Mobius would settle for no less.

The High Lord reclined upon a great throne, surrounded by half a dozen serving girls that catered to his whims. And Mobius had many whims. One of the girls, a young dark-haired beauty that reminded Mobius of Clemeta, now three thousand years dead, was busy applying glistening oil to his bare chest. He smiled beneath his hooded cowl, letting her fingers play exquisite sensations across his skin.

"You do that very well, my dear," came the muffled voice from beneath the brown hood. "Perhaps this

36

The Dark Realm

Bob Dvorak

evening you can show me what else you do well?"

"Whatever you wish, my Pharaoh," she smiled seductively and gently traced a pattern with her long fingernails.

"Of course."

One of the eunuch guards approached, bowing low and waiting to be recognized. Mobius let him wait, suddenly angry that his game had been interrupted. He watched as the guard strained to hold himself perfectly still, and marveled at the pain and stiffness that the eunuch must be experiencing. A few more seconds passed, then Mobius spoke.

"What is it?"

"The High Priest and the Chief General wish an audience with the Pharaoh," the eunuch stammered, obviously uncomfortable in Mobius' presence.

"They wish an audience, do they?" Mobius giggled, and the serving girls shivered — except for the one who looked like Clemeta. Mobius liked that.

"What is your name, girl?" he asked.

"What would you like it to be, master?"

He liked that as well. "You shall be called Clemeta. And you shall receive a wardrobe according your new station."

"New station, master?" she asked, her eyes suddenly wide with anticipation.

"You shall be Clemeta, the Royal Escort."

"Thank you, my master," she bowed and began kissing his sandaled feet.

He liked the feel of her full, wet lips upon his toes. "You may continue to do that, Clemeta." He sighed and rested his head against the back of the throne. Then he remembered the eunuch. "Oh yes. You may send in the Royal Advisors."

Ahkemeses, the High Priest, and Teth-Net, the Chief General, climbed the steps of the platform that overlooked the construction site and stood beneath the palm leaf covering that blocked out the sun. They ignored the young woman at Mobius' feet.

"What can I do for you this day?" Mobius asked.

"Hail Pharaoh Mobius! Hail the divine ruler of the Ten Empires!" Ahkemeses proclaimed.

"Yes, yes, I know who I am," Mobius said impatiently. "What news do you bring me?"

Teth-Net spoke first. "The axiom wash did its work very well, Pharaoh. Most of the Earthers have acclimated so well that they do not realize that their world was not always like it is now. The others have accepted the situation and look forward to your promises of glory in the new Egyptian empire."

"Yes, they are so gullible," Mobius laughed, "just like the other worlds before them."

"We are in the process of building our forces and spreading the stelae into new areas. The expansion will proceed as you planned."

"Good. Good," the Pharaoh said. "And what of our neighbors?"

"We are poised to take Libya, and our armies are preparing to strike out at Israel and Ethiopia."

"Fine," Mobius said. "Continue with the preparations. And what news do you have, High Priest?"

Ahkemeses stepped forward. "I have finished the calculations that you requested. This world is slowing down. If the current decline continues, then the Nile Empire will be plunged into eternal night long before we have taken the possibilities that we have come for."

"Then the Gaunt Man spoke true," Mobius muttered to himself. "That is all, my advisors. I have much work to do before the palace is completed."

As Ahkemeses and Teth-Net departed, Mobius signaled for Clemeta to rise from her work, though he regretted the loss of her lips and tongue upon his feet.

"Go to my head steward and tell him to help you prepare yourself for an evening of finery," Mobius gently ordered, letting his fingers linger in Clemeta's silky hair. "Tonight, Clemeta, you and I shall celebrate the establishment of the Tenth Empire. But first, I have some errands to attend to."

14

Christopher Bryce approached the room where Coyote, Rat and Tal Tu were resting. The boys had grown attached to the edeinos since the events at the canyon, and had seemed to adopt him in light of Rick Alder's death. Hopefully, that would make what he had to tell them easier — on them as well as on him.

"How are you feeling, Tal Tu?" Bryce asked.

The edeinos shrugged in his lizard way. "The wounds heal, but I am not ready to travel yet. Lanala will not answer my prayers of healing in this dead land. I have never remained hurt for so long, Christopher."

"I need you to do something for me, Tal Tu," Bryce started to explain. "And Coyote and Rat, too. Someone has to stay here and watch over Congressman Decker, and since Tal Tu can't travel anyway ..."

The edeinos lowered his spiny head. "I understand, Chris. I would be a burden on the journey you must make. But here, beside Decker, with my former Saar's tribes marching toward us to attack, I may be able to help. I will do as you ask."

Coyote stood up and glared at Bryce. Here it comes, the priest thought, the confrontation I expected. The teen moved closer.

"You want to leave us behind? After all the things we've been through together? Man, why didn't I see this coming?" Coyote's voice was full of anger and pain, full of rejection.

"Coyote, you and Rat are my friends. You saved my life. I am not deserting you. But we are going into the very heart of the evil that has come upon our world. I don't know what we'll face there, and I can't spend my time worrying about you."

"No, don't bother, Father," Coyote spat, "you don't have to worry about us any more."

"Coyote ...?" Rat began, but the older boy cut him off.

"Be quiet, Rat," Coyote ordered, "it's just us now. Like it used to be. Like it always was."

Coyote left the room. Rat hesitated a moment, then followed after his friend.

"He is angry, Christopher, head strong," Tal Tu said. "But he will come to understand your decision."

"Watch over them, Tal Tu," Bryce said. "And watch over Decker, too. They need you."

"I will do my best. But make sure you accomplish what you set out to do, and then come back to us, because we need you as well."

And then Tal Tu went to find the boys, leaving Bryce alone to contemplate the coming days.

15

"The colonel has certainly provided us with sound transport — even if it is a bit outdated," Mara exclaimed as the group approached the aircraft. Bryce still marveled at her childlike sense of wonder, and was constantly taken aback when she started spouting mathematical calculations and scientific theory.

"The colonel was very cooperative because of our affiliation with Decker," Bryce said. "Having presidential clearance sure has worked in our favor so far."

"Your president's power means nothing where we are going," Kurst declared.

Tolwyn studied the airplane with nervous trepidation. "This is another of the magical flying wagons?"

"It's a plane," Bryce said.

The warrior woman shook slightly, then steeled herself. "I will endure," she said, checking the dress saber that hung at her side. It was the blade Decker had given her, the blade that had belonged to his companion Teagle. The blade that had killed the Carredon.

From the far end of the hangar, Colonel McCall approached the four companions. He greeted them with a nod. "Are you sure I can't assign some men to you, Father Bryce?" he asked.

The priest shook his head. "You heard what happened to the men that started out with Congressman Decker. None of us want more deaths on our consciences. I really won't feel comfortable until we've been dropped off and your pilots are safely on their way back here. Besides, with the edeinos army marching toward you from the north, you'll need every able body you can find."

The Colonel agreed. "These are damn strange times, Father. There hasn't been any change in Decker, and I wish the doctors could figure out how to remove those daggers."

"Do not attempt to remove them, Colonel," Kurst explained. "To do so would immediately kill Decker, as well as the person performing the operation."

"You really feel that Congressman Decker's mission is best served by going to Australia?"

"Yes, Colonel," Bryce said, uncomfortable with his slight stretching of the truth. "The last information we came across pointed us to occurrences in the South Pacific."

"President Wells asked me to comply with Decker's associates, and that's what I've done. Good luck, Father, Kurst, ladies." Colonel McCall shook hands with the four, then stepped back to watch the plane exit.

Tolwyn removed the heart-shaped stone from her pack and handed it to Bryce. "You will carry this, Christopher." Then she entered the aircraft, followed by Mara and Kurst.

Bryce slipped the blue and red stone into his pocket and started up the steps. A familiar voice halted his progress, however, and he turned to see Tal Tu and the boys entering the hangar.

"Be careful, Father Bryce," Rat called.

"Take care of yourself, man," Coyote added. "And keep the women safe."

Bryce smiled, touched that the three had come to see them off. He raised his hand in farewell, then boarded the airplane.

16

Thratchen cautiously approached the great hall of Illmound Keep, responding to the Gaunt Man's summons as soon as he arrived back in Orrorsh realm. Thratchen was from the cosm of Tharkold, and once served as chief lieutenant to the High Lord of that techno-horror realm. But Tharkold suffered two recent defeats: one to Kadandra and the brat Mara, and one to the Soviet Union of Earth. Subsequently, the Tharkold realm was never attached to Earth. It could take his old master decades to regain the power necessary for another cosm raid.

But Thratchen was on Kadandra when that world destroyed the maelstrom bridges connecting the two cosms together. The Kadandrans used every bit of their cybernetic knowledge to build weapons of war to defeat the remaining Tharkold invaders—who the Kadandrans called Sims. Thratchen discovered that the reason for his master's defeat was that the Kadandrans were ready for their arrival. A young scientist — a child prodigy! — named Dr. Hachi Mara-Two had discovered the existence of the cosmverse, and her studies revealed the approach of the Sims.

Stranded alone on the hostile world, Thratchen tracked down the young woman, killing her friends and associates along the way. But Mara eluded him by actually stepping into the cosmverse and disappearing from Kadandra. She had gained this power of transportation by using the energy of stormers, and while Thratchen was enraged by her escape he was also intrigued by the possibility of gaining this new power for himself.

Using her own transference cylinder, Thratchen followed Mara to another cosm. And then came the cruelest turn of all. Mara had discovered their plan to raid Earth as well, and she sent herself to this cosm to aid its people. While that enraged Thratchen even more, it also made him more anxious to catch up with the stormer and pry her secrets from her. Once on Earth, however, she teamed up with other stormers and suddenly the possibilities stretched before Thratchen like an unending highway. He pledged his service to the Gaunt Man and went about ensuring the safety of Mara and her companions until both they and he could discover all of the implications of their burgeoning abilities.

He moved through the corridors of the keep at a steady pace, neither hurrying nor slowing. The great hall was ahead of him, its double doors opened slightly as if in wait for some intended prey. Two more paces closer, and then a large form stepped out of a shadowy alcove. Thratchen, startled by the near silent emergence, expanded his claws and dropped into a combat ready stance.

"Nervous?" the large form asked. It was Scythak, one of the Gaunt Man's hunters, and his tone had a definite mocking quality to it.

"Step aside, Scythak," Thratchen ordered. "I have business with the Gaunt Man."

"Yes, you do," the giant agreed. "I don't know what you've done, but the master has been in a dreadful rage. Perhaps when he's done with you, I'll be given your rank."

"Don't count on it, shapeshifter," Thratchen said as he shoved his way past. He could feel the glare of Scythak's eyes upon his back as he moved into the great hall. He shut the doors behind him.

The hall was dark this day. The heavy curtains were drawn tight, and only the dancing flames in the fireplace provided light. Sitting in a high-backed wicker chair was the Gaunt Man, flickering shadows played across his skeletal features. Across his knees rested his ever-present cane. It had a dragon-head top (the Carredon's head, actually, Thratchen noted), its jaws opened wide. Caught firmly in those jaws was a small blue and red stone — a piece of an eternity shard.

"You summoned me, master?" Thratchen asked, dropping to one knee and bowing his head before the being who claimed the title, Torg.

"I am disappointed, Thratchen," the Gaunt Man said, his voice like the fetid gust of an opening tomb. "I have felt the failures in Core Earth, but you must tell me the details."

Thratchen swallowed hard. He had to be careful with this game he played. His position was not as secure as he liked, and the wrong word or phrase could spell his destruction at the High Lord's hand.

"The Carredon is dead, my lord, killed by Tolwyn of Aysle and an Earth priest named Bryce," Thratchen explained. "Her sword and his use of an eternity shard were more than the dragon could withstand."

"I do not understand this!" the Gaunt Man raged, slapping the cane across his lap. "The Carredon has never failed, never even been seriously injured. Who is this woman that she frightens Uthorion and slays the Carredon? Who are these stormers that can use raw possibilities without the aid of a focus device?"

"Perhaps they do have a focus, master," Thratchen said quietly.

"Explain yourself."

"Perhaps they are able to focus the possibilities through themselves."

The Gaunt Man dismissed the notion with a wave of his elongated hand.

"There is more, High Lord," Thratchen continued. "Malcolm Kane is dead, as well. And the stormer from Kadandra still lives."

"What were you doing during all of this, Thratchen? Tell me why you survived so that I may kill you for your cowardice."

"I arrived too late to help either the Carredon or Kane," Thratchen lied. "All I could do was observe as the battle came to a conclusion. But the runes of never life and never death were placed within one of the stormers. The one called Decker, I believe."

"So, he must have refused my gracious offer," the Gaunt Man mused, obviously trying to sort through the recent events and all there possible consequences. "I shall enjoy studying his life as it enters my machine. But what of Kurst? What was his role in all of this?"

Thratchen thought for a moment, deciding on the best way to salvage the situation he found himself in. He decided that redirecting the Gaunt Man's anger could buy him the time he needed to finish his observations.

"I cannot be sure, since I arrived so late, but I believe that your hunter was helping the stormers," Thratchen finally said. "He shifted into wolf form and battled at their sides."

The fire that erupted in the Gaunt Man's eyes was more intense than the heat from the flaming hearth. When the High Lord spoke next, the tone caused a chill that effected even Thratchen's cyber implants.

"Leave me, Thratchen," he said with menace and implied destruction. "I must determine the next course of action. But know this: the stormers shall pay for these affronts. They shall pay with their very souls."

17

Julie Boot looked up, startled, and realized she had been dozing off in the muggy warmth of the Twentynine Palms Marine Hospital, baking as it was in the heat of the double-length day. Somewhere off, she heard the roar of a plane engine, which signaled the departure of the strange group that had arrived over a week ago. She eased her back from the stickiness of the chair, crinkling vinyl as she stood and stretched out the kinks of several hours straight work with a slow T'ai Chi routine. Nearby, lying still and deathlike on the bed, was Congressman Andrew Jackson Decker, who she had come to consider her patient, even though she was only a nurse and not a full-fledged doctor.

Decker's face was pale and gray, and his eyes were closed, the muscles flicking with little convulsions. A light cover was drawn up to his waist, crisp and white and still military clean, despite the emergency setup. But in his chest were the two staves of metal, glowing rods that resembled twin daggers thrust into his dying body.

He probably should have been in ICU, but the beds were full and his companions had flown him all the way from the Grand Canyon without killing him. The tall one, Tolwyn her name was, had said something about his not being able to die, even if he had wished. "The runes," she had said, pointing to the shafts in Decker's chest. "He will never die; he will never live." Then she had said no more, until the priest, the only unwounded one among them beside the teen, had gone to comfort her.

So they had taken a chance and put him in a regular room, and either she or a doctor or one of the companions had had him under observation since he was brought in, the metal staves glowing obscenely in his body like electric eels feeding at carrion.

Julie crossed to the window, looking out over the compound and beyond, north to where one of the local marine units was even now driving back an invading army. They'd been doing well, but just lately, as though the attackers were running out of momentum after their incredible initial surge. Julie shuddered, squinting into the ash-dimmed sun as if she could see a hundred miles and judge the marines' progress. She'd seen some of the attackers — nightmare creatures out of a museum, bipedal dinosaurs and ape-men and other things too horrible to name. She shuddered again, remembering that one of the invaders had arrived with Decker and was now a guest of the base. Tal Tu, the companions called him, and the lizard man actually used human speech.

She checked on Decker again, but of course there was no change. She gazed at him for a long time, something about him troubling her aside from the obvious facts of his injuries; something about the set of his face, the feelings emanating from him. Even in his coma-like sleep, he was handsome and dashing looking, but there was something ... a sadness, a pain that was not related to his wound. It was etched in his face as if by long years of use, like laugh-lines that ran in the wrong direction.

Decker's eyelids pulsed, the eyeballs moving quickly back and forth in REM, Rapid Eye Movement, a type of sleep that indicated the dream state. She wondered what a man who was dead and not dead could be dreaming of.

18

Andrew Jackson Decker dreamed he was walking along a beach, listening to the waves wash against the shore. He knew he was dreaming, but it was the most realistic dream he could ever remember having — very much like his dreams of the Heart of Coyote. With every step he took, he felt the sand shift beneath his shoes, felt the salty spray of the ocean upon his face. And still he walked, choosing to climb one dune or to go around another, content to simply let the dream run its course.

He reached the top of the next dune and paused, tilting his head back to catch the sun. The warmth felt good against his cheeks and forehead, and he closed his eyes and sighed. But his reverie was short lived, for a strange voice broke through the calm.

"Come, come, Mr. Decker," said the accented voice. It reminded Decker of a British accent, but there was an undercurrent of some older, darker brogue. "You've made scores of choices to get to this beach, and now the true work must begin."

The voice belonged to a man sitting in the sand some few yards off. He wore a Puritan-style coat and shoulder cape, and a wide-brimmed hat rested on his head. His outfit was totally black, and Decker wondered how he could stand the heat in such garb. Then he remembered this was a dream, and that made the scene more understandable. As Decker walked closer, the dark-cloaked man stood up. He was skeletal thin and very tall, and he grinned evilly from the shadows beneath his hat. He carried a walking stick with an ornate head carved in the shape of the Carredon, the creature that had wounded Decker and caused him to be trapped in this unending dream.

"How can you wear such clothing in this heat?" Decker asked.

"Heat does not concern me, Mr. Decker," the tall man replied, twirling the cane so that the congressman could see the blue and red stone that the carved Carredon held in its open maw.

"What does concern you, mister ...?"

"Lord Byron Salisbury, Earl of Waterford," the tall man said, mocking Decker with a slight bow. "That is one of the names I am known by. Others call me the Gaunt Man. But you may refer to me by my newest title."

"And that is?"

"I am the Torg."

"A unique title. I'm surprised my mind conjured up such an image for this dream. When the Carredon mentioned you I pictured someone much … different."

"This is a dream, stormer," the Gaunt Man laughed, "but it operates by my rules, not by the feeble workings of your paltry mind."

Decker didn't like the direction this dream was taking. He tried to conjure up a different setting, but the scene refused to change.

"You should have accepted my offer, stormer," the Gaunt Man declared. "Instead, you chose the runes."

The Gaunt Man gestured and Decker looked down. Twin staves of metal jutted from his chest, and he remembered the last moments of his battle with the Carredon. There was no pain associated with the staves, only a draining feeling as though they were letting something slowly leak out of him.

"Those make you mine," the Gaunt Man continued, obviously pleased with Decker's sudden discomfort. "They connect you to a very important device of my own creation. A machine that sorts possible outcomes for later use. Much too technical for you, I'm sure. But with those staves, you become an integral cog in the mechanism. Behold!"

The Gaunt Man nodded toward the beach that stretched past the dune. As he did so, dozens upon dozens of doorways appeared. The doorways looked out of place without any walls, just standing in unorganized rows along the sand. But they beckoned to Decker, taunting him with their hidden secrets. Open us, they seemed to say. See what lies beyond our closed doors.

"They call to you, Decker," the Gaunt Man teased.

"Each door wants you to choose it over the one standing beside it. As for me, I really don't care which of them you open. Just as long as you do open one."

Decker tried to hold himself in check, tried to turn away and walk back across the beach. But his legs stepped forward and his hand shot out to grasp a door knob.

"Yes, Decker," the Gaunt Man laughed. "Yes, stormer. Choose!"

And Decker swung the door he chose wide.

And the dream of choices continued.

19

James Monroe stepped off the bus into the heat of a Californian desert. Even with the ash cover, the temperature was soaring. Along with the rest of the passengers, Monroe was directed toward a long, one-story building. He hoped the air conditioning was working.

He was a tall man, on the young side of forty, and he had left his home in Philadelphia to escape the invaders that had taken New York. But it was just his luck that his flight had been one of the last commercial planes allowed to land in San Bernadino before air traffic had been prohibited. Now he found himself in the Mojove Desert, impressed into military service on a base not all that far from where the same invaders were attacking in the west.

He glanced around at the other people that had ridden with him, all professionals from a dozen different fields. But he hadn't gotten to know any of them during the brief indoctrination and the drive into the desert. He had other things on his mind.

Specifically, his thoughts kept returning to a woman

with emerald eyes.

Monroe entered the building, relishing the brief burst of cold air as it hit his skin. But the relief it provided didn't last long. While the interior was cooler than outside, it was far from comfortable. Even military air conditioners designed for use in the desert couldn't keep up with the simmering heat. He stood for a moment, looking around the large room that had been converted into a reception area, when a uniformed soldier with a clipboard approached him.

"Your name, sir?" the soldier asked.

"Monroe. James Monroe."

The soldier scanned the list on his clipboard, then made a check mark with his pen.

"Welcome to Twentynine Palms Marine Corps Air Ground Combat Center, Dr. Monroe," the soldier said. "Your personal belongings will be transferred to your sleeping quarters. Is there anything I can do for you?"

"Yes, you could get me a ticket on the next plane out of this war zone," Monroe said, hoping that he was making it clear how much he detested being here.

The soldier ignored the sarcasm and calmly replied, "Twentynine Palms isn't in the war zone, Dr. Monroe. It is being used as a staging area and as a backup hospital, however."

"Look …" Monroe started to say, but a woman was suddenly standing beside them, clearing her throat. She wasn't decked out in full uniform, like the soldier. Instead she wore a green T-shirt and pants to ward off some of the heat. Her brown hair was cut short, and she was pretty in a frazzled sort of way.

"Private, did I hear you say this gentleman is Dr. James Monroe?" she asked the soldier with the clipboard.

The soldier saluted. "Yes, Major Boot."

"Doctor, if you'll follow me ...?" the woman asked, but her tone indicated that it was an order.

Monroe nodded to the soldier and followed the woman. She led him back out into the heat and across the compound to another building. When she opened the door to the building, Monroe was assaulted by the familiar smell of antiseptics that marked all hospitals the world over.

"Funny, you don't look like a major," he said at last.

"That's all right. Drenched in sweat, you don't exactly look like a Philadelphia doctor," she shot back casually. Monroe liked that.

She stopped in front of a door and gestured for Monroe to enter. He looked at her questioningly.

"The locker room and showers, doctor," she sighed, somewhat perturbed that she had to explain it to him. "Get cleaned up. Then I'll take you to meet your patient."

He started through the door, then paused. "You're putting me to work already?"

"Dr. Monroe, there is a war going on out there."

He started forward again, then turned to her once more. "I don't even know who you are."

"Major Julie Boot," she introduced herself, "head nurse of this facility. Now please, doctor, go get ready."

20

Dr. Hachi Mara-Two was in the cockpit of the transport, watching the pilots manipulate controls. She had a learning chip in one of the slots beneath her ear. It was recording every movement the pilots made so that she would have a textbook to refer to later. Or she could download the data during sleep to facilitate learning. Probably, Mara thought, she would do both.

She asked a question, and the copilot answered her.

As she listened, her hand went to the data plate in the pocket of her jumpsuit. On the plate were microcircuits filled with her memories, images of the world she left behind. Plugging in the chip allowed her to ease her homesickness for a time, and adding memories to it kept her occupied during lulls in their activity. But there was no lull now.

"Might I try?" Mara asked.

The pilots glanced at each other, shrugged. Then the copilot rose and offered his seat to the teen.

"Well, little lady," the pilot said, "if you can fly half as good as you know the theories behind it, you shouldn't have any problem."

Mara smiled. Data flowed across the inside of her eye, calling up details she had recorded earlier. Then Mara did as the pilot had done …

… and the plane jerked and bucked like an ornery animal. Mara's eyes went wide. She had done just as the pilot had. She replayed the data and tried again. And the plane jerked again.

"You can't just imitate me," the pilot explained. "Flying requires the right touch as well. Here, try this."

The cabin door swung open and Father Bryce pushed his way into the cockpit. His face was red and sweat had gathered on his bald forehead. He looked nervous, and his voice was filled with anxiety.

"Who's driving this contraption?" he shouted. He saw Mara seated at the controls, and she smiled at him. The red left his cheeks and he paled considerably.

"I should have guessed," he moaned. "Do you have any idea what you're doing?"

Mara began to say something, but the priest waved her off.

"No, don't answer that," he sighed. "There are some

things I'm better off not knowing."

21

Monroe let the water wash over him, rinsing away the day's sweat and grime. It would return, of course. The heat would see to that. But for the moment, the cool water felt good against his skin. He knew that Major Boot was waiting for him, but he allowed himself a few seconds more under the shower spray.

As he washed, he thought back to his last days in Philadelphia, to a scene that was forever etched in his memory. It was just a few days after New York had gone silent. Refugees were pouring in, and the hospitals had called in every available doctor to work the emergency rooms — even the high-priced specialists like himself. He was in the ER in fact when the cop and priest wheeled in the young woman.

She had been hit by a car and was in very bad shape. He remembered fighting to save her life, remembered the pang of defeat and sadness as that life slipped away. The monitors flatlined. He lost her. Then the priest was shouting at the woman, telling her to live. He tried to calm the man, tried to help him cope with his grief.

And then the monitor resumed its normal pattern of beeps and the woman sat up. Most of the damage he noted was gone, and what few cuts remained were healing rapidly. To this day, Monroe had no explanation for what happened. He supposed it could have been a miracle. Perhaps the priest's prayers had been answered.

But there were some strange events related to the incident. The young woman, whose driver's license identified her as brown-eyed Wendy Miller, claimed her name was Tolwyn of House Tancred. And her eyes were a sparkling emerald green.

The hospital officials released her before he could finish all his tests, claiming that she was healthy and they needed the bed space for those who weren't. She left then, off to chase the dream she had spoken of to everyone who would listen. The priest went with her, of course, and the cop. But Monroe could not get her out of his mind, and he left Philadelphia shortly after they did.

He turned the faucets and cut the flow of water to the shower. Once he stepped out of the stall, he would again be dealing with life and death. He wondered what he would discover this time.

22

Major Julie Boot was waiting when Monroe emerged from the locker room. While it was evident he had cleaned himself up, she could see the heat already beginning to work on him anew.

"Look at this," he complained. "I'm sweating again."

"Come on, doctor," she said, grabbing his arm and leading him down the corridor. "It's time to meet your first patient."

She led him to a private room, and she noted his surprise when he saw that there was only one patient within. He walked over and stood at the foot of the bed, not asking any questions, not examining the chart. He only stood there, staring at the staves that jutted from the patient's chest, then glancing at the patient's face. After a time, the doctor walked over to the chair that rested in the corner and collapsed heavily into it. His head dropped into his hands and Julie could hear him sigh.

"Doctor, is something wrong? Aren't you even going to look at his chart?" she asked.

The doctor looked up, and his eyes had a hollow cast

to them. "I can't take this case, Major."

"Excuse me?"

"I think my words were clear," he said. "I cannot work on this patient."

"And why not, doctor?"

Monroe stood and walked back over to the bed. He had grown weary since entering this room, and his shoulders sagged noticeably. She felt pain coming from him, an unspoken sorrow that she didn't understand. Finally, he spoke.

"He's my brother."

23

Bryce marveled! True, he had been nervous at first, but his long love affair with flying finally overcame his trepidation at seeing young Mara at the throttle. (And it didn't hurt that she had gotten the hang of it — at least somewhat — and the plane was no longer responding like a bucking bronco.)

Flying was one of those things, he believed, that a person just can't get enough of. Like a great-tasting meal: even if you numbed your taste buds by too much indulgence, all you had to do was stop for a while and let your nerves recharge. Then you could go right back and eat some more, and enjoy it just as much as that wonderful first bite. How some people could be frightened by being up in the air he didn't understand. That kind of thinking was alien to his nature, to his inborn curiosity.

It was a thrill being in the cockpit. For Bryce, it was a boyhood thing, a dream of sorts — all those switches, dials, lights and power bars waiting to be flicked, read, noticed and adjusted. It was so ... exciting! And then there was Mara.

No, thought Bryce, excuse me, Dr. Hachi Mara-Two. The longer he knew her, the more the name really seemed to fit the sixteen-year-old girl who sat so determinedly in the copilot's seat, reaching up and down, flicking switches and tapping dials like a seasoned pro. Bryce grinned and left the cabin, marveling at the contradiction in teen's clothing.

Even with the loss of Alder and Decker, and with having to leave Coyote, Rat and Tal Tu back in California, Bryce figured they were in better shape then they had been when they departed Philadelphia. They now had a destination. They had transportation. They had pilots. And with any luck they had contacts waiting for them in Australia. It was amazing what kind of clout Congressman Decker had provided them with. Bryce sobered when he thought of Decker and his plight. Offering up a brief prayer, he followed it with a quick thought to Decker. "Hold on," he thought hard, trying to send the message by willpower alone. "We're on our way to help you."

In the cabin, Bryce noted that Tolwyn had finally pried herself away from the window and had fallen asleep in her seat. Once she got over her initial fear of "the magic flying wagon," she became enraptured of the view outside. Now, however, after countless hours in the air, she let rest take her mind and body. Like a child, she looked beautiful in sleep. The usual hardness left her features for a little while. Even the mottled bruises left by the Carredon could not hide her innate loveliness, and the patch on her forehead made her look dashing. She was radiant in repose.

Kurst, on the other hand, was in sleep as he was awake, his body coiled and ready to spring at the slightest sound. There was something about the man that disturbed Bryce, and only a little of it had to do with the fact that Kurst was a werewolf. But the priest couldn't make a list or put his finger on exactly which of Kurst's traits bothered him. Perhaps it was his lack of comradery, or his secrecy, or the way he seemed to watch everyone and everything.

Suddenly his good mood was gone, and Bryce sat down heavily in one of the vacant seats. He missed the others — Alder, Coyote, Rat, Tal Tu. They had been with him from the beginning, and now it seemed unfair and wrong that they were not with him now. Instead, it was just Father Christopher Bryce as the representative of Earth, traveling along with three people from other — cosms was the word Mara used. With dark thoughts troubling his mind, Bryce drifted off to sleep.

24

President Jonathan Wells sat in his office in Houston, Texas, trying to get comfortable in his new surroundings. It still bothered him that he had to order the evacuation of Washington, D.C. They ran, and there was only one excuse for it. Wells tried not to dwell on the fact that the lizards had beaten them, at least temporarily. He sighed. They were in the worst period of American history, with actual invaders on American soil, and it fell to Jonathan Wells to keep the country alive. He wished he was someone else right now.

But he wasn't, and as president he had a job to do. He shuffled through the piles of paper on his desk, dismissing each in turn as he scanned for those items that needed his immediate attention. A dispatch from Twentynine Palms caused him to pause. It was from Colonel Arthur McCall, informing the president that there had been no change in Congressman Decker's condition. In addition, the group that accompanied Decker had departed for Australia aboard a military transport, as per the president's request.

"What happened to you, Ace?" Wells thought. "Did you find the Heart of Coyote? Are those companions you told me about even now rushing to use it to save the world?"

It sounded so far-fetched to believe that a few people and a blue and red stone could make any difference, but something deep inside Wells told him they could. He remembered his recurring dream, the one that forced him to send Decker on his fatal quest. Wells would have gone himself — if he had been younger, if he didn't have the responsibilities of the country weighing him down.

He looked at the report again, going over the details of Decker's condition. Wells decided that he had to know what was going on. He had to see Ace for himself. Perhaps then some of this would start to make sense. He placed the dispatch carefully into his "In" basket, then continued shuffling.

The next document that drew his attention was an Executive Order awaiting his signature. Wells read the words and felt rage building within him. The order, once signed, would grant the Delphi Council the ability to raise its own army. Yes, the document called them agents, but the intent between the lines spoke of the need for power that was answerable directly to the new agency.

Perhaps he had been wrong to establish the Delphi Council. Already the so-called think tank had recruited some of the most formidable scientists, politicians, and military personnel in the country. It was churning out policies and plans to be implemented in case of any contingency. And while the council was supposed to report directly to the president, much of the time it was handled directly by Vice President Dennis Quartermain. What policies had been passed by Wells seemed extreme, but not out of the question considering the state of the nation. But the council would have to be monitored more closely.

He placed the document into the basket as well. He would have to talk about that piece of paper with Ellen Conners, one time senator who now headed the Delphi Council. He didn't relish that talk. Wells reached for another stack of papers to sort when a knock sounded at the door. Startled, Wells almost dropped the papers.

"Come in," he called as he carefully set the documents down.

The door swung open and Dennis Quartermain entered the room. "John," the Vice President asked, "have you signed that document I left with you this morning?"

"Not yet, Dennis," Wells replied. "Is there anything else? I am rather busy."

Quartermain ignored the brusque tone in Wells' voice. "There is someone outside to see you, but ..."

"Since when did you take on the duties of my secretary?" Wells asked as he stood up. "Who's out there?"

Before Quartermain could answer, a figure filled the doorway. He was rough looking, tough. Not the sort commonly seen associating with someone in Wells' position. He wore a leather jacket, dark glasses, and a three-day-old beard.

"You sent for me?" the man spoke, his voice strong and solid.

"Come in, Quin," Wells called, trying to sound friendly. "I'm glad you could make it. It's been a long time."

"Not long enough," the man named Quin said as he pushed past the Vice President.

"Are you going to introduce us?" Quartermain asked at last.

"No, Dennis, I'm not," Wells replied. "In fact, you never saw this gentleman. Now leave, I have work to do."

Rage flared in Quartermain's eyes, but he held himself in check. He glared at Wells for a moment, then turned and left the room, closing the door behind him.

"That man doesn't like you, John," Quin said.

"The feeling is mutual," Wells said. "But he does his job and he does it well. Enough of him. How are you, Quin?"

Quin Sebastian, soldier of fortune, slid onto the fine leather couch across from Wells' desk. He propped his hands behind his head and leaned back comfortably.

"I'm here, and I still don't know why. You know, I don't work for you or for the government anymore."

"Let me make a call, and then we can get down to business," Wells said as he lifted the telephone receiver. "Get me General Powell."

25

"Your brother?" Julie Boot shouted. "What do you mean he's your brother?" But as she asked the question, she knew that it was true. Monroe had the same features, the same eyes. He was younger than the congressman, not as tall. But there was definitely a resemblance.

"My name used to be James Monroe Decker. I had it legally changed," Monroe said, not looking at Julie as he spoke. "A good joke my parents had, naming us after presidents. I wonder what they would have named a daughter had they had one. Betsy Ross Decker?"

"Why ...?" But he didn't let Julie finish.

"Why didn't I keep the name? I had a falling out with my family at an early age. Ace was the shining star, the apple of my parents' eyes. He excelled at everything he did. All I ever heard was why couldn't I be more like Ace, and look at what Ace accomplished today."

There was bitterness in Monroe's voice, and sorrow. But Julie couldn't decide which was the prevailing emotion.

"I didn't come home from college when my parents died, and I think that was the straw that finally made Ace accept my absence. I didn't go to see him play pro ball. I didn't attend his wedding. I never even acknowledged that he was my brother." Monroe laughed then, but there was no humor in the sound. "My brother the congressman!"

He got up and walked over to the bed. Decker was lying still. Only the constant beep of the monitors and the slight rise and fall of his chest showed that he still lived. "I was a bastard," Monroe continued. "God, I hated Ace. He was so ... perfect. But for all of my snubs, he showed up at my graduation from medical school. We didn't talk. But I saw him standing at the back of the auditorium, watching me. His wife died a few weeks ago, just before the storms began. I didn't go to the funeral. I never even met her."

Julie came and stood beside Monroe, placing her hand gently on his arm. "You've got to help him, Dr. Monroe. You're the best chance he has right now. I've read your file. You're a brilliant surgeon."

Monroe looked at her, catching her with his steady gaze. "I'm the best. Okay, let's examine the patient."

Julie smiled. "I knew you'd come around."

"Just remember," he said, seriousness creeping back into his voice, "my name is Monroe, not Decker."

26

Angus Cage tracked his quarry through the twisting tunnels beneath the temple, confident that he would catch him before long. Cage was a bounty hunter and a hero of sorts on Terra, the cosm that had produced the villainous Dr. Mobius. It was five years ago that Cage had battled Mobius in this very temple. Five years ago that Mobius fell into a seemingly bottomless pit, ending his threat to Terra forever. But there were other villains, like the one Cage tracked now.

Purple Haze was a second-rate crook with a flashy gizmo that provided him with a fog screen. It wasn't the most powerful weapon, but it helped the Haze slip out of his grasp on more occasions than he cared to remember. This hunt, he promised, would be the last.

Cage checked his own weapon, making sure his tommy-gun's ammo drum was snapped in. He adjusted his hat so it sat low over his eyes. Then he stopped to listen. There was talking coming from up ahead. From the sounds, Purple Haze wasn't alone. Great, thought Cage. Why do these little adventures always wind up getting complicated?

He proceeded cautiously, expecting a trap around every bend. His nerves tensed when each turn produced nothing more threatening then clinging cobwebs. The voices were louder now, as though the speakers didn't care who heard them. Up ahead was a lighted opening. That's where the voices were coming from. Well, Angus, he thought, you always wanted to go out in a blaze of glory. This could be your big chance.

Steeling himself with a couple of deep breaths, Angus

The Dark Realm

Bob Dvorak

Cage leaped through the portal and into a large chamber. The chamber, he noted, was full of costumed characters — including many that Cage had met and dealt with over the years. He lowered his tommy-gun, shifted his hat back, and cleared his throat.

The costumed men and women stopped talking and turned to regard Cage. He smiled.

"That's better," Cage said. "Now, does someone want to tell me what the hell is going on in here?"

An elderly gentleman stepped forward. Standing beside him was a man in a long, dark coat who wore a dark blue mask and carried a diamond-tipped cane. Cage knew both of them — Dr. Alexus Frest and the Guardian.

"Ah, I'm glad you're here Angus," Dr. Frest said in his frail, aged voice. "We've been trying to contact you for the past few weeks."

"I've been busy," Cage replied. "As a matter of fact, I was just finishing a job when I happened upon your little gathering. Anybody seen a nasty little villain named Purple Haze run through here?"

The Guardian snapped his fingers and the crowd parted. There, held fast between a Rocket Ranger and a gadget hero, was Purple Haze.

"This isn't fair, Cage!" Haze screamed. "You tricked me! You had all these heroes waiting for me! Scared to face me on your own, huh?"

Cage ignored Purple Haze, turning to Dr. Frest. He and the scientist went way back. Frest had been forced by Dr. Mobius to construct the gizmos that made Mobius so formidable. Forced by threat of harm to his family — a wife and daughter that Mobius had spirited away as insurance of Frest's cooperation. It was ten years ago that the Guardian rescued Frest's family, allowing the scientist to finally turn against his villainous master.

"I'll ask again, Frest," Cage said. "What's going on?"

"Mobius is not dead, Angus." Frest's words cut through Cage's rough exterior, striking his heart like cold ice. "All those gadgets and weapons he forced me to construct over the years, they were never meant for use against Terra. Mobius has left our world and is even now attempting to conquer other worlds."

"I don't understand ..." Cage stammered.

"I have located him on another world, Angus," Frest emphasized. "He has left our planet to spread his evil elsewhere. And what evil it is! He has destroyed at least six worlds over his thirty-year career. But we have him now!"

Cage looked around at all the costumed heroes. These were the Mystery Men, as the tabloids called them, the heroes that fought to keep the world safe from the madmen like Mobius. In fact, each of the men and women here had battled Mobius at one time or another.

"What are you planning to do, Alexus?" Cage asked softly.

"That is what I am here to explain, Angus."

The Guardian helped Frest up onto a large crate so that the scientist could be seen by everyone in the chamber. Then he addressed his audience.

"My friends," Frest began. "For years I toiled in the labor of the villain Mobius, helping him gather wealth and power. It was always my impression that I was helping Mobius further his plans on Terra, but I was wrong. Records we found in this very temple, hidden in a secret chamber, reveal that Mobius is in possession of a device that allows him to travel to other dimensions! And he is using this device to conquer these dimensions with impunity. We have all fought against Dr. Mobius at some point in our careers, and we have all failed to stop him. So, we each must share a portion of the blame for what has befallen these innocent worlds."

A murmuring started, quickly spreading through the chamber. The Guardian tapped his cane on the stone floor three time, loudly cutting through the noise. The chamber fell silent again.

"I have devised our own way to travel to this newest dimension," Frest continued. "But the systems are fragile, untested. At best, this will be a one-way trip. I'm not sure if I can duplicate the process once we reach this new world."

"Why us?" called a woman Cage recognized as Miss Freedom.

"Because," the Guardian answered, "someone has to do it. Afraid you can't cut it, lady?"

"No one is required to make this trip," Frest interrupted quickly. "But those of you who do decide to accompany us must make a pledge. That is my only request."

"What kind of pledge?" Cage asked as he weighed his options.

Dr. Frest stood as straight as he could, and his voice rang out with a power it never had before. "We, the Mystery Men of Terra, must pledge ourselves to each other and to our quest. We must fight to end Mobius' reign of terror, even at the cost of our own lives!"

Cage glanced from side to side, noting that while not all of those present had raised their hands, more than half of them did. He added his own to the group and let his voice join the others.

"We, the Mystery Men of Terra, do pledge ourselves to each other and to our quest. We will fight to end Mobius' reign of terror, even at the cost of our own lives!"

Dr. Frest smiled. "Help me down, my boy," he said to Cage. Cage did so, then followed the scientist over to a weird machine.

The machine was all controls and dials, connected to a frame that was attached to one wall of the chamber. When Frest threw a switch, blue and red light filled the inside of the frame.

"This is our gate to another world," Frest called above the hum of the machine. "Step through while you can, before the machine burns out and the gate closes."

Not waiting to see if anyone else was coming, the Guardian stepped into the light and disappeared. With a shrug Cage followed him, letting the light engulf him in its crackling embrace.

27

"Very good, Mara," the pilot said. "Very, very good."

Mara was pleased herself. She was finally handling the plane on her own, not through repetition via chip replay. Forced-learning drugs, administered to her throughout her days in school, made her mind more susceptible to new ideas and processes. She laughed out loud with the sheer joy of flight.

"That's Australia down there, so we'll have to start our approach," the copilot explained.

"I guess that means you want me to get up, huh?" Mara asked. The copilot nodded, and Mara slid out of the seat.

"H.M.A.S. Nirimba, do you copy?" the pilot said into his headset, trying to raise the control tower that would guide him into Australia.

A voice came back over the radio, welcoming them to Australian airspace and giving them heading directions.

Mara took it all in, trying to digest everything at once as her internal computer recorded the scene. But her joyous mood was cut short when she saw what was happening outside the cockpit. The dark ash clouds had been with them since they left California, but now a small storm was forming in front of the plane. Black clouds swirled together, connected by flashing lightning. Driving rain pelted the windshield, and then the plane was submerged in the dark cloud.

"What's going on?" she shouted above the static that had replaced the control tower voice on the radio.

"Damndest storm I've ever seen," the pilot called back. Then he cried out, "My God!"

On the other side of the window, out of the rain and swirling mist emerged two vaguely human shapes. Banshees! Mara thought. Like the monsters the Sims threw at us on Kadandra! These banshees were ghostly, with long, flowing hair that framed their heads, and transparent torsos which faded away below their stomachs. They raised spectral arms and floated toward the windshield, apparently intent on crashing into the plane — or through it.

For a moment fear gripped at Mara's heart, and she backed away from the horrors. But as the banshees slid through the windshield and into the plane, she shook off the paralyzation and moved forward. She wasn't fast enough, however, to save the pilots. The banshees reached into the pilots' chests with incorporeal fingers, opening their spectral mouths wide to let loose their screams.

Mara fell back, rocked by the supernatural sound. The pilots own screams joined that of the banshees, and Mara could only watch as the men began to wither and die. She watched their life force drain away, a thin mist leaving their mouths and entering the banshees. With each departing breath, the pilots became thinner, more corpselike. The banshees, in contrast, became fuller, less vague.

The door behind Mara swung open and Father Bryce was there. "Sweet Jesus," he muttered. The banshees stopped their death call as the pilots collapsed into dust and bone in their seats. Then they turned toward Bryce and Mara, their hands outstretched to deliver another death-cold touch. Mara, still weak from the effects of the previous scream, could barely get her body to move. But Bryce was there, brandishing his cross before him to intercept the ghostly hand.

The banshee kept sliding forward, reaching out to touch Bryce's cross. Upon contact there was a flash of blinding light, and the banshee screamed. But this was not a death call so much as a scream of pain. The light rolled from the cross and up the banshee's arm, disintegrating the spirit as it traveled. In seconds, one of the creatures was destroyed. The other, more cautious now, held its distance and regarded the priest warily.

"Banish the monster, Chris," Mara demanded as she weakly unholstered her laser pistol. "Do it before it can scream again."

Bryce thrust his holy symbol at the spirit, trying to put as much faith as he could muster into the act. The banshee darted back and forth, remaining out of Bryce's reach. It opened its mouth wide, and fetid breath filled the cockpit. Then it screamed.

The blast of sound was like an icy wind. It knocked the priest back, stunning him, causing him to drop his cross. The banshee drifted forward, ready to finish off Bryce. Mara started to rise, hoping to place herself between the monster and the priest, but a strong hand gripped her shoulder and pushed her back down.

"No weapon you have can stop a banshee, girl," Kurst growled. "The priest is on his own. If he fails, we are all dead."

"If I don't get to those controls," Mara reminded him, "then we're dead anyway."

28

Dr. James Monroe entered the operating room. His patient, Congressman Andrew Jackson "Ace" Decker, had been prepped and Monroe had examined the X-rays. The strange metal staves produced a shadow on the film that made it hard to see detail, but it appeared that they weren't lodged too deeply in Decker's chest. When Monroe physically examined the pieces of metal, he was intrigued by the arcane symbols carved into them, and by the weird patterns of light that ran along the staves. But more so, he was confused by the lack of blood, by the cleanness of the wounds. The staves simply appeared to have passed through Decker's flesh without puncturing it. The strangeness of the whole case bothered Monroe's logical mind, reminding him of his mental struggles with the Miller/Tolwyn case.

Monroe acknowledged the attendants with a curt nod. There were two nurses, Major Boot, and a doctor who was a general practitioner. All had their surgical masks in place.

"Is everybody ready?" Monroe asked lightly.

"I don't think we should try this, doctor," the general practitioner said. "His friends repeatedly warned me against trying to remove the staves. They said it could kill him."

Monroe turned his strong gaze on the general practitioner. "Were any of these friends doctors, doctor?

Were any of them a surgeon with my qualifications? I can see why they wouldn't want you to attempt this, but surgery is what I do. Now, either take your place to assist me, or get out of my operating room."

The GP stood indecisively for a moment, then he lowered his head and took his place beside the operating table. Monroe nodded.

"Good," he said. "Unless anyone else has any problems, let's get this operation over and done with."

Monroe began with a simple clamp assembly, attaching it to one of the staves. He applied pressure, but the staff refused to budge. "Must be lodged in the rib," he reasoned. "We'll have to open him up."

He asked for a knife, and Julie handed him one. She had moved in to replace the nurse as soon as the operation became more complicated. She dabbed Monroe's forehead with a cool sponge, wiping away beads of sweat before they could fall into his eyes. Then he lowered the blade to Decker's chest.

As the gleaming tip touched the patient's skin, Monroe screamed. Fire leaped from the glowing staves into the knife and up, engulfing Monroe in burning agony. He fell back, vaguely aware that the lights in the operating room were exploding. Julie used her own body to protect the patient as glass shards rained down. There was an electric screaming that seemed to come from every piece of machinery in the room at once. It mingled with Monroe's own scream.

He dropped to his knees, sure that the fire had melted away his flesh and was now working on his nerves as it ate toward his bones. The fire crawled over him like a thing alive, bubbling the soft tissue so that he could smell himself cooking. He closed his eyes and screamed again, praying for death to take him so that he didn't have to suffer any more of this pain.

He wasn't sure how long he went on screaming, but a gentle hand finally roused him from his pain. Julie was standing beside him. There was worry in her eyes. He blinked, realizing that the pain had stopped and the fire was gone. He carefully looked at his hand and saw that his flesh was whole, unscarred.

"Decker?" he managed to ask.

"No change," Julie answered.

"Then let's get him back to his room," Monroe said. "I've got to think about this before we resume the operation."

29

Andrew Jackson Decker's dream of choices continued. He walked through another door and found himself in a barren field of crumbled rock. Next to him, standing where only a second ago nothing stood, was the Gaunt Man.

"I'm getting tired of this dream," Decker said, kicking a stone across the field.

"But it has only just begun, stormer," the Gaunt Man laughed. "And I must say, you are doing extremely well."

"Doing?" Decker asked. "What am I doing?"

Before the Gaunt Man could answer, a burst of flame erupted from Decker's chest — from the metal staves, actually — flashing brightly before it dissipated into the air.

"I see someone tried to remove the rune staves," the Gaunt Man said. Decker turned to him, concern etched deeply in his face. "Oh, don't worry," the Gaunt Man said with a dismissing wave of his thin-fingered hand. "They would need to rip them out of you before any harm would befall your body. The person who attempted the action, however, may not be so lucky."

"What are you after?" Decker demanded. "What do you want with me?"

The Gaunt Man gestured and more doorways appeared in the barren field. "I need your choices," he explained. "I need you to distinguish one possible event from another. Take this field for example. In mere minutes the ground will start to shake, fissures will appear, and you will more than likely be swallowed into a deep, rumbling pit. Unless, of course, you choose which door does not have this outcome behind it."

Decker couldn't believe it. He was stuck in a dream obeying the dictates of a madman! No, he decided, I will not let my subconscious mind turn me into someone's slave!

"Make your own decision," Decker shouted above the rising wind. Somewhere in the distance a deep rumbling began to build. It rolled like a wave beneath the ground, shaking the landscape as it passed by.

"Very well, Mr. Decker, this is your dream," the Gaunt Man said, straightening his long coat and adjusting his wide-brimmed hat. "If you have no regard for your own life, who am I to tell you differently?"

The Gaunt Man started to walk away as the ground shook and cracked wide. Long crevices split open, releasing foul, long-trapped vapors into the air. Decker lost his footing and hit the shaking ground hard. He remained that way for long seconds, trying to regain his breath. When he did move, a fissure opened in the place he departed.

On his feet again, Decker watched as the Gaunt Man walked across the field as though the ground was not shaking violently. Decker, meanwhile, was doing everything he could to stay upright and avoid the ever-widening cracks. He turned back to the doors. Already a number of them had been knocked down or swallowed into the dirt. If he didn't move soon, he wouldn't have any choices left to make. He turned again to the Gaunt Man.

"It is your choice to make, Decker," the Gaunt Man called above the roar of the earth. "It is your decision. Choose a door and life, or choose to stand where you are and die."

Decker stepped back as the earth shifted in front of him, throwing up a mound of rock. Then, without another moment of hesitation, he dashed through one of the remaining doors.

30

The banshee floated closer, and Father Christopher Bryce tried to control the fear that raged through his body. He was shaking badly, acutely aware that he had no weapon with which to battle the specter. His cross, which handily dispatched the other banshee, was lost somewhere on the floor of the cockpit. Even if it were close by, he doubted he could reach it before the grave-cold hand touched him and drained away his life force.

The ethereal arm reached toward him, spreading ethereal fingers wide. Bryce desperately forced his mind to think through the problem facing him. What was the cross that it was able to destroy spawns of hell? What power did it possess? Perhaps, he reasoned, it only possessed what he gave it, focusing his faith into a tangible field of good that no evil entity could withstand. Did he need the cross to duplicate the feat? Rationale told him no, but faith was a leap beyond the rational.

The hand was closer still.

Bryce began to pray aloud fervently, imagining the power of the words cloaking him with holy armor. "Though I walk through the valley of the shadow of death, I will fear no evil ..." he shouted, and the banshee flinched. He continued the prayer, each word striking the ghostly creature as if bullets from a sling. He stepped forward, filled with the power of his faith, and the banshee shrank away.

"In thee, O Lord, do I put my trust," Father Bryce said with conviction and power. "Let me never be ashamed; deliver me in thy righteousness." He saw that the banshee was growing smaller, less substantial. He was doing it! His prayers were being answered! He could stop this monster!

The plane took that moment to jerk wildly. Bryce lost his balance and hit the cockpit wall with his shoulder. His concentration dissolved with the shooting pain. Before he could clear his head and resume his prayer, the banshee struck. Floating as it was, the rocking plane was no obstacle. It touched Bryce's arm with its ghostly fingers and the priest screamed. Never had he felt such cold! In that touch was his death, and Bryce's faith crumbled only to be replaced with a numbing fear.

"Back, creature of the night!" a strong voice called out. "Back in the name of Dunad!"

The touch was gone then, but the cold remained. It raged through his arm and shoulder all the way down to his hand, causing it to hang limply at his side. Bryce opened his eyes to see Tolwyn standing between him and the banshee. She held her sword before her, commanding the monster with the authority of her god, Dunad. She did claim to be a paladin, Bryce thought detachedly, a holy knight. Of course she would have some miracles to call upon. Didn't Lancelot have such powers in the stories of the Knights of the Round Table? Oh the cold hurt so bad! But Tolwyn and the others needed him. He had to shake off the effects of the banshee's touch.

"Dunad add power to my sword!" Tolwyn called as she swung her blade at the banshee. The power her own faith granted her was limited, however, and the sword passed through the insubstantial form without doing any damage. The banshee screamed then, aiming the full fury of its voice at the paladin. She doubled over, attempting to protect herself from the painful sound. But Bryce could see on her face that it hurt her terribly. And the banshee was drifting forward, intent on bringing its death touch to bear on Tolwyn.

"Here, Chris," Mara said, handing him his cross. "I found it. Hurry. I have to reach the controls and I can't do that with the banshee in the way."

Bryce took the holy symbol with his good hand and advanced on the ghost. Already he felt the power returning. He shoved the cross into the specter and shouted loudly. "Begone!" With a terrible wail, the banshee collapsed inward and vanished with a popping sound. Bryce looked down at the cross with amazement. He barely noticed Mara leap past him to grab the controls of the descending plane.

"You handled yourself well, priest," Kurst said from beside him. "If not for you, we would have died like the pilots."

Bryce nodded weakly. He had much to think about. Was his faith, even after all that had happened, dependent on relics and symbols? Could he only manifest it through a metal cross? And, if that were the case, would he really be able to provide the others with the help they needed in the place they were going?

As usual, Bryce had no answers for himself. Doubt began to gnaw at his newfound resolve, and he was suddenly very afraid.

31

Coyote sat by the window, looking out into the compound of the base. On his lap sat the gray cat with the red collar. It was Tal Tu's pet, but right now the youth needed its companionship more than the edeinos did.

"You've been through a lot, huh fella?" Coyote asked the cat. It regarded him with big eyes, then rubbed its head against his hand. "I hope they're all right, cat," he whispered. "I wish we were with them."

Outside, there was suddenly a lot of activity. Coyote glanced around, trying to see what was happening. He notice Major Boot coming toward him from down the corridor.

"Julie," he called, "what's going on?"

"Casualties," she said. She looked dishevelled and sleepless. "Incoming casualties," she repeated. "We were hit really hard up north, and there are too many for Edwards, China Lake, and Fort Irwin to handle."

Coyote pictured the map he had been studying and recalled the three military installations to the north and west. He saw something in the nurse's eyes as she spoke, something that hadn't been there before. It looked like fear. "We're losing, aren't we?" he asked.

She shook her head. "No, we're not losing. But we're not winning either. Look, I've got to go. Casualties ..."

"Can I help?" Coyote asked, gently placing the cat down.

Julie smiled. "If you think you're up to it."

"I helped Father Bryce in Philadelphia," he said

proudly.

"Philadelphia?" Julie asked. "We just got in a new doctor who's from Philadelphia."

"What's his name?"

"Dr. Monroe."

A wide grin spread across the teen's face. "Dr. Monroe! That was Tolwyn's doctor! Maybe he's the same guy. Come on, let's go see him!"

"First let's go help the wounded," she suggested.

Coyote's smile disappeared and he nodded. He followed Major Julie Boot toward the helicopters landing in the compound, wondering why Dr. Monroe had come all the way to California.

32

In the steamy jungle clime of central Borneo, there was a shallow valley that stretched leisurely down into a great depression. A canopy of rain forest kept the area hot and moist — perfect growing weather. Thratchen walked beside the master planter, inspecting the field. The trees had been cleared away in a small swath that ran down the side of the depression; it was a place the master planter had judged to be perfect for rainwater drain irrigation, and it also was near enough to the keep to make harvest easy.

"The field looks fine," Thratchen commented. "But what about the crop?"

The master planter of this Orrorshan field was a small man with hard eyes that never seemed to move. He spoke to Thratchen without looking at him, as though he had more important matters to attend to. "The crop is ripe, and I was planning an early harvest of this field anyway. You get a stronger crop with an early harvest."

Thratchen knew the theories of gospog planting, but

it wouldn't hurt to let the man babble about his work. It could even gain the misplaced raider from Tharkold an ally in the inevitable struggle. "Why is that, master planter?"

The master planter stepped over to the side of the field where a large group stood waiting. Letting Thratchen's question hang in the air unanswered, he placed his hand on the smooth, cold flesh of the creature before him and petted it gently. The creature was an Other, one of the huge, shambling octopus-like monsters that were particular favorites of the Gaunt Man. Nearly three dozen of the many-tentacled beasts waited beside the field with growing anticipation.

"If you reap early, Thratchen," the master planter finally said, "there will be more ill-formed and weak gospog, but those that survive will be strong and healthy. They will be the best of the lot, and they will thrive."

The Others grew exceedingly restless. The Caretakers, ghoulish creatures assigned to control the Others, were having a hard time keeping the shamblers from charging the field. The master planter smiled. "This will be a wonderful harvest. The Gaunt Man will be pleased."

He sounded a bell and the Others began to shamble forward, their great tentacles writhing and flapping as though they were trying to fly. The Caretakers stood by with their blunderbusses, but there seemed to be little need for the short guns with flaring muzzles. All was progressing smoothly.

Thratchen and the planter watched as a gospog emerged from the ground. It was humanoid in appearance, a fusion of plant and flesh. This particular gospog was slow. It did not even react as an Other drew close. Strong tentacles flared out, catching the gospog. It struggled weakly, but could not break free. The Other dragged the gospog toward it, then under it so that it could be consumed by its gaping maw. This event allowed three sturdy gospog to shamble to safety behind the Other, where it could not turn to see them. Somewhere a blunderbuss discharged, and the Others set up a low, wailing dirge.

Several strong gospog struggled past the obstacle course of tentacles, with only an occasional one stumbling and falling beneath the inexorable march of the Others. The master planter smiled, pleased with the reaping. Only the best and strongest would survive; only the toughest and most fully-formed would join the Gaunt Man's army.

Thratchen watched for a time, then turned to the planter. "When it is over, prepare for the next planting."

The planter nodded, then turned back to regard the field, savoring the slow, satiated mewling of the Others as they crawled through the blooming rows. He did not notice as Thratchen spread his metal wings and took to the sky, flying back toward Illmound Keep.

33

Within the dark forest of Rec Pakken, Eddie Paragon held vigil. He sat beside the High Lord of the Living Land, waiting for the darkness device to finish its healing work. Without Baruk Kaah, Paragon was sure he didn't have a chance. The High Lord's favor was all that had spared him back in New York, and it was all that kept the battle-crazed lizardmen from tearing him apart. But except for two brief periods, the High Lord had remained unconscious since trying to spread his reality into Silicon Valley.

The first time he awoke, he called for the ravagon. The winged demon entered the dark forest and Baruk Kaah ordered him to fly to Aysle. "Uthorion promised to assist me," the High Lord said weakly. "Tell him to send the Wild Hunt." The ravagon nodded, accepting the assignment of its own accord and not because Baruk Kaah demanded it. At least that was the attitude the demons seem to portray, as far as Paragon understood it.

The second time the High Lord awoke from his fevered dreams, he called for a gotak. He told his priest to keep the tribes moving, to press the attack in the areas that had succumbed to their reality. Then he lapsed back into his healing sleep, and Paragon sat down to wait.

Paragon must have nodded off himself, for he snapped awake when he heard his name called. "Singer Paragon," Baruk Kaah said weakly. "How do my tribes fare?"

"The war proceeds, High Lord," Paragon explained, remembering the last words the gotaks spoke. "The tribes do well within the stelae bounds where they can work the miracles of Lanala, but they fall back from the Earthers weapons in those places still strong with Earth reality."

The High Lord let out a long breath. "Your reality is strong, singer," he said. "I have never been hurt like that. Never wounded so gravely. But Rec Pakken heals me, and soon I shall rise to lead the tribes to victory."

Baruk Kaah paused, turning his lizard eyes to regard the human sitting beside him. "Why are you still here, singer? Why did you not run when you had the chance? The edeinos would not harm one protected by the Saar."

Eddie Paragon shrugged. It had never occurred to him that he could simply leave the camp. And even if it did, he didn't believe he could reach civilization. He had no skills that would help him in the wild. He was just a rock'n'roll singer — nothing less, but certainly nothing more.

Black leaves parted and a ravagon entered the sleeping area. It was the silent one, the one Baruk Kaah had dispatched to Aysle some days ago. He acknowledged the High Lord and spoke. "It is good to see you improving, High Lord. Lord Uthorion sends his greetings."

"And his assistance?" Baruk Kaah demanded. "Does he send that?"

"The Wild Hunt is on its way," the ravagon said. "It cuts across this continent even now, landing here and there and leaving destruction in its wake."

"Good, good," Baruk Kaah muttered sleepily. "Soon the tide of battle will turn and that dead spot within my realm will be no more." His lizard eyes closed then, and the High Lord fell back into his healing sleep.

Paragon regarded the ravagon, realizing that it wouldn't let him leave like the edeinos might. He had lost his opportunity for freedom. He would just have to be more conscious of other opportunities as they arose. With that thought, he tilted his head back against the black bark of a black tree branch and drifted to sleep.

34

France had changed since the miracle of Avignon. The Church had grown powerful, more influential. Technology was banned, heresies were crimes, and the whole nation had taken a step back toward the Dark Ages. No, it was more than a step. It was a leap, a slide, a great jump into the past that made centuries disappear. It was madness, and Claudine Guerault was caught in its terrifying grip.

She had been running and hiding since the golden arch of light had descended to Earth in Avignon.

Religious fervor raged through the streets, but it was an unhealthy revival as far as Guerault was concerned. Monks called for people to give up the sins of the modern world and go back to simpler times. And, for the most part, they embraced the words and took them to heart. Modern conveniences were considered evil, technology was the tool of the devil. There was talk in the streets of miracles, of the Second Coming, of Armageddon. And beneath it all was a constant murmur that rippled through the countryside. She had heard the prayer-like chant of the coming of the Holy Father of Avignon. She had heard the name of Pope Jean Malraux whispered in alleys, shouted in cathedrals. But unlike her countrymen, the name did not fill her with hope. It filled her with dread. If he represented the ideals of this "revived" religion, then he was not someone she wanted to put her trust in.

Guerault was a reporter, but she couldn't find a way to let the world know what was happening in France. Her colleagues had disappeared, her office closed. All news was the province of the Church now, and monks spread the words of faith and miracles everywhere. And that seemed to be the extent of the news offered to the people, the totality of available information.

If she was found, she would have to proclaim her devotion to the unseen Malraux — and the monks and priests seemed to know if people were sincere. She did not want to face the newly-instituted Inquisition with lies, for she felt no devotion to the returning pope of Avignon. If anything, she felt anger and hatred toward him for the changes he caused.

She had been hiding in basements and sewers, moving from one haven to another as she tried to find a way out of the country. This particular basement had been quiet when she arrived, but now from somewhere far off she heard noises. She ignored them for a time, content to sit and rest. But eventually her curiosity got the better of her. She went in search of the sounds.

Father Herve regarded the man on the rack with a critical eye. "He won't survive another pull," he said to the monk who stood by his side. "I think now is the time for the Faith of our Church to take a hand."

The monk, a large and well-muscled man who could not have weighed less than two hundred pounds, paled and backed away as the priest spoke. The priest rolled up his sleeves and approached the whimpering prisoner.

"Francois," he whispered. "Francois, why do you persist in this heresy? Your memory is a tool of the devil, as are the technological horrors you continue to make use of. Admit it and let me drive him out, and you will be saved for all eternity. The Eternal Father is going to descend to Earth soon, and when he does, all his followers will be known to him. Those who are not of his flock will sicken and die. Do you not wish to live?"

The man on the rack stirred, rattling his chains like some literary ghost. He whimpered a reply that Herve could not understand.

"Eh? Eh, Francois? You must speak up. Do you accept the word of the Vicar of Avignon as the one true word? Will you give up your will to mine, and let me help you?"

A new light of energy came into Francois' eyes, and the broken man looked up, his tear-streaked face twisted into unfathomable sorrow. "What is it you want of me?" he cried, his voice cracking with the effort. "Why are you doing this? Who are you? Why does my work with machines bother you?"

The priest made no response. He simply regarded the man with contempt and waited for him to continue. Francois sighed. "I believe whatever you say," he finally shouted. "I will do whatever you say! Stop it, just stop it, won't you?"

"Ah, Francois," Father Herve said, clicking his tongue like he was admonishing a child. "Your words are hollow, as is your belief in the Eternal Father. I must fight the devil within you before you can truly come to accept Pope Jean Malraux, I see that now."

He placed the ornate box that he carried on the table that held the tools of the Inquisitor's trade, opening it reverently. Inside was a small piece of wood, plain and unremarkable looking. But as soon as the box was opened, an aura seemed to rise around the priest and his subject like a cloud. Father Herve began to pray, his French turning to Latin and rattling off his tongue forming a powerful web of energy that could not be dampened. Francois writhed beneath the stinging words and the aura of the powerful relic.

Father Herve made a three-fingered gesture once, twice, three times. Now he could see the blue and red light radiating from the heretic on the table. As he suspected, Francois was a stormer. That explained his ability to continue to use modern machinery even though the reality of Magna Verita had replaced that of Core Earth. He could feel energy, as heat, surrounding the stormer. So much power! Some of it was his for the taking, and the rest belonged to the land, for High Lord Jean Malraux to take for his own when he descended. And he was coming soon, so soon.

Herve invoked the miracle that would empty this vessel of its possibilities, sending some into the priest and the rest to the hidden stelae spread throughout the land. With each word of the prayer, he felt the energy flow out of the stormer in waves. It was as refreshing as water from a cold spring, as nourishing as a mother's milk. And Herve drank in as much as he could.

Father Herve felt himself practically begin to glow with the joy of it, and he laughed long and loud just as Francois screamed. The tortured man's wail took a long, long time to die away.

Claudine Guerault closed her eyes, but she couldn't block out the sound of the man's scream. What had that priest done to him? She had no idea, but she knew that it was awful. Then, before the man's cry died away completely, she ran back into the far reaches of the basement. Back there, in the darkness, she could hide from the priest and his inquisitors. She could remain free.

35

"Good job," Bryce said casually to Mara, but the screeching noise from the undercarriage striking the tarmac was just now beginning to die away in his ears. Still, she had brought the plane down safely and more or less intact. He winced as Tolwyn probed the flesh of his right arm where the banshee had touched him.

"I am sorry, Christopher," Tolwyn said. "But we must see how badly you have been hurt."

He watched as she examined his arm. It was still numb, but the cold was lessening. The skin where he had been touched was white and bloodless, like the skin of a corpse. The dead patch was the size of a baseball, and around it the skin was black and blue.

"The banshees must have drifted across from Orrorsh," Kurst said matter-of-factly. "I do not think they were sent after us in particular. We were just the luck of the draw."

"Luck," Mara muttered. "I don't believe in luck."

"We will encounter worse creatures as we get closer to the Gaunt Man's domain," Kurst continued. "And once we enter the dark realm, the nightmares shall truly begin."

Tolwyn finished her examination and gestured for the priest to put his shirt back on. "I can dress normal battle wounds, Christopher, but that wound is not from a normal battle. If I were a priest, perhaps ..."

"What do you mean?" he asked.

"In Aysle, priests can heal wounds and invoke miracles, much like you banished the banshees," she explained. "Have you tried to heal yourself?"

He looked shocked. "What kind of powers are you attributing to me? Except for rare cases, priests of Earth don't go around healing people or banishing demons."

"Why not?" Tolwyn asked, confusion clouding her features. "And you did banish the banshees."

Now it was Bryce's turn to be confused. Did she have a point? He clutched at his bruised arm as he tried to make sense of the changes in reality.

"Christopher?" Tolwyn inquired, concerned about his state of mind.

"I'm okay. Really." He rose, steadying himself against his chair. "Really," he said faintly. Static crackled over the pilot's discarded headset, startling everyone in the cockpit. It had been silent since the banshee attack, but now the noise was back. And underneath the static, a voice broke through.

"Bit of a rough time, mates," the voice said. "Welcome to Nirimba Airfield. If you're all right I suggest you get yourselves in gear and move out. That show of fancy flying scraped your undercarriage pretty badly. Looks to me like you're leaking fuel."

"Triple damn," Mara yelled. "Let's get out of the plane. Now."

Kurst grabbed an M-16 from the plane's store and headed for the exit.

"Can we at least get ourselves organized here?" Bryce asked impatiently. "There's gear to unload, there's —"

"Now!" Mara shouted, her voice snapping with command. "A fuel leak means the possibility of explosion. We'll get the gear later, if the plane doesn't go up in flames. Let's move!"

It was a credit to the group that when necessity demanded they moved together well, with little wasted motion in the cramped confines of the plane's interior. Tolwyn shot Bryce a glance and he detoured to pick up the pack containing the Heart of Coyote. Kurst, too, watched the priest's actions carefully. What are you all about, Mr. Kurst, he wondered. But the thought was fleeting as he followed the others off the plane.

36

It was like listening to a storm that moved closer and closer so that the thunder was a continuous roll. It was like the constant wash of the sea on the shore, only deeper in pitch and more powerful. It was like the bass line of a church organ playing Handel's Messiah on a long, extended note. It was like all of these things, and none of them. It was the sound of action — every last tank, every last APC, every last vehicle the army had in this area converging on one strategic point. On the other side of the storm front that formed the current battle line, lizard men and dinosaurs converged as well.

Lieutenant Charles Covent knew that when it was over, only one side would be in any shape to fight again.

His radio crackled, and he answered in the brisk code of the U.S. military. He always imagined himself as part of the most powerful fighting force on the face of the Earth, but they found themselves helpless before the spears and unexplainable magic the primitive invaders possessed. Even their own weapons refused to work at critical times, and that scared Covent more than he dared admit.

"Disperse your unit and begin choosing fire alleys, Blue Leader," Red Leader ordered over the radio. Covent complied, dispatching the lead squad with a few practiced sentences. Men leaped from the back of an armored vehicle and crunched off across the scrub in tight, precise formation. Then they scattered for cover. Faintly, over the now-muted roar of the other vehicles, Covent could hear the clatter of last-minute checks on personal weaponry. He counted off twelve seconds, scanned the horizon for danger, and lifted the radio to his mouth.

"Blue Four, do you copy?"

The receiver crackled. "We copy."

"Go up thirty past Blue Three, set up a kill zone stake on their mark," he said quickly.

"Confirm that, Blue Leader." The radio static died out and another squad peeled away from its vehicle, advancing quickly past the position the first squad now occupied. Satisfied, Covent looked down into the belly of his own vehicle, where his sergeant was busy with the tie-in to HQ.

"What's the word, Joey?" he asked.

"That's confirmed, HQ," Sergeant Joey Houston said into his radio. Then he looked up. "We've got us a horde coming in just where HQ said they would." He grinned a big Texas grin. "Unless there's something tricky going on, I'd say we got us a turkey shoot."

"Good, we need one," Covent muttered. He dispatched Blue Five to the left flank to set up another kill zone. "What kind of trick could they be pulling, Joey?"

"They say we're out of the Dead Ring here, that the lizards are getting overextended," Houston said. "Maybe they got booby-traps rigged up to make this area go dead too, once the fighting starts."

Covent felt his nerves tingle with fear, but he held the sensation in check. The Dead Ring was what the soldiers called the three-hundred mile area around Sacramento where practically nothing high-tech worked. Like the Zone of Silence on the east coast. There had been a couple of real bad slaughters initially. Then HQ stopped ordering units across the storm front. Since then they had been holding their own; now the lizards were trying to break out.

"Hell," he said. "What kind of trap can a lizard set?"

Houston grinned at him, that funny gap-toothed smile that could look so kind or so deadly. Right now, Covent wasn't sure which it was.

"Charlie," Houston laughed, "if they were plain old lizards, we wouldn't be sitting here right now."

Eyeing Houston, Covent had a sudden thought. "Listen up, Blues. I want to know about anything that looks out of place, anything ancient or primitive looking that's not connected to a lizard or a caveman. You copy that?"

He saw Houston nod in approval. He put down his radio to wait.

37

Number 3327 soaked in his private hot tub as the two young women worked the tension out of his neck and shoulders with practiced fingers. A screen on the wall flashed the news of the day, and a line running across the bottom provided the latest stock information. Kanawa Corporation stock, and all its myriad subsidiaries, was up. It was always up. That was the way of reality in the cosm of Marketplace. A gentle beep sounded at the sliding door. Information immediately flashed across the inside of the dark glasses Number 3327 always wore, relayed from sensors in the floor mat and scanners in the door frame. Number 3327 read the digital words as they appeared.

"Enter, Nagoya," he called.

Nagoya walked into the room, bowed, and sat in one of the lounge chairs beside the tub. He briefly let his eyes wander to the young women, but then snapped them back to Number 3327.

"I have returned from Earth cosm with information for you, Kanawa-sama," Nagoya began.

"Proceed," Number 3327 nodded.

"The Gaunt Man has successfully attached enough realities to Earth to circumvent the possibility of a reality backlash," Nagoya reported. "We had hoped to delay or prevent a number of realities from arriving. While Tharkold was prevented from making the connection, the Nile Empire decided to drop its bridges before the Earth could repel the other invaders."

"Mobius is a fool," Number 3327 said.

Nagoya agreed. "Still, with Orrorsh, the Living Land, Aysle, Magna Verita, and the Nile all attached to Earth, the Gaunt Man's immediate problem of handling Earth's massive energy surges has been solved. Tharkold's loss

The Dark Realm

Francis Mao

alone was not enough to hinder his plans."

"And each of these realities are firmly established?" Number 3327 asked.

"Only Orrorsh has absolute power in its region, but the other realms are working toward that. Baruk Kaah suffered a slight setback, but Uthorion has sent him assistance. Mobius is already conquering vast areas of the planet, and France does not even realize it has been invaded."

"Of course it doesn't," Number 3327 smiled. "That is the subtlety Malraux is known for."

"Neither he nor Uthorion have descended into their respective realms yet, master."

"That is the way Malraux works, cloaking himself in the myths of his religious trappings. Uthorion is just frightened. He still hides from a meaningless threat made by an overzealous stormer."

"Kanawa-sama," Nagoya interrupted. "There is evidence that the prophecy he runs from has finally come true."

Number 3327 laughed. It was a brief laugh, humorless. Then he spoke. "Since we cannot stop this merger, we must find another way to profit from it. Send word to the Gaunt Man. As we have previously accepted his generous offer to share in the spoils of Earth, he can expect our realm to be established within the next few Marketplace cycles. Then see to the bridges."

Nagoya stood, bowed, and went to perform his master's bidding. Number 3327 sank back into the tub to soak.

38

The three lead squads were in position, and Covent quickly scanned the surrounding area to make sure there was no better observation site for the command vehicle. Ahead of him was a zone of death, with sighted-in kill-stakes laid out for the gunners along the lines they were to lead the attackers through. They were outside of Little Lake, between the China Lake Naval Weapons Center on the east and Sequoia National Forest on the west. The last sighting of the enemy was due north, on the other side of the storm front. But the storm's intensity had increased, and for the last eighteen hours they could see nothing through the swirling clouds and driving rain.

"Lieutenant," Sergeant Houston called from inside the vehicle. "I've got HQ on the radio."

Covent dropped into the APC and took the headset Houston offered. He listened, nodded, said he understood, and handed the set back to the sergeant.

"What's the word, Charlie?" Houston asked curiously.

"HQ has received some reports from the east formations. The storm is clearing enough for them to see through and the lizards are gone."

"Gone? What do you mean gone?"

Covent shrugged. "Maybe they've fallen back. Who knows how a lizard thinks?"

The two men went top side and scanned the horizon with their binoculars. The storm front had calmed, and they could catch images through brief openings in the weather. The lizards, the dinosaurs, the primitive men and women — none of them were anywhere to be seen.

"What happened to the massive buildup?" Houston asked. There was an edge of panic in his voice. "That's how they increased the Dead Ring, isn't it? By sending a massive force across the storm front? So where'd they go?"

Covent tried to think the situation through. He had

orders to stop the lizards from advancing, to keep them on the other side of the storm front. But now they were gone, and not a shot had been fired.

"Hand me the map," Covent ordered.

Houston complied.

"What are you looking for, Charlie?"

"Just a hunch, Joey," Covent said, handing the map back to his sergeant. "Get HQ back on the horn. Tell them we're moving out."

"What?" Houston shouted in surprise. "We don't have orders …"

"They're trying to outflank us, Joey. If they get their forces past the storm front, then we're going to find ourselves in another Dead Ring. Remember what happened to the National Guard units in New York? We've got to forestall that."

"But where are they going to make their move? The storm front cuts across the entire state."

"You've got to think like a primitive on this one, Joey," Covent said. "I think they're going to make their rush through the Sequoia National Forest."

39

Bryce and the others sat in the terminal, sipping coffee and explaining their mission to the Australian officer who had greeted them on the tarmac. At least, they explained as much of their mission as they could without getting into too great a detail. The officer, who said his name was Captain Jeremy Albury, listened without comment, as did the other people with him. When the four finished speaking (three, actually, as Kurst remained quiet throughout the exchange), Albury spoke.

"We've been asked to cooperate with you as a favor

to your government," Albury explained. "I don't know how much of your story — sketchy though it is — I believe, but we've been having troubles of our own. We've lost contact with Indonesia. There's a massive storm front surrounding the islands that we've been unable to fly through. And worse, there are reports of ... things attacking people along the coast. These are damn strange times we're living in."

"We need transportation across the continent, captain," Bryce said. "And then, if possible, some kind of vehicle to get us to Borneo."

"Like a gyroplatform or a jump boat," Mara added.

"Well, yes," Albury said, throwing Mara a strange look. "Perhaps you didn't understand me. We cannot contact or get near Borneo or any of the other islands. The storms, you know."

"I'll take them," said one of the men who was with Albury. Bryce looked at the man. He was around the priest's age, but taller and in better shape. He dressed like a mannequin from a Banana Republic clothing store, but his clothes looked more functional than stylish.

"Now listen, Tom," Albury began. "I let you sit in on this because you seemed to know what was happening, but I can't just let you ..."

"Who are you?" Tolwyn asked the man, cutting off the Australian officer curtly.

"My name is Tom O'Malley, ma'am," he offered, extending his hand. "The aborigine sent me to fetch you and your companions."

"Aborigine?" Tolwyn asked, confused.

"An aborigine is a native of this continent," Bryce explained quickly. "A black-skinned person who ..." He stopped, realizing what he just said.

"A black man? With white hair? And a missing tooth?

And a hole in his tongue?" Tolwyn asked excitedly.

"Yes, ma'am," O'Malley nodded. "That sounds like Djil to me."

"You will take us to him," Tolwyn said, gripping Tom with strong hands. It was not a question.

Albury stepped between them, shaking his head. "This is damn irregular," he commented. "I can't let you go off alone with a civilian. What would my superiors say? Hell, what would your country say?"

"Then you will come with us," Tolwyn decided. Without further comment, she reached for her gear.

"But …" Albury started to say.

Kurst leaned close to Albury. "It is for the best, captain."

Bryce grinned at the exchange. Finally, someone else for the group to steamroller. He walked over to O'Malley. "How do you propose to do this, Tom?"

"I have a plane, Father," Tom explained. "It's fueled and ready to go."

"Then by all means," Bryce said, "lead the way."

40

Covent and his men entered the Sequoia National Forest carefully, expecting lizards to leap out of the tall, massive trees as they walked beneath them. But the forest was quiet, and nothing leaped out to attack them.

"Okay, Houston, have the units range out in close patrol patterns. If we keep the storm to our right, they shouldn't be able to sneak up on us," Covent said.

"Roger, Charlie," Houston shot back. "Do you think the rest of the units will reach us before the dance begins?"

The dance. Houston had such a way with words. Covent, however, did not have the ability to mask meanings under less offensive language. So he told the truth. "I don't know, Joey. But as of now, it's just us, so let's keep it together."

The lead units ranged ahead, moving on foot because the forest wasn't designed to allow heavy vehicles to move through it easily. Between the ash-filled sky and the nearby storm front, it was dark in the forest. This made the men nervous, but they concentrated on the task before them and seemed to be handling it okay.

An explosion sounded in the distance, and Covent tried to see what was happening through his binoculars. "Raise the units, Houston," Covent ordered. "I want to know what's happening."

More explosions sounded, and Covent could hear screams coming from his men. Damn! What had they blundered into?

"I've got Blue Three on the horn, Charlie," Houston informed him as he passed over the radio.

"Blue Three, what's your situation?" Covent demanded.

"We're in some kind of mine field, lieutenant," the voice on the radio said. "Blue Two's taken the brunt of it, but the rest of us are sitting tight until we can figure a way out of this."

"What kind of mines, soldier?" Covent asked. "Surely the lizards aren't using land mines?"

"I don't know what they are, sir. But they seemed to be tied into some strange plants. As a matter of fact, I think the plant is in a small Dead Ring because I can't raise Blue Two on the box. I can see a few survivors, but their radio isn't responding."

"Hold your position, Blue Three. And keep me informed if anything changes." Covent replaced the radio and scanned the area with his binoculars.

"Exploding plants? Small Dead Rings? How can we fight this stuff, Charlie?" Houston asked.

"As best we can, sergeant," Covent replied. "As best we can."

41

Angus Cage felt himself emerge from a tunnel of light, felt the cascading energy roll off his body like water when he emerged from a swimming pool. He felt disconnected, light-headed. It took a moment for his vision to clear, for his senses to resume their job of telling his mind what was going on around him. When they did start working again, Cage found himself in a large warehouse filled with endless rows of wooden crates. The Mystery Men were sprawled around him, each shaking off the effects of the strange form of travel.

"The gate has collapsed, Cage," the Guardian said, suddenly appearing beside him. "Dr. Frest was one of the last ones through."

"How many?" Cage inquired, speaking through numb lips and deadened tongue.

"Approximately three score made it here," the Guardian answered.

Sixty? Only sixty of them? Cage sighed. Was that enough to dismantle Mobius' operation? He didn't have a clue.

Suddenly bright overhead lights snapped on, and Cage heard the sounds of several rifle bolts being thrown. It sounded like they were surrounded, but it was hard to see through the glare.

"Halt!" ordered a deep voice. It was a man, and he had a Middle Eastern accent.

"We're sorry for intruding," Cage heard Dr. Frest call out. "We did not mean to trespass."

Angus Cage checked his own weapon, desperately blinking his eyes so that they would clear. He could see shadowy forms now, perhaps a dozen men standing upon a catwalk above them.

"I do not want to hear your excuses," the Middle Easterner shouted. "You can save them for the shocktroopers!"

"I'm sure that won't be necessary," the pretty Raven Wing yelled back. She was standing about five feet from Cage, wearing that black outfit he had always dreamed about. He pushed the thought out of his mind as she continued. "If you'll just direct us out of here, we'll be about our business."

"And what business is that, woman?" the man laughed, and his cohorts picked up the evil sound.

The Guardian decided to answer the Middle Easterner. "We seek Dr. Mobius."

The Middle Easterner laughed harder. He made a brief motion and his companions leveled their weapons on the Mystery Men.

"Look," Cage yelled up, deciding to cut through the tension before guns started blazing. "We don't want any trouble."

"It is too late, my friend," the Middle Easterner shouted. "You have found much trouble. Where do you think you are? This is one of Pharaoh Mobius' Royal Warehouses."

Angus Cage smiled. This was Mobius' property? That was all he needed to hear. He would figure out what this Pharaoh business was about later. "Okay, Mystery Men, you heard our hosts. This place belongs to Mobius."

"Then let's trash it!" Power Lad suggested. Cage wholeheartedly agreed.

The Middle Easterner and his goons, of course, had no say in the matter whatsoever. They didn't even put up that good of a fight.

42

Lieutenant Charles Covent approached the strange plant cautiously, placing his feet carefully into the moist soil. The forest was so alive, full of living noises that almost made him forget the situation he and his men were in. He had a walkie talkie, but as he got closer to the plant it had stopped working. He was sure his pistol and rifle were similarly incapacitated.

"Be careful, Charlie," Houston called from somewhere behind him. He had not agreed with Covent's tactics, but the lieutenant couldn't order any of his men to undertake this mission. It was something he had to do himself.

The plant was a lush, green color. It was about three feet high, with broad, four-pointed leaves. The leaves had an unusual pattern of orange dots that distinguished it from any other plant in the forest. Covent had been about twenty feet from it when his walkie talkie failed. The closer he moved toward it, the more he had to fight the urge to discard his clothing and howl at the storm. The plant's scent called up primal images in the lieutenant's mind which he was finding harder and harder to ignore.

"This is very weird, Joey," he shouted back, but the words seemed to lose meaning right after he said them. He was beginning to forget what he was coming to do. The grass felt so inviting beneath his feet. He paused, imagining himself rolling in it, getting its fresh smell all over his body.

"Lieutenant?" Houston called. "Are you all right,

Charlie?"

Charles Covent blinked once, twice. He ran his hand over his face. Did someone call him?

"Lieutenant?" Houston said again, louder this time, more forceful.

"I hear you, Joey," Covent said at last. He reached down and drew his knife from his boot sheath. He had to do this quickly, while it was fresh in his mind.

He had to kill the plant.

He wasn't sure if that was what he had set out to do. He thought maybe he had come to examine it, to see what effects it would have on him. Now he knew. It was a dangerous plant. It was the lizards' plant.

The knife led him forward, its sharp point held before him at the ready position. One step. Then another.

"I'm going to kill it, Joey," he yelled.

"Charlie, come back here," Houston shouted. "We can blast it from here. Don't go any closer!"

A third step. Covent kept going. Joey didn't understand the effect the plant was having on him. If he didn't kill it now, he might not be able to get away from it. A fourth step.

Then the ground exploded, and all of Charles Covent's thoughts ceased.

43

Mara sat in the rear of the plane, adding more memories of Kadandra to the data plate she had carried from her world. When complete, the data plate would be able to invoke sensover memories of her homeworld, memories so real that she could immerse herself in them for hours at a time. She called up an image in her mind, then transferred it to her internal computer. There it was converted to data that she could laser onto the plate. The plate would enhance the image and connect it to the other images already placed upon the plate, forming a longer, more complete picture. It was hard work, but it gave her something to do during the slow periods.

This was a slow period.

Kurst sat across the aisle from her, staring out the window intensely. He didn't show it, but she could tell that he was growing more tense the closer they got to Orrorsh. Something over there frightened him, perhaps something he didn't even remember. But his subconscious remembered, and it was sending him vague, undecipherable warnings. At least that was her guess.

Tolwyn was asleep in the seat in front of him, conserving her strength for when it would be needed. Christopher was in the cockpit, talking with Tom O'Malley and Captain Albury. She hoped the two newest members of their group weren't doomed to suffer as the other pilots had. Or as Alder had. Or Decker.

She shivered when she thought of Decker. She had never seen such a state before, although it did remind her of the volunteers at the institute. When plugged in to provide their energy to the transference cylinder, they were in a coma-like state much like Decker was in. But they volunteered to enter such a condition. Decker had been forced into his by the Carredon.

Mara put away the data plate and strolled toward the cockpit. She had had enough of memories for the time being. O'Malley was at the controls of the plane, and Father Bryce was standing behind him. Albury was in the copilot's chair, but he didn't appear to be helping in any way.

"How much longer?" she asked.

"We've still got a ways to go," O'Malley said. "But we

will be stopping in the Northern Territory to take on fuel."

Mara regarded the pilot with curiosity, adjusting her lens filter to discern the Storm Knight energy. As she supposed, Tom O'Malley glowed with the blue and red energy.

"Why are you helping us, Tom O'Malley?" she asked.

O'Malley considered the question briefly. Then he answered Mara. "A feeling, I guess. First, when the aborigine strolled in from the Outback, I felt he needed my assistance. Then, when I finally met you and your friends, I felt that it was important that you get to where you want to go."

"Do you always trust your feelings?" Bryce asked.

O'Malley smiled. "Always. Don't you?"

The plane began to descend then, dropping quickly as O'Malley guided it toward the ground.

"Sorry about that, but I prefer to fast drop. That's when you know you're really flying."

Mara edged closer to Father Bryce, placing her arm in his. "I like this guy," she whispered. "I think he's going to get us to Orrorsh."

"Yes," Bryce agreed, holding tight to the pilot's chair as the plane angled wildly. "But I'd like to get there in one piece!"

44

Sergeant Joe Houston gave Lieutenant Covent the once over. There was shrapnel all through his right leg and in his stomach, and he was unconscious. But he was alive, and that counted for something.

"Get him out of here," he ordered the soldier driving the jeep. "Make sure he's on a helicopter and being evacuated to Irwin or Twentynine Palms before you come back to the unit."

The soldier confirmed the orders and drove off. Houston watched after the vehicle for a time, then turned to deal with his current situation. "I never wanted to be in charge, especially in a war-time engagement," he complained. "Hey, private. Did I ever tell you I was related to General Sam Houston? Of Texas?"

"Once or twice, sergeant," the private replied.

"Oh," Houston said, disappointed.

"Sergeant, we've got company!" the private shouted.

Houston grabbed his binoculars and looked toward the storm front. Emerging from the bizarre weather pattern were flying creatures, winged reptiles and hovering starfish that looked to be tough and mean. Below them were lizard men and a handful of primitive-looking men and women riding weird dinosaurs. Houston wondered if the dark forest would inhibit the enemy, or if they were better equipped for this terrain than his men were.

"Wait for it," he told the private, who was now manning his radio. He counted off, watching the lizards advance. "Have Blue Three start firing."

The battle began then, as Houston ordered Blue Platoon to attack. It was their job to keep the invaders from taking the forest — to keep them on the other side of the storm front. He just hoped the other squads made it to the site quickly, because he had a bad feeling about this combat situation.

The battle was a series of bright flashes to Houston, like something under a strobe light, stop-action scenes melding one into another with punctuations of darkness in between. There were starshells and flares, and the hordes of nightmare attackers from out the dark, and the constant hammering of machineguns, and the explosions of artillery shells and grenades. One moment he remembered was a whoosh of anti-tank fire that brought down one of the huge dinosaurs, its side an exposed cavern of bloody tatters that brought others of its kind to feed. Cries of pain and fury arose from the attackers, and through the little blinks of battle Houston realized they were winning. The bastards were falling back across the storm front, falling like scythed wheat as they ran.

But then the scene changed. The storm front advanced toward Blue Platoon, rolling forward through the mighty sequoias. Through his binoculars, he watched as a dark cloud broke away and transformed into black armored riders atop black foaming horses. "My God," he whispered. "Who are they?"

He watched a moment longer as the riders cut into his men with flaring swords and metal-shoed hooves. A new slaughter had begun, and this time the soldiers were on the receiving line.

"Call in, private, call in!" Houston shouted. "We need back up!"

And over the screams of his men, the discharge of their weapons, and the thundering hooves, Houston heard a horn sound. It was the sound of a coffin opening, the sound of the deepest night.

It was the sound of death.

45

The Horn Master sounded the great horn and ordered the Wild Hunt forward. The Hunt arrived in Baruk Kaah's camp as the battle to the south started, and the High Lord quickly dispatched the Hunt to assist his troops at the storm's edge. The edeinos did not expect to meet such staunch resistance in the forest and, without their reality to protect them, the Earthers' weapons cut the lizards down. But the Wild Hunt was not as hindered by varying realities. Its magic was strong wherever it traveled, for it carried its own reality with it.

Now the huntsmen cut through the Earthers with swords and spears. The wolf hounds ripped at them with sharp teeth. The ravens tore at them with deadly talons and pointed beaks. The forest ran red with rivers of blood. As the Hunt passed by, the squires followed behind. They gathered the souls of the dead so that they could be bound to the Hunt. Thus the Hunt grew.

The Horn Master watched a moment more, then turned his fiery eyes upon a chariot further back in the Earther line. That was the command chariot, the Horn Master knew. The Earth warriors were directed from there. A cannon mounted on the chariot fired burst after burst into the Hunt, bringing down a few of the Horn Master's cherished huntsmen. That could not be abided.

The Horn Master whirled his jet-black mount and galloped straight for the command chariot. When the warriors within it noticed him, they turned the cannon his way. Fire spewed from the open mouth of the weapon, but the first shots went wide, missing their mark. The next blast was more accurate, but the Horn Master raised his shield and deflected the shot. Then he was upon the chariot, his great sword slicing through the cannon as his horse sliced through the tall grass.

"It's no good, Houston!" he heard one of the warriors shout.

"Order the men to fall back!" the other said, raising his personal weapon to defend himself.

The Horn Master cut them both down quickly, cleaving the men in two with his mighty sword swipes. He watched them fall to the forest floor. The cries around him told him that this engagement was drawing to a close. But a voice behind him made him whirl, his sword at the ready.

"Blue Company, do you copy?" The voice came out of a small black box atop the chariot. "Please respond, Blue Company."

His sword slashed downward. The box exploded into a dozen shards. Blue Company was no more! Its warriors would now run with the Wild Hunt, forever responding to the call of the horn. The Horn Master raised his sword triumphantly, then led the spectral host back into the raging storm.

46

Pharaoh Mobius entered his temporary sleeping quarters that overlooked the site where his palace was being built. Muab, the Royal Builder, was working the slaves throughout the night to complete the palace according to Mobius' schedule. He had never failed his Pharaoh yet.

The temporary quarters were splendid, full of rich silks and fluffy pillows. A tray of fruits awaited him, as well as a decanter of fine wine. He fell upon the pillows, sinking into their softness. Yes, he liked being Pharaoh. He liked it very much. He reached for his goblet when a soft hand touched his and a soft voice spoke.

"Allow me, master," the voice said.

"Ah, Clemeta," sighed Mobius. "I had forgotten that you would be here."

"Where else would I be, master?" she asked as she handed him the goblet.

She had been with him since he had taken a liking to her that day at the construction site. He had her promoted from serving girl to Royal Escort, and she was now dressed accordingly in gold and silver. She was so like

Bob Dvorak

the original Clemeta, the Clemeta of his court some three thousand years ago in Terra's Egypt.

"Remind me to one day tell you about ancient Egypt, Clemeta," he said after sipping the wine. "About how I took the throne."

She was beside him now, holding a bunch of grapes. Without a word, she pulled one grape from its stem and placed it in her mouth. She rolled it within her lips, moistening the fruit so that it shined. Then she reached toward the Pharaoh's hood, offering the grape to her master.

Before Mobius could take the fruit, the door swung open and a priest marched in. Mobius remained seated, barely turning toward the man. He was a lesser priest, one of Mobius' faithful from Khem, and it appeared that he had ridden hard to get here.

"Pharaoh, I am sorry to disturb you, but I have urgent news that cannot wait," the priest blurted out, trying to catch his breath.

"Very well," Mobius said, his tone ice cold. "Tell me this urgent news."

"The Mystery Men are here, master," the priest explained.

"More," Mobius demanded.

"One of the Royal Warehouses in Cairo. It has been demolished. Witnesses say the destruction was caused by an army of costumed men and women."

"And?" Mobius urged.

"They left a message. They carved it into the wall of the warehouse ..."

"With a diamond-tipped cane," Mobius finished. "The trademark of the Guardian. What did the message say?"

The priest gulped nervously. "It said, 'We will bring

you to justice, Dr. Mobius. Your games of conquest are over.' It was signed, the Mystery Men."

The Pharaoh took the moistened grape from Clemeta's delicate fingers and popped it into his mouth. Then he gulped down his wine and tossed the goblet aside. Standing, he said, "You did well to bring me this news, priest. However, you did disturb my evening of relaxation. I hate that." He took Clemeta's chin in his hand and gently tilted her head so that he could look into her soft eyes. "I was so looking forward to relaxing. Ah, well. The duties of the Pharaoh do not end at sundown."

Mobius giggled at that, since such ways of reckoning time no longer worked. The sun rose and fell apparently at will now, due to the change in the planet's spin.

He turned and walked quickly to the door, but he stopped when he got there. "Oh, yes. We have ruined your evening, dear Clemeta. To make it up to you, I present you with a gift." Mobius gestured in the direction of the priest. "He is yours to kill for ruining your pleasure. I just require that his death be slow and agonizing."

Clemeta's mouth dropped open, but when she saw that Mobius was serious her lips curved into a wickedly delightful smile. The priest began to protest, but a look from the Pharaoh silenced him.

"Remember, slow and agonizing. Have fun, my love," Mobius said. He directed his guards to assist Clemeta and hurried off to deal with the new development in his empire.

47

Father Bryce held on to the back of Tom O'Malley's chair as the plane landed. He needn't have bothered, for

Tom brought the plane down smoothly, with barely a bump.

"A big difference from your landing, Mara," he joked. But she didn't pick up on the humor. She seemed serious all of a sudden.

"They didn't answer your call, Tom," she said. "Why didn't the tower guide you down?"

The pilot shrugged. "It's a small air strip. Maybe no one's around."

It had started to rain as they made their approach, and now the rain was falling heavily. Great drops bounced off the plane and splattered upon the tarmac. O'Malley grabbed the pistol and holster that hung behind his chair. He strapped on the holster as he walked out of the cockpit.

Bryce and Mara followed him, but Albury remained seated. "I'll wait here," he offered as they walked away.

Tom exited the plane first. Kurst and Mara followed behind him, then Tolwyn. Bryce, pulling up the collar of his jacket to ward off some of the rain, exited last. Tolwyn and Tom were waiting right outside the plane when he emerged, getting soaked to the bone.

"Don't just stand there!" Bryce shouted over the drum beat of the rain. "Get inside. Let's go." Tolwyn put out a hand to stop him, and pointed across the runway to the opposite side of the small airfield, and then to the lone building beside a small hangar.

At the door to the building, two men with pistols stood, watching them. And over there, in the pouring rain, a group of at least six was moving toward them at a steady pace from across the runway.

"What's everyone so nervous about?" Bryce asked, his voice nearly a whisper. "They could be friends, you know."

The rain was heavy, very heavy, and it slapped the top of his head like a man playing bongos. The water ran in rivulets down to his eyes and into his beard, and pooled into a little stream that ran off his chin. His clothes were baggy and wet as well, and hung like lead from his body. He really didn't want to get into a fight in these conditions. He wished that they could go inside the building, where it looked warm and bright and dry.

Unfortunately, the way was blocked by the two men with pistols. The men did nothing; they just stood in the doorway and watched. And that would have been fine, if not for the larger group moving across the tarmac, coming toward them out of the rain.

"The Devil and the Deep Blue Sea," Bryce said softly. "Okay, now what?"

Tolwyn growled deep in her throat, and for a moment he thought it was Kurst. But Kurst was gone, into the shadows without a sound. Mara, too, had vanished. Tolwyn took Bryce's arm firmly.

"As you say, either or both groups could be friends," she said, leading him in slow-cadence steps toward the open door of the building, eyes locked forward and unafraid. "But until we find out for sure, let us move on the smaller group first."

Tom nodded and walked with them, also trying to appear calm and unafraid. They continued to stride, step by step, away from the plane and toward the building. The group across the runway began moving faster, and Bryce fancied he could hear a shout come from out of the beating rain. Fear took him, and his breath grew short. There were too many of them! He didn't even have a weapon! He started to run, but Tolwyn's strong arm held him back.

"Easy," she cautioned. "Do not give them cause for

alarm."

The two men in the doorway were motionless, still with their pistols held up, at the ready but not aimed. Bryce was aware of the pounding rain drumming on his head and back, and he wondered where Kurst and Mara were hiding.

Thirty feet from the door, at the point Bryce judged was as close as they wanted to get and still have a chance not to be shot, Tolwyn stopped. She glanced at Tom and he nodded.

"We need fuel for the plane," Tom called. "Is Old Jake around?"

The two men laughed. "Old Jake don't own this place no more. It's ours now," one of the men called back. "And I think that fine airplane out there is ours now, too."

From behind them, another shout arose.

"Please let us pass," Tolwyn said to the men in the doorway, her voice loud over the driving rain. "We have a vital mission to perform to save a friend's life."

"Come over here, little lady," the second man said. "If you're nice to us, maybe we'll help you." He did not move as he spoke, and his pistol did not waver.

"Who are these people, Tom?" Bryce asked.

"Looters would be my guess," the pilot replied. "Things are a little wilder out here, especially since the days and nights got longer."

Tolwyn continued to walk closer to the two men, finally stopping once she was within arm's length of them. "Will you let us pass?" she asked again.

Bryce waited to hear the answer as though simply asking a person was sufficient for finding out his intentions. And yet, that almost made sense for Tolwyn. She seemed to be able to look inside people sometimes and know their true selves in a way he never could — and he considered himself a very perceptive person.

One of the men grabbed Tolwyn then, wrapping thick fingers around her forearm and pulling her toward him. The other man raised his pistol and aimed it at Bryce and O'Malley, freezing them in their tracks. But the priest noticed that Tolwyn wasn't resisting. She hadn't even reached for her sword. Instead, she let the man pull her close. She tolerated his touch, waiting until he stuffed his pistol back into his jacket pocket.

"Now," he urged, "isn't it nicer in here with me, out of that rain?"

"No," Tolwyn answered truthfully. And with that, she made her move. Her free hand shot out and smashed the pistol away from the other man, then her knee came up to meet the soft flesh between her would-be suitor's legs. She silenced his howl with a shot to the throat that crushed his windpipe.

The second man attacked then, using his greater weight to drive her against the wall of the building. His large fist connected with the side of her head, snapping it back. Bryce gasped, sure that Tolwyn would be injured — or worse. But then her elbow caught the man in the chest, and he staggered back to catch his breath. That's when Tom got involved.

The pilot planted a heavy punch in the man's side. As he spun to ward off the pilot, Tom delivered two quick shots to his face, then decked him with a vicious uppercut. The man, his face a bloody mess, dropped to the ground.

"Are you all right?" Tom asked Tolwyn.

"You let him live," she said, surprise filling her voice. "You are a more generous adversary than I am."

Before Bryce could comment on the exchange, Kurst and Mara were beside him. Both appeared out of the rain silently. He noticed that metal claws were extended from Mara's cybernetic arm. The claws were covered with blood.

"The others have been taken care of," Kurst said.

"How?" Bryce stammered, not sure if he really wanted to know.

"We do not have time for this, priest," Kurst continued. "We must take the supplies we require before any others show up."

"There might be more?" Bryce asked.

"There could be, Chris," Mara answered. "These kind usually travel in packs."

Without any further discussion, Tom went in search of the fuel his plane needed.

48

Quin Sebastian listened as General Clay Powell outlined the facts. President Douglas Kent and Vice President Gregory Farrel had been in New York to attend a special session of the United Nations when the world suddenly changed. New York and a large portion of the east coast had been cut off from the rest of the country, engulfed in a zone of silence that disrupted all forms of modern communications. To add to the problem, the area was crawling with organized armies of dinosaurs and lizard men that were establishing some sort of staging ground for an expanding invasion.

"Recently," continued General Powell, "we discovered that the island of Manhattan had not completely fallen to the invaders. Reports of an interim government being established by the deputy mayor seem to be true, so some form of resistance has been mounted. We have also learned that the street gangs have taken parts of the city for themselves. While these are two very different types of settlements, they both represent order in an area we once took to be in total chaos."

"And?" Quin urged, trying to get to the point of all this.

"One of the refugees, the ex-mayor of New York himself who fled before the first week of the invasion was over, claims to have seen President Kent alive."

Quin sat up in his chair, looking from Powell to Wells for confirmation of what the general was saying.

"That was a few weeks ago, Quin," Wells said. "We only found out about Mayor Green's claim ourselves. After checking it as best we could, I called you."

"And what do you want me to do?" Quin asked.

"I want you to go into New York and find Douglas Kent," Wells said. "And if Kent is alive, I want you to bring him back out of there in one piece."

Quin studied the maps that Powell had brought with him more carefully now, examining the marks that indicated what refugees had reported as far as conditions in the Zone of Silence. "What are these triangles overlaying the map?" Quin asked, pointing at the gray and white triangles that covered the map from New York to the Great Lakes.

"Those are the areas where the lizards have taken control. The gray triangles are areas where our weaponry works occasionally but has an annoying tendency to cut out," Powell explained. "The white triangles are the areas we call the Zone of Silence."

"I want to talk to a few of these refugees," Quin finally said. "And I'll need some special equipment."

"There's a refugee relocation camp in Kentucky," Powell said. "Most of the New Yorkers wind up there sooner or later."

"And Quin," Wells added, "I want this kept quiet. If certain parties discovered that President Kent might still be alive, your mission would be in jeopardy."

"I'm surprised you don't feel threatened by this news, John," Quin smiled.

But Wells returned him a serious look. "I didn't want this job, Quin. I still don't want it. But someone has to do it, and I guess I'm the best one there is right now. Certainly not Quartermain. Kent is my friend. If he's alive, I want him brought out of there."

The soldier of fortune studied the map again, tracing the outline of Manhattan with his eyes. "I'll take the job, John."

"Very good," Wells said, sighing with relief. "Clay, give the man anything he needs."

49

"I do not believe this!" Lord Uthorion, who wore the body of Lady Pella Ardinay, raged. "What do you mean she killed the Carredon?"

The ravagon held its own temper in check as it repeated the words the Gaunt Man had sent it to convey. "Again, the Carredon confronted Tolwyn of House Tancred in a place of Core Earth power. Using that power, an Earth priest provided the paladin with the means to deliver a killing blow to the dragon. The Gaunt Man is as upset as you are. The Carredon was among his most favored."

Uthorion looked out of Ardinay's eyes, suddenly feeling trapped within the soft, feminine flesh. "The Carredon," the words slipped past large, red lips. "The Carredon helped me conquer Aysle. It was invincible. It killed Tolwyn once! It should have killed her a second time! Why didn't it kill her?"

The ravagon stepped toward the open window of Uthorion's tower. "I do not know why the dragon fell. I do know that the Gaunt Man is not pleased. Tolwyn will die. The Gaunt Man has already made preparations to assure that." Then, without waiting for leave from the High Lord, the ravagon flew into the Ayslish night.

"The prophecy does not bode well, Angar Uthorion," Pope Jean Malraux said. The false pope, High Lord of Magna Verita, sat with the High Lord of Aysle. Both were waiting for specific events to occur before entering their realms on Earth — Uthorion for the death of Tolwyn, Malraux for all the signs and portents of his arrival to be revealed.

"No, no, all is well," Uthorion decided. "The Carredon grew old, careless. That is the explanation for its demise. But the Wild Hunt is strong, powerful. It will destroy the paladin with ease. Then I can claim my new realm without worry. Then the prophecy will be over."

"As you say, Angar," Malraux returned, but he could not help staring at the single bead of sweat that hung on Ardinay's exquisite upper lip.

50

Eddie Paragon looked up as Baruk Kaah emerged from the black forest, stretching his body and breathing deeply of the ash-filled air. He turned to one of the nearby optants, the priests of life, and motioned for him to attend him.

"Yes, Saar," the optant said as he genuflected before the High Lord. "How may I serve you?"

"Gather the optants and start the prayer," Baruk Kaah ordered, twitching excitedly at his decision. "It is time for Lanala to send the Deep Mist to this world."

The optant made the signs of obedience, then set off

to carry out the High Lord's wishes. Baruk Kaah then made his way over to where Paragon sat.

"When the Deep Mist flows down the bridges and fills this realm, then it shall truly feel like Takta Ker," Baruk Kaah declared. "That will be a glorious day, singer."

Paragon nodded, still unsure of his part in all of this. He thought again of asking, but he didn't want the High Lord to realize he was useless. He didn't think he'd live much past that realization.

There was activity in the camp today, Paragon observed. Edeinos scampered to and fro like ants around a crumb. Some attended to the large dinosaurs that lounged along the fringe of the camp. Others cared for the wounded. Paragon knew of the battles happening around them. A benefit of being so close to the leader, he mused. From the large number of wounded, Paragon imagined that the battle had not gone exactly as Baruk Kaah had envisioned it.

A group of arriving edeinos carried the spoils of war — handfuls of machineguns and rifles. They dropped them into a growing pile, obviously glad to be rid of the dead things. Paragon wondered what Baruk Kaah wanted with weapons of Core Earth. From what the singer had observed so far, the majority of the lizard men refused to use anything that wasn't alive. Except for the gotaks, but they did not seem plentiful enough to waste as front-line soldiers.

As Paragon thought about these things, a gotak rushed over to examine the weapons. Baruk Kaah, as was his practice, went over to examine the gotak.

"These are the weapons for the gospog?" Baruk Kaah asked as he hefted an M-16.

"Yes, Saar," the gotak replied. "While our warriors

cannot use these instruments of the dead, the gospog will have no trouble wielding them against the Earthers."

The High Lord shook in anticipation. "Very good. I understand the crop will be ready shortly."

A commotion arose on the other side of the camp. Edeinos leaped aside as a black cloud rolled past them. Stepping out of the cloud was a huge man in an antlered helmet. His fire-red eyes paused momentarily upon Paragon, then shifted to Baruk Kaah.

"Your warriors were driven back, High Lord," the Horn Master said. "But the Wild Hunt destroyed the army that opposed them. Still, there were not enough of your edeinos left to activate the next stelae boundary."

Baruk Kaah rocked back on his tail as he contemplated this news. His lizard eyes darted from side to side nervously, and his head twitched. But he settled himself as the ravagon approached, unwilling to show weakness and indecision before the Gaunt Man's emissary.

"You did well, Horn Master," Baruk Kaah said. "I thank you for the assistance you and your force provide. Now I must regroup my own forces before we attempt another strike."

The High Lord waved one clawed appendage and a stalenger approached. It reached out with its tentacles to establish a communications link with the High Lord.

"Return to the Eastern Land and inform the master planter that he must harvest his crop now. Then lead the gospog back here over the maelstrom bridges," Baruk Kaah ordered.

"As you wish, Saar," the stalenger replied. Then it spread its starfish-shaped body and glided into the air. Soon it was gone from sight.

"Can we expect any attacks from the Earthers?" Baruk Kaah asked the Horn Master.

The leader of the Wild Hunt shook his antlered head. "No. It will take them time to regather their warriors. And I do not believe they will attempt to cross the storm front. But they will be ready for when you make another push into their reality zone."

"Yes," Baruk Kaah hissed happily, "but they won't be ready for the gospog."

The High Lord motioned for the Horn Master and the ravagon to follow him into the black forest that was Rec Pakken. Eddie Paragon hesitated, his gaze returning to the growing pile of automatic weapons.

"Come along, singer," Baruk Kaah called impatiently.

Sighing, Paragon followed them into the black forest.

51

Julie Boot rushed out to meet the incoming helicopter. For a change, there was only one wounded soldier aboard it. She had become distracted in the last few hours, and that was not a good state of mind when so much depended on her. But she couldn't get Doctor James Monroe out of her mind. And she couldn't stop herself from subconsciously putting the "Decker" back on the end of his name.

The chopper touched down and two medics unstrapped the stretcher that held the wounded soldier to the landing gear. Julie quickly checked the soldier's condition. He was unconscious, and shrapnel riddled his leg and stomach, but he didn't appear to be in too bad a shape. She turned his dogtags over and read the name imprinted in the metal: Lieutenant Charles Covent.

"Okay, get this soldier inside and prepped," she ordered the medics. "And tell Dr. Monroe we'll need him in surgery."

She thought again about the doctor and his

relationship to the congressman who was still in a coma. Was that why she was attracted to Monroe? Did it have something to do with switching feelings from one Decker to another? She didn't know, and she was too tired right now to care. With a wave to the helicopter pilot as he lifted his chopper off the tarmac, Julie Boot turned and followed the medics toward the base hospital.

"Welcome to Twentynine Palms, Lt. Covent," she whispered, jogging to catch up with the stretcher.

52

Mara sat with her knees hugged up to her chin, and felt very much the little girl at that moment. She was tired, and the gentle rise and fall of the plane was comfortably lulling her to sleep. Tom was a good pilot, keeping the plane as steady as possible even though the weather wasn't cooperating. She looked out her window, watching the rain drops splatter upon the wing. The constant patter of the rain on the metal hull around her was almost like music now. It no longer seemed harsh and angry as it did aboard the military plane.

After she and Kurst had taken out the gang at the last air field, Tom had moved quickly to secure the fuel he needed for his aircraft. She recalled his tall, lanky frame as he directed them to help him. He laughed a lot, trying to make the grim situation they were in seem more normal, and he constantly brushed red hair from his eyes. He claimed to know the man in Tolwyn's dreams, but even if he didn't Mara would have trusted him anyway. He just felt right. Maybe that was the kid in her, the trusting I-believe-everything part of her. But she liked that kid. The kid just didn't get out enough anymore.

Mara dozed for a time, then awoke as the plane started to descend. She looked around. Tolwyn was asleep, as were Father Bryce and Captain Albury. She quietly made her way to the cockpit, moving like a gentle breeze through the cargo hold. In the cockpit, Tom O'Malley and Kurst sat in the command chairs. She stepped behind Kurst and watched as the ground rushed toward them.

"We'll be down in a few minutes," Tom said cheerfully. "Then I'll introduce you to the Wee Folk and the aborigine shaman."

Mara looked questioningly at Kurst, but the Orrorshan shrugged. She would have asked Tom what he was talking about, but the pilot was working the controls with an intensity that refused to be disturbed. He was very good, she noted again, and she clicked on her recorder so that she could later study his movements and techniques.

The plane landed in a place Tom called Victoria River Downs. The rain was still falling, but it had changed to snow as the long night that gripped this part of the world continued and the temperature dropped. They all bundled up in whatever was available — blankets, mostly — and followed Tom out of the plane and across the snow-covered landing strip.

Mara was tempted to grab a handful of snow and toss it at Father Bryce. His bald spot made such an inviting target, she thought with a smile. But she held herself in check. There would be time for fun and games later. She hoped. Tom led them to a small building that looked warm and cozy. He opened the door and ushered the group in out of the cold.

"Shut that door!" came an angry shout from within the building.

"Yeah, you're letting the warm air out!" came still another voice.

Tom smiled, shaking the snow from his jacket. He motioned for the group to join him, and the six entered the room beyond the vestibule. Sitting around a roaring fire, some in seats with their short legs not reaching the floor, others reclining on the floor, were seven little people.

"Oldchilds," Mara blurted without thinking. Their size did make them appear as children with aged faces.

Tom laughed. "No, Mara, Wee Folk."

The seven looked up with hurt expressions, apparently unsatisfied with the labels Mara and Tom assigned them. They were dressed in old-fashioned clothing — breeches, leather jerkins, and vests. The males among them, of which there were five, were stocky, and four of them wore long beards. The fifth was clean-shaven, and looked younger than the rest. The two females, also of stocky build but obviously of the opposite gender, smiled at Tom. All were busy with the pile of items stacked between them. Mara noticed engineering manuals, magazines, a piece of a motor, tools, and a few digital watches among their treasure.

Tolwyn stepped up beside Mara. She had a look of bewilderment on her face, like there was a question fighting to come out.

"Is something wrong?" Mara asked, but Tolwyn dismissed her and stepped closer to the strange group of little people.

"So let's introduce everyone," Tom suggested, looking at Father Bryce expectantly. The priest still had bits of ice in his beard, and he shook with a slight chill. But he walked over to the fire and smiled at the group.

"I'm Father Christopher Bryce," he said softly. "I'm a Jesuit priest."

"We know of your type," one of the little people said,

pointing at the cross that hung around Bryce's neck. "You are a follower of Dunad."

Tolwyn, who had been examining the oldchilds fiercely, suddenly gasped. "Hai Dunad!" she cried. "Sintra vas Dunad?"

"Tolwyn, what's the matter?" Mara asked, concerned for her friend.

"These are not Wee Folk or oldchilds, Mara" Tolwyn said. "These are dwarves from the land of Aysle."

"That's what we've been trying to tell Tom since we found him," said the youngest dwarf.

One of the females leaped to her feet and yelled, "Tolwyn? Ge stettsu Tolwyn vas Tancred, gee telliber?"

The other dwarves started chattering, and they stood and ran to Tolwyn. They clustered around her like children, yammering away in nonsense syllables, hopping up and down first on one foot, then another. Two of them did cartwheels. Then they formed a circle about her, and they called out in unison, "Ho, Tolwyn!"

Bryce put out a hand and gave Kurst a look to stop him from advancing. The dwarves were touching Tolwyn's hands, smiling up at her, stroking her clothing, laughing.

"You are dressed like an Earther," one of the females laughed.

Then a dwarf fell to one knee and held a metal spike (that Mara assumed to be both weapon and walking stick) above his head, obviously offering fealty of some kind. Another barked something and waved his own spike, wagging it dangerously near the face of a third, who fell backward onto the floor. Then they were all doing it, bowing solemnly with downcast faces, offering Tolwyn their weapons. There was a moment of silence.

"Well I'll be," O'Malley breathed.

Tolwyn stood there, looking mystified and a little frightened, holding in a breath as though about to say something.

"Tolwyn," Bryce said slowly. The dwarves did not move a muscle. "You'd better do something or we'll be here all day."

She turned to look at him and her face cleared. She laughed, a clear and lovely laugh. "Kanta!" she said proudly. "Kanta *noch*," she corrected herself and turned back, touching each dwarf's hand individually and repeating the strange phrase, "Kanta noch." Each one padded back to his or her seat, smiling, except the one who had started it all. He sat with Tolwyn in the middle of the floor, where she stayed, sinking down with heavy legs. The dwarf moved around her to sit with his back propped against hers, like mismatched bookends. He held his spike up over his head and waved it, and said something that made the others laugh.

"It seems," Bryce said dryly, "that Tolwyn needs no introduction."

Tom grinned. "They seem to know each other, by the looks of it. Why don't you finish the introductions, and then we'll see what the Wee — excuse me — what the dwarves will tell us about all that."

The dwarves smiled smugly, and one said, "It'll cost you." They all laughed and said, "Heh!" in unison.

Bryce introduced Kurst, Mara, and Captain Albury, but there was no reaction from the dwarves other than a curt nod of the head. Then it was O'Malley's turn, and he pointed to the first dwarf and started to speak, but the dwarf interrupted him.

"My name is Braxon," said the first. "And this is my sister …"

"… Praktix," chimed the second, a female of obvious

beauty (at least to another dwarf).

"I am Grim," said the third, who smelled of things arcane.

"Gutterby," muttered the oldest of the lot.

"Pluppa," said the other female. She had the look of a leader.

"Tirad," said the sixth, a powerful-looking warrior.

"And I am Toolpin!" proclaimed the one seated with Tolwyn. "The only one who remembered the legend of Tolwyn of House Tancred!"

The other dwarves started protesting at once, in both English and their strange language. Mara laughed at the spectacle, which got rather loud before O'Malley shouted for quiet. Through it all, Tolwyn stared straight ahead, as if trying to see something in the faces of the assembled dwarves.

"Are you going to explain yourselves?" O'Malley asked. "This is a new one even for me, and I've been listening to your tall tales for the past few weeks!"

"What tall tales?" Gutterby asked with genuine hurt.

"With Tolwyn's permission ..." Toolpin began, turning toward the paladin.

"Please. Speak," said Tolwyn softly, nodding to the young, beardless dwarf.

Mara noticed that Bryce was leaning forward in the seat he had found, his hands clutching at the armrests.

"I'll tell it as a story!" Toolpin crowed.

"A story!" shouted Praktix.

"A story!" agreed Braxon

"Don't let Toolpin tell it," said Triad. "I'll fall asleep."

"Fine friend you are," Toolpin said.

"Friend? Did I ever give you reason to believe I was your friend?" Triad asked indignantly.

"Let Grim tell it," suggested Pluppa with a laugh.

"*I'll* tell it, for I was the only one of us to witness the great event," declared old Gutterby with great finality, and all the dwarves fell silent for a beat.

Sheepishly, Toolpin whispered, "You told the last story." Then they all started talking again, each suggesting someone else tell the story, or vetoing someone's suggestion.

"Enough!" yelled Tom at the top of his lungs. "Gutterby," he ordered, "tell the story."

"You know, you don't have to be so nasty," Toolpin complained. But his words were cut short by a sharp rap on his helmet from Pluppa's spike.

"Go ahead, Gutterby," she encouraged, before the dwarves began to argue again.

Gutterby, aged, round and plump, stood on a chair (which brought his head about level with O'Malley's chest) and scanned his audience for effect. The other dwarves settled comfortably and turned to watch him, looking for all the world like excited children. Mara felt a giggle coming on, but stifled it when she saw Tolwyn's expression. This was important to her. Perhaps it was the key to her missing memories.

Gutterby cleared his throat.

The dwarves, in unison, shouted, "Hey!"

53

"My name is Gutterby," Gutterby said, "and I've seen five hundred and eighty Aysle years come and go. If the gods (who we as a people have very little to do with) are willing, I'll probably see another hundred."

"Hoy!" shouted the other dwarves with one voice.

"When I was a young lad of seventy-five," Gutterby continued, "Aysle was enjoying a Golden Age of sorts. The War of Crowns had been over for some three years,

The Dark Realm

Valerie Valusek

peace finally secured by the formation of the Delegate Legacy. This feudal system was set in motion by the Great Houses of Aysle and spearheaded by Pella of House Ardinay. But Pella wished to speak for more than just one House. She wanted to fully embrace the ideals of the Delegate Legacy. So she gave her land and titles to House Tancred and became one of the simple people. With House Ardinay dissolved, she became Speaker for the People, the leader without a House.

"In this time of great freedoms and opportunities, we never expected another war. But one grew out of a raging, unnatural storm. This war was not fought between the Houses, or between humans and dwarves, or giants, or elves. It was a war against invaders from another place, another world. Pella Ardinay was quickly elevated to Lady of the Houses and asked to lead the defenders of Aysle. She accepted this post, asking for the greatest warrior of each House to join her as Knight Protectors and military advisors. And so were gathered Kwev of House Daleron, Abonon of House Gerrik, Seris of House Liandar, Hoger of House Vareth, Candal of House Bendes, and Tolwyn of House Tancred."

Tolwyn drew in a great breath, held it, then let it out in a slow hiss. But she did not say a word. She just waited for Gutterby to continue.

He did.

"The invaders were horrific beings — monsters and undead warriors, specters and moaning ghosts. They slashed through our defenses, cutting their way to Lady Ardinay's keep. For the most part, our weapons were ineffective against these supernatural beings. Only those of us with true magic or magic items at our disposal were able to launch effective counter-assaults. But the invaders didn't seem interested in wiping us out to the man. Instead, they pushed on for Ardinay's stronghold.

"I was of House Vareth then, the only dwarven family recognized by the human Houses as being of royal blood. I was in the courtyard when the vile Uthorion arrived, riding atop a dragon that called itself Carredon. We were scared, the boys and I. Shivering in our boots we were. But we held our ground. It helped to see the Knight Protectors on the ramparts above us, waiting to take their turns against the invaders. So, being brave, we cast our spears and arrows, hacked and slashed with our swords, and fell before the onslaught of the Carredon.

"Nothing hurt the beast. Nothing slowed it. To it, we were nothing more than wheat in a field. And its claws cut us down. I still bear the scars delivered by its vicious attack, welted lines across my chest and belly. I watched from where I fell as Tolwyn of House Tancred leaped down to face the monster. Her weapons of magic worked better than ours, but in the end the Carredon was too strong for her. As she fought the beast within the garden of crys flowers, Uthorion slipped into the keep to find Ardinay. Tolwyn cursed him, pledging to see him dead before this was all over. Pledging to return from the grave if necessary to fulfill her promise.

"The Knight Protectors prayed then, concentrating on Tolwyn. They tapped the power of their own souls to perform a miracle of legend. As the Carredon's claws struck and blood splattered the blue and red flowers, the Knights sent Tolwyn's spirit someplace else, and a new legend was born. The legend of Tolwyn Neverdeath, who would one day return to Aysle to stand at Lady Ardinay's side."

Gutterby motioned to Toolpin, who hurriedly tossed him a jug of Earther ale. (Foster's Lager, they called it, served in a small metal jug called a can.) He popped it open (as Tom had shown him) and drank thirstily, not caring that some spilled onto his jerkin.

"What happened then, Gutterby?" Tolwyn demanded, knocking the ale from the dwarf's hand.

He stared at her angrily, then wiped his beard on his sleeve and laughed. "Always was an impatient sort, weren't you, Lady Tancred."

"Your story ...?" she pressed.

"Of course," he nodded, and continued his tale.

"Something awful occurred within the walls of Ardinay's keep. None of us who were there ever found out exactly what. But the Carredon and the other creatures withdrew, retreating back over the terrible bridges of tortured bodies they had descended. When Lady Ardinay appeared atop her tower, she claimed victory over the forces of evil, and those of us that survived cheered.

"But all too soon things began to change in Aysle. The land became a darker place, and new creatures roamed the land. Ardinay herself was different, less compassionate. She abolished the Delegate Legacy and reinstituted the old laws of rank and privileges. We went along with her in the beginning because she had saved us from the invaders and we believed that everything she did was for our own good. By the time we knew differently, we went along with her because she was too powerful for us to oppose. Soon we were crossing bridges of stone into other worlds, to bring enlightenment to these places our Lady said. But all we brought was death.

"When we arrived on this world, me and my fellows decided we had had enough of enlightenment. So, after meeting up with Tom O'Malley and his magic flying machine, we find ourselves here, talking to a legend."

Gutterby, his story finished, collapsed heavily into the chair he had been standing on. "Telling stories always takes a lot out of me," he said, motioning Toolpin to toss him another Foster's.

Pluppa took Tolwyn's hand and raised her head so that she could look directly into the paladin's eyes. "Have you come here to gather us? Is it time to go back to Aysle?" the female dwarf asked.

Tolwyn, her jaw set in determination, replied, "Soon, but not yet my friend. First we must go to Orrorsh and find Uthorion. Then, when I have repaid a debt to a man named Decker and fulfilled my pledge to Uthorion, then we can return to Aysle and discover what has changed in my absence. You say all this happened over five hundred years ago, Gutterby?"

"Aye," Gutterby nodded, "give or take a year or two."

"And Lady Ardinay still lives?"

"Correct again, Lady Tancred."

Bryce looked from Tolwyn to Gutterby and back to Tolwyn again. "Is something wrong?"

"I do not know how things work on Earth, Christopher," Tolwyn said, "but in Aysle humans do not live much longer than one hundred years."

And, for the first time that evening, the dwarves had nothing to say.

54

Julie Boot watched as Dr. James Monroe worked on

the wounded soldier. Monroe was very good, she decided, as good as his reputation had led her to believe. But reading reports is one thing. Seeing the man work was quite another. His hands moved with speed and grace, and there was a confidence about him that made every subtle movement a work of art. To Monroe, medicine was his talent. Like a musician plays a concerto, Monroe performed an operation.

"You're in good hands, Lt. Covent," Julie whispered to the soldier on the table, and even though he couldn't hear her, she felt better for letting him know.

Monroe finished removing the shrapnel from the soldier's leg and stomach. Then, when he finished closing the patient and finally turned him over to his assistant for recovery, he took the metal tray and motioned for Julie to follow him.

"What's the matter, James?" she asked, suddenly concerned for the soldier.

"Nothing terrible," Monroe replied, slipping the surgical mask away from his mouth. "Lt. Covent will be up an around in no time. But take a look at what I pulled out of him."

Julie examined the material on the tray. She expected to see pieces of metal. Instead the tray was full of bone slivers and long thorns. She looked up at Monroe, her eyes full of questions.

"The lizards make some strange land mines," Monroe said. "Maybe we should go have a talk with the friendly lizard you told me about. What was its name?"

"His name," Julie corrected. "His name is Tal Tu."

55

Christopher Bryce was astonished by the tale of invaders and miracles. Could it be true? Is that what happened to Tolwyn before she appeared in the body of Wendy Miller? And did it really happen five hundred years ago? His mind reeled. The dwarves were asking questions again, and Bryce cut off his own thoughts so that he could concentrate on the fast-talking little people.

"How long you been here on this strange world?" asked Toolpin.

"How does the Quest end?" Praktix chimed in.

"I do not know," Tolwyn said, taking one of the spikes from the dwarves and staring at it intensely.

"Tolwyn," Bryce said. "Memories return slowly. Give it time. You've had a wonderful push here. I'm sure the rest will come soon. Meanwhile," he turned to Tom O'Malley. "We still have a mission to complete. Where is the shaman you told us about?"

Tom shrugged. "He was here when I left. In fact, he told me where to go to meet you. Pluppa, where'd Djil go?"

Pluppa jumped up when Tom spoke, smiling at the sound of his voice. At least, that's how it looked to Bryce. Could the dwarf lady have some feelings for the pilot? Bryce smiled at the thought. Well, he decided, it's no more strange than a priest having feelings for a five hundred year old paladin from a different world.

"Djil went for a walk," Pluppa declared.

"Terrific," Bryce muttered.

"We are running out of time," Kurst announced, and Tolwyn nodded in agreement.

"Do you have a map, Tom?" Bryce asked.

The pilot led him to the far wall, where a map of the area hung. Kurst followed, examined the map for a moment, then pointed out the route.

"We need to travel across the Timor Sea to the interior of Borneo" Kurst explained.

"We have a companion who's dying," Bryce added quickly, "and the only way to save him is to confront the Gaunt Man and ... and then what?" The priest asked Kurst, but the resulting dwarven clamor cut off any possible answer.

"The Gaunt Man?" asked Grim.

"The Gaunt Man!" exclaimed Triad.

"Tough nut," said Gutterby.

"Very tough," agreed Braxon.

"Dangerous," added Praktix.

"Tough," said Toolpin, just so he could add to the conversation.

"Of course we'll go," decided Pluppa. "If that's where Tolwyn Neverdeath wants to go, then we'll go. Eh, Tom?"

Tom O'Malley nodded. "That's what Djil told me we'd be doing. But we'll have to cross a storm front. There's no guarantee we'll make it through that."

"You'll get us through," Pluppa smiled.

Bryce hoped that the dwarf's faith in the pilot was all they would need. But he had a feeling that it would take more than that to get them into Orrorsh realm and back out again.

56

James Monroe was surprised to see the two boys in the room with the lizard. They were the same boys that had been with the priest and the cop back in Philadelphia. The same group that had departed with Wendy Miller — who called herself Tolwyn since "returning" to life. He desperately tried to remember the boys' names, but he couldn't. However, he knew how to fake his way through a conversation until the names came back to him.

"Well, well," he said, smiling his best bedside manner smile. "I didn't know you boys had moved out west."

"That's right," Julie said, "Coyote mentioned that he knew you, doctor."

Coyote! Of course, thought Monroe. Thank you Major Boot! That makes the younger boy Rat. Odd names. Gang names. He had tolerated their presence back in Philadelphia because they had grown so close to Tolwyn. He would have to pretend to like them again. At least they appeared to be cleaner now, and he couldn't smell them from across the room. Perhaps if he kept his distance ...

Rat stroked the gray cat that sat on his lap. "Hi, Dr. Monroe."

Coyote laughed. "Just like old times! Dr. Monroe saved Tolwyn. Did I tell you about that, Julie?"

"Briefly," Julie smiled at the boy. "You'll have to give me all the details later on. We've come to talk to Tal Tu, if that's okay with you guys."

Coyote looked at the edeinos resting on the floor of the room. Apparently, the bed wasn't comfortable for Tal Tu's strange proportions. He turned to Julie. "Sure. Me and Rat have to go visit Congressman Decker anyway. Come on, Rat."

The boys knew Decker? Monroe decided that he would have to hear their stories before too long. He wondered if Tolwyn, the cop, and the priest were here at Twentynine Palms, too.

"Nice to see you again, Dr. Monroe," Rat said as he followed after Coyote, the cat clutched firmly in his arms.

"Leave the cat," Julie ordered.

"Okay," Rat said with disappointment, but he placed the cat on the floor. Once free of the boy, the cat raced over to cuddle against the edeinos. Then the boys were gone.

"Tal Tu, this is Dr. James Monroe," Julie said, introducing the two. "He wants to show you something."

Monroe felt silly treating the lizard as though it were human, but he didn't want to upset Julie. He placed the metal tray full of shrapnel beside the lizard without a word and waited to see what it would do. Probably try to eat some of it, he imagined.

Tal Tu carefully lifted a piece of bone from the assortment of items. He turned it over a few times, smelled it, and placed it back on the tray. "That is the bone of a lokritosk," Tal Tu said. "And those are thorns from a hessi bush. These items are dead, yet they are from Takta Ker. Where did you get them?"

Monroe, taken aback by the lizard's capability of speech, couldn't find the words to answer him. How could this ... thing ... speak? And worse, how was he expected to tolerate such behavior in a ... thing?

Julie looked at the doctor expectantly, but when she saw that he was not going to answer Tal Tu, she filled the gap. "These were in some kind of bomb that injured one of our soldiers. Have you ever heard of such a weapon."

Tal Tu shook, and looked away from Julie and Monroe. "It is the shame of my world you ask about, abominations. It is a thing of the gotaks, the priests of the dead. These are the contents of a pain sack. It bursts open to release these items, causing pain and perhaps death to those within range of the burst."

Monroe swallowed hard, then forced himself to speak to the lizard. "Then ... this is a weapon?"

Tal Tu nodded.

"What kind of people use such things?" he asked.

"The people of the Living Land," Tal Tu answered,

"who have embraced the ways of the dead."

57

Kurst stood outside the building, knee deep in fresh snow. The frozen whiteness was still falling around him, and the long night gave no sign that it would soon be over. The hunter knew he should rest, gather his energy. For soon would come the challenges and tests he craved. They had made it easier for him, though. The stormers were accompanying him to the Gaunt Man without a struggle and of their own accord. It was almost amusing. Such confidence this group had! With the Aysle renegades beside them, they might make the final leg of the journey interesting. But in Orrorsh, nothing they did would be enough to deter the Gaunt Man's power.

He thought about the group and his place in it. Decker had accepted him on face value, as had Tolwyn. But Mara and Bryce still had a healthy caution where Kurst was concerned. That made them the more dangerous of the group. Mara was off in the corner, doing what she had done during every idle moment she could find. She was working on the metal plate she carried, inscribing it with her beams of light. Bryce, on the other hand, was sitting inside by the fire, staring at the eternity shard they called the Heart of Coyote.

Coyote. That was the name of one of the boys they left behind with Decker. The other was Rat, the boy who had asked him a disturbing question. The question continued to nag at him half a world away.

"I am a hunter for the High Lord of Orrorsh," Kurst had told the boys, "a common servant who is treated well because of his skills."

And then the youth asked his damning question.

"What were you before that?" Rat inquired.

Kurst had only one answer for the boy. "I do not remember. My memories were taken from me."

The thought turned his blood cold. What did you take from me, Gaunt Man? he wondered. Do I really want to know the answer to that question? Or am I satisfied with my station, content to do my master's bidding until a stormer finally takes me down?

"Stormer," he said aloud, watching the breath trail as the word left his lips. He was a stormer. Tolwyn, Bryce, and Mara were stormers. Tom O'Malley was a stormer. Each had the ability to retain his or her own reality no matter what realm they walked.

"Storm Knight," he said, wondering what difference a word made. But as the frosty air puffed into the night, he realized that it did make a difference.

The door of the building swung open then, caught by a cold breeze and slammed against the wall. Captain Albury, who opened the door in the first place, struggled to close it before the noise and cold awoke the others. Breathless, he finally managed to secure the latch. He did not see Kurst, who was standing within the shadow of the building. Albury stepped over to a bench beside the airstrip and placed one booted foot upon it. Tom's plane was in front of him, waiting patiently for them to board.

Kurst watched as the captain produced a pipe from his jacket pocket. So the fool had come out into the cold to smoke, the hunter mocked silently. Kurst sensed something then, an intense sensation that screamed for him to shift to wolf form. But he held the urge in check, refusing to succumb to his animal instincts if he could help it. After all, shapeshifting outside of Orrorsh, even for one such as he, was not without risk. He tried to focus on the unseen danger, but nothing revealed itself. He again turned to watch Albury, who was now puffing contentedly on his pipe.

Was that a movement off to Albury's right? Kurst wondered. Or were his senses playing tricks on him in the cold, snowy night? Kurst stepped out of the darkness into the light cast by the small bulb over the building's entrance. Albury looked up at him, startled. Then the captain smiled.

"I was wondering where you disappeared to, Mr. Kurst," Albury said. "Come out for a bit of air, did you?"

Kurst saw the shadow behind Albury move, but he was too far away to intercept it. Black tendrils snaked out and wrapped around the captain. Where they touched, Kurst saw the flesh dissolve. He smelled the stink of Albury's burning skin. He leaped forward, seeking to release the captain before the creature finished him off. A tendril cracked like a whip across Kurst's arm, searing his flesh and knocking him to the ground. He rolled through the snow, out of the tendril's reach. Albury's screams filled his ears, and he realized that his own were mixed with the captain's.

Intense beams of light cut through the darkness. Kurst saw Mara standing a few feet away from him, firing her energy weapon at the creature. It dropped off of Albury, a black mass of thin, wispy limbs. She gave it no chance to escape, pumping shot after shot into the black form until it stopped moving. Then, with a burst of flame, the creature was gone.

Bryce ran past Mara to kneel beside Albury. He examined the man for a moment, then turned his head away. "My God," Bryce said, "what did it do to him?"

Kurst started to rise, but Mara stopped him with a gentle hand. "Let me look at your arm, Kurst," she said.

The hunter nodded and ripped away the smouldering cloth of his jacket sleeve. "That was a shaden, Bryce," Kurst explained. "A creature from Orrorsh. Its tendrils are coated with an extremely powerful acid. This allows it to liquify its food so that its main body mass may absorb it."

"Giga-gross," Mara said as she used snow to cool Kurst's burns. "Is Albury all right?"

"Albury is dead," Bryce blurted. "His face, his chest, they're ... melted."

Kurst noticed the crowd that had gathered in the doorway. Tolwyn and Tom were there, as well as the dwarves. "I suggest we go inside," Kurst offered. "Shaden do not hunt alone."

Bryce helped Mara get Kurst to his feet. "What about Captain Albury?"

"Leave him," Kurst said. "It will be safer to deal with his remains when dawn breaks and the shaden are not up and around."

"How do you know they won't be around when the sun rises?" Bryce demanded.

"Because," Kurst told him fiercely, "the sun's rays burn them just as their acid burned Albury."

"And how long before dawn arrives?" Bryce asked. "Do you have any idea how long this damned night is going to last?"

The hunter ignored the priest as something else caught his attention. He wasn't certain, but he thought that the pool of darkness where he had been standing, the one beside the building, moved. Whether the dead creature behind them was the only shaden that had drifted over from Orrorsh or the airstrip was full of them, Kurst knew they didn't have a chance out here in the open. Another movement, and Kurst's senses screamed out their warning cries. "Get us inside, Father Bryce. And make sure all the lights are turned up bright."

58

Major Julie Boot felt as if her life was lately defined by three places. The first of these places was the operating chamber, where she and her staff had been tending the wounded for the past twelve hours, ever since the first helicopter had touched down, loaded with casualties from the northern front. The second place was at Andrew Jackson Decker's bedside, where she came to do what little she could for the congressman, usually simply talking and hoping that he would eventually respond. The third place was in Dr. James Monroe's quarters, finding comfort and release in the arms of the talented surgeon.

She was in with Decker at this time, coming to sit with him since she had neglected him throughout the long bout in surgery. There had been no change in his condition, but she thought she detected a paleness around his eyes. How long could he go on like this? The staves in his chest glowed with a faint blue light that shimmered and crept like tiny snakes around the carved runes. The glow was growing dimmer daily.

Decker's face was strong, handsome. It was very much like Monroe's face, though older, more seasoned. What were the runes sucking from you, Ace? she wondered. And how long before it was totally sapped?

It wasn't fair! All the wounded she treated, all the dead she buried — where was the sense of all this? Where was the purpose? And this man, lying in a coma with metal stakes driven into his body … it made her angry. She could feel the rage inside her, growing in response to her questions. But there was no one to vent the rage upon, no single enemy to strike out at.

She leaned over Decker, her lips almost touching his, staring at his closed eyes.

"Live, damn it," she whispered fiercely, putting all her anger into the words. "Live."

Feeling helpless, she turned and strode from the room, leaving a whisper of hospital cloth in her wake. Had she lingered a moment longer, she would have seen the staves begin to glow just a touch brighter. She would have seen Decker's eyelids snap open before they closed again.

59

"How very interesting," the Gaunt Man commented as he monitored the instruments on the machine.

Thratchen, standing beside him, tried to understand what the dials were telling him. But he had no clue as to the workings of this machine. He only knew that it stripped and sorted possibilities from stormers (and anything else containing the precious energy).

The Gaunt Man looked at Thratchen from the corner of his eye. "You appear confused, Thratchen. Ah, of course! You cannot see what I can see. But I assure you, if you could it would interest you greatly."

The Gaunt Man stepped around Thratchen and threw a number of switches, craning his neck to watch as energy played across the gridwork of the machine. Satisfied, he again turned to Thratchen.

"As you know I have been using Decker's possibilities to sort through the possibilities of this world," the High Lord explained. "I need him to show me which to keep and which to use up. That is not a talent that our kind possess. But Decker has it, and even now he is making choices for me."

"What has that to do with what you saw?" Thratchen asked impatiently.

"Careful, son of Tharkold. I am not someone you want to become angry with," the Gaunt Man cautioned. "However, I think you will find this tale amusing. You see, Decker is close to being used up. The machine is stripping him faster than his body can replenish the energy. That means we are close to the solution I seek, so I dare not dampen the machine's work. But Decker is such a perfect battery, as it were. I hate to lose him."

More dials were turned, more switches toggled.

"Now, however, it appears he will be around long enough to finish the task I have placed before him," the Gaunt Man said. "It appears that another stormer has given him support, helped him slow the process that is eating away his possibilities — helped him heal himself, you see. If she continues to provide him with support, he will continue to do my sorting for me. Isn't that grand?"

"Ironic, I should think," Thratchen replied.

"Yes, and I love irony," the Gaunt Man decided. "It leaves such a bitter taste."

60

Father Christopher Bryce and Mara helped Kurst into the building. "Shut the door, Tom," Bryce called behind him as he moved Kurst to a chair. Then he turned back to see that the door was firmly closed. The dwarves started talking at once, but the priest ignored them. "Lock it, too."

Tom did as he was told, securing the bolts that held the door shut. Tolwyn examined Kurst's arm, noted the burns, then looked at the priest.

"What has happened here, Christopher?" she asked, her hand moving to grip the hilt of her sword.

"Creatures from Orrorsh," Bryce said. "Kurst calls them shaden. They drip acid."

"Oh!" shouted the dwarves.

"They've tasted blood," Kurst explained. "If there are any more of them out there, then we can expect them to try to get at us."

"You make it sound as if they're intelligent," Bryce protested.

"In a way, they are."

"What do you …"

But Bryce's question was cut off by a loud thump. They all turned to look at the far window, the window on the dark side of the building. The light from the bulb over the doorway did not reach that far, and the shadows were deep there. At the window, attached like a snail to the side of a fish tank, was a black shape that Bryce figured must be a shaden. It hung on the glass, its tendrils splayed and throbbing, as acid dripped hotly down the pane.

"Lights, Tom," Bryce shouted, "turn on all the lights!"

More thumps followed, and the building started to shake as unseen things hammered into it.

"They're trying to get in!" Mara shouted.

Tom ran toward a metal box that hung on the wall beside a window. Bryce assumed that the box contained the switches to the exterior lights. As Tom reached the box, he fumbled with the latch that opened it. Faster! Bryce thought. A violent crash sent vibrations throughout the room as something smashed into the side of the building.

"Hurry," Bryce called out. "Let's get our gear and be ready to head for the airplane. I don't think we want to remain here under these conditions."

"Be careful, Tom," Braxon called out.

Bryce turned as the sound of shattering glass filled the room. A black tendril snaked in through the broken window beside the switch box, reaching for Tom. He finally got the box open, but before he could flip the switches the tendril wrapped around his hand.

Tom's screams were loud inside the building. The shaden's acid was already eating through his glove to get at the tender flesh beneath it. But then Braxon was there, swinging his battle-ax in a tight arc that sliced through the creature's limb. Severed, the tendril fell from Tom's hand and the creature retreated back outside.

"Hurry, Tom," Braxon urged.

Using his uninjured hand, Tom flipped all the switches in the box. Outside, the runway lights flared to life, as did the flood lights all along the building. High-pitched squeals sounded in the night. It was the sound of shaden crying.

"Now what?" Mara asked.

"Now we head for the plane," Bryce answered as he examined Tom's hand. The acid had burned it badly, but it had not melted through to the bones. "Mara, bandage this up," he said.

The priest went to the window beside the door and looked outside. It was still snowing, and he could see the large flakes dancing in the pools of light the floods threw across the field. While the runway and the airplane were bathed in bright light, the path between the tarmac and the building was a pattern of dark spots and light. The floods were not situated to provide a continuous, uninterrupted area of light, so shadowy pools rested between each pool of brightness.

"We will be vulnerable as we move from light to dark," Tolwyn said, appearing at Bryce's side. "We will have to fight our way to the flying machine."

"And risk more injuries? There must be a better way," the priest demanded.

"Would you rather stay here and risk all of our deaths?"

"Hey, look out there!" Toolpin shouted as he pushed between Bryce and Tolwyn.

Standing beneath the airplane, holding a flaming torch, was a man. The man was dark-skinned, with a patch of white hair. He was wearing furs to protect him from the cold, but he did not appear comfortable in the confining garments.

"That's Djil!" Toolpin exclaimed.

Bryce strained to see the man better. Yes, he could be an aborigine. The man walked toward them, stepping off the tarmac and onto the path of light and darkness. But as he took each step, his torch flared brighter, forming a circle of light around the man that banished the shadows as he strode forward. In seconds he was in front of the door.

"Sorry, I'm late," he said. "Too bad about the poor fellow out there. But we're all alive, and there's still a trip to be made. So let's get on with it. Time for our special walkabout."

The man did not wait to see if they would agree with him. He turned and made ready to return to the plane. With no other options, Bryce motioned for the group to gather around the strange man. Then, safely bathed in the light of his extraordinarily bright torch, they all walked to the tarmac.

Bryce expected the shaden to attack as they moved down the path. With every step he expected some dark creature to leap upon them, its limbs dripping acid and its squeal loud and terrifying. But no attack came.

Tom opened the plane's hatch, and he and the dwarves

climbed in. Bryce, Tolwyn, Kurst and Mara waited outside, however, looking over the small black man dressed in furs. He doused his torch in the snow, all the while his eyes were locked on Tolwyn's. Then he smiled, showing white teeth — except where one was missing.

"I am Djilangulyip," the man said. He drew a long, knotted rope from out of the folds in his furs. "But you can call me Djil."

"Jill?" Mara asked.

"Close enough," Djil laughed. He pulled the rope through his strong, callused hands, lingering on each knot in turn. "Tolwyn Tancred," he said, touching the first knot and smiling at the paladin. "Christopher Bryce, Hachi Mara-Two, Kurst," he said, moving over the next three knots and nodding at each of the companions.

There were two knots left on the end of the rope. Djil touched the fifth knot and his expression saddened. "Andrew Decker," he sighed. "Such pain he must endure. But that is his part in this, his burden." His hand moved to the final knot. "And this is me, Djilangulyip. Now we are ready."

"Ready for what?" Bryce asked, confused by the proceedings. How could this man know them? The priest didn't understand.

"Ready to finish the dream," Djil laughed. Then he ushered them onto the plane, out of the snow.

Out of the night.

61

"How long has it been night, Ahkemeses?" Dr. Mobius asked his High Priest. They were standing together atop the monolith constructed beside his as-yet uncompleted palace. The monolith was a mobile structure, great fitted stone blocks atop four huge wheels. Hieroglyphics were carved across the stones, pictures proclaiming the majesty of the Tenth Empire and the greatness of its Pharaoh.

"We have been without the sun for the past forty-three hours, Pharaoh," Ahkemeses replied. "Already the temperature has dropped to below freezing and the masses grow worried."

Mobius smiled beneath his cowl. "Good, I want them to worry. I want them to be so frightened that when they see what I can do for them they will fall down and worship me."

The Pharaoh looked down into the monolith, through the large opening on the top where he stood. He was on the lip of the monolith, looking down into its hollow interior. Within, a great framework of wooden beams and riveted metal formed a resting place for a gigantic golden sphere. The sphere was constructed of riveted metal as well, with a coating of gold that made it sparkle. It was one of Mobius' greatest creations. He smiled proudly.

"Have there been any further sightings of the Mystery Men?" he asked his High Priest.

"No, Pharaoh, not since the first incident in Cairo," Ahkemeses said.

The Pharaoh nodded, pleased. The he turned to the crowd below.

"Let the people know, Ahkemeses, that their Pharaoh will provide them with light when the darkness falls, with heat when the cold becomes unbearable!" Mobius shouted. "Let the light of Mobius shine across his realm!"

The monolith began to shake as the great sphere started to roll up the framework tracks. Slowly, it emerged from the top of the monolith, a golden ball against the black of the sky. But it did not stop there.

Magno-repulsors of Mobius' own invention lifted the sphere higher into the sky. A gasp rippled through the crowd, and Mobius could feel their excitement and wonder — and their fear.

"When Muab finishes the Grand Temple of Ra in Luxor, then we shall move the monolith there," Mobius explained to Ahkemeses as the sphere continued to rise. He noted that it did not rise smoothly. There were a few slight jerks and bounces as the repulsors compensated for the weight. "I will have to fix that, Ahkemeses," the Pharaoh noted.

And still the golden sphere rose. High into the sky over Thebes it climbed, eventually coming to rest some forty miles above the city. Mobius laughed with glee.

"Now, Ahkemeses," he cackled, "let there be light!"

The golden sphere flared with energy, becoming a small sun in the night sky. The light it cast filled the realm with heat, banishing the darkness with its powerful glare. For long moments, there was only stunned silence from the crowd below him. Then a cheer started up. It was a cheer for the Pharaoh. It started as a small ripple at first, gradually swelling like the waves of the ocean. Mobius let the sound wash over him. He smiled.

"Let the Gaunt Man work his plots," the Pharaoh laughed. "Let him stop the world for all I care! We shall have light in the Nile Empire! We shall have warmth! Then, when I am ready, I shall take the possibilities from the cheering cattle and move on. What do you say to that, Ahkemeses?"

"I say, Hail Pharaoh!" the High Priest proclaimed.

Mobius, content with his exalted station in life, looked up and basked in the sunlight he had created.

The Dark Realm

My realm is a dark labyrinth. And only I know what lurks beyond the next corner.

— The Gaunt Man

We've entered the darkness of our own accord. Are we very brave, or just very stupid? Whichever, God help us to reach the light.

— Father Christopher Bryce

62

Major Julie Boot sat at Andrew Jackson Decker's bedside, studying his face in the dim light cast by the monitors. It was a fine face, she thought, a movie star's face. Or a sports figure's. Or a congressman's. She smiled. What is it with you, Major Boot? she asked herself. Are you falling for the man in the coma? He did look stronger, though, more healthy than he had since they brought him in. Maybe her little visits were helping. Maybe …

The instruments monitoring his vital signs showed no change. According to them, he had gotten no worse, or no better. Slowly, hesitantly, she reached out and took his hand. It was cool in her own, dry. She rubbed it slowly, gently, wishing that it would grip her back with the strength she knew it possessed.

"Wake up, Ace," she whispered. "I need to speak with you." She leaned forward, putting his hand to her cheek. "I need to know who you are."

She sat like that for a long time, holding Decker's hand and whispering words of comfort to the unconscious man. Did she really think that her voice and nonsense words could bring the man back to them? Even Dr. Monroe had given up on Decker. It was too dangerous to try another operation, he said. And the only way to give him a chance was to remove the strange metal shafts imbedded in his chest. But Julie felt deep within her that her visits were helping him. She didn't know how that was possible, or why, but as long as the feeling remained she would come and sit with Decker.

Then it happened.

Decker's hand squeezed hers.

It wasn't a strong squeeze, and it lasted only a second before his fingers went limp again, but it was the most wonderful feeling she had ever know. She laughed with the joy of it.

"What are you doing sitting in here in the dark?" Monroe asked from the doorway.

"James, he responded to me," Julie said, unable to keep the joy and excitement out of her voice. "He squeezed my hand."

"It could have been nothing more than a muscle spasm, or an involuntary response to your touch," Monroe said as he came closer to examine Decker.

"Or it could have been a sign that he's getting closer to us, that he's fighting off whatever it is that caused his condition," Julie snapped back, immediately sorry that there was an edge to her words.

Monroe looked at her, anger flashing briefly in his eyes. "You'll have to get a hold of yourself, nurse," he warned her. "Where's your objectivity?"

"Damn objectivity!" she screamed. "Where's your compassion, Dr. Monroe? He is your brother, after all."

"I asked you not to bring that subject up."

They were silent after that, her standing and watching as the doctor listened to Decker's heart, checked his pulse, and peered into his eyes with a light.

"He's just as he was earlier," Monroe said finally. "His vitals are stable, but there's nobody home. I think we're all going to have to face the facts."

"And what facts are those, doctor?" Julie demanded.

"Andrew Jackson Decker is not coming back, Julie," Monroe said, his expression softer than it had been, more human. "His mind is gone."

63

"Very odd," the Gaunt Man said, musing over his machine. "It appears the stormer aiding Decker is stronger than I anticipated. During the process, Decker almost pulled himself out of the dream I have him in. I had to increase power before I got him to settle back into the dream state." He turned another dial. "Now he is back to sorting possible scenarios for me. But for a brief moment … very odd."

Thratchen regarded the Gaunt Man. This machine gave the Gaunt Man an edge over all the other High Lords, an edge beyond even his eons of experience and almost unlimited personal power. The machine gave him the ability to eradicate possibilities. And, with Decker attached to it, it gave him the power to use specific possibilities to his own ends. It was a power unthinkable to those who called themselves Possibility Raiders. It was power akin to creation — power clearly in the domain of Apeiros the Creator, daughter of Eternity. It was a power that frightened Thratchen, and fascinated him.

"Decker," Thratchen said carefully, "is he the only one who could serve you in this fashion?"

The Gaunt Man turned to Thratchen curiously. "No, but stormers of his power are rare. Perhaps the woman called Tolwyn, the one Uthorion fears so much, could be used. Or even the young woman you seek. What did you call her?"

"Mara," Thratchen replied. "Dr. Hachi Mara-Two."

"Of course," the Gaunt Man smiled. "Why do you ask?"

"You do not yet have either of those stormers in your possession. We do not know Kurst's status, but from his last reported actions he has turned against us," Thratchen explained.

"I know all of this," the Gaunt Man growled. "What are you getting at?"

"We have Decker, High Lord. But there seems to be a stormer with him who can interrupt the workings of the runes. We could wind up losing him."

Worry played across the Gaunt Man's skeletal features. "This must not occur," he said. "Decker is more powerful than any other stormer I have yet used. I must keep him until the process is finished." The Gaunt Man stood by the control banks, practically crackling with power. "He must be brought here, to Orrorsh realm," the Gaunt Man decided. "He must be brought to me."

Thratchen waited, forcing the smile from his thin lips. His ability to manipulate situations was working again. Was it a wonder that one day soon he would be the Torg, and not this ancient, skeletal relic beside him?

"I have sent others to intercept Kurst, but there is still Scythak," the Gaunt Man said. "It is Scythak's turn to hunt. He will keep others from helping Decker. He will bring Decker's physical form to me."

Thratchen nearly howled his excitement. Scythak would be even easier to manipulate, he knew. He would complete his mission for the Gaunt Man, but he would do it in the manner Thratchen decided. Yes, all would work out for the best, Thratchen thought as the plan developed in his mind. He let the details fall into place as he followed the Gaunt Man up the stairs to find Scythak.

64

Eddie Paragon sat beneath a tree, watching the activity in Baruk Kaah's camp. Baruk Kaah was still locked in conversation with the Horn Master and the ravagon, but the edeinos were not wasting time waiting for their leader. They were gathering the plants they used as weapons — hrockts, Paragon remembered they were called. Others were involved in elaborate rituals that Paragon could not fathom. They danced and twitched in large numbers, singing praises to Lanala, their god.

He had been within Rec Pakken for the beginning of Baruk Kaah's meeting, but as the discussion grew more heated the three lost interest in him. After a time, he simply slipped out of the forest of black stone.

Paragon grew bored watching the lizard men. Their rituals were tedious, nothing more than a series of oft-repeated movements that agitated and excited the edeinos into a state of frenzy. Still others stood totally quiet, looking out over the fields around them. These contemplated the swaying grass, finding evidence of their god in such simple occurrences. He had spoken to one of the edeinos about these things, and he envied their spiritual existence. But he could not embrace their way of life as other humans had. There was too much modern man in him, he decided.

He moved through the camp lazily, looking for something to break his mood. He found it when his wanderings brought him to the pile of weapons the edeinos had taken from their last battle. Spoils of war, he knew. There were machineguns, rifles, pistols—Paragon couldn't put a name to any of them. He didn't know an M-16 from a Beretta. If he grabbed one, could he get it to work?

His breathing was quicker now. What was he contemplating? Did he think he could take out the entire camp? No, he told himself. Calm down. Not the camp. But with a weapon, he might be able to make it to the front and back into his own reality. He might be able to make it home.

His hands was sweating. He was a singer, a performer. What did he know of combat and survival techniques?

Jeff Menges

The answer was not a thing. But the guns were right there, unguarded. No one was paying any attention to him. He was just another part of the camp. His gaze returned to Rec Pakken, and he expected to see Baruk Kaah come storming out after him in response to his thoughts. But the black forest was the same as before; no one emerged from its depths to stop him.

Even the Wild Hunt was gone, the black cloud dispersed until the Horn Master gathered it again. Paragon wiped his hands on his jeans. If he was going to try anything, it would have to be now. Without thinking, he grabbed a pistol and a rifle from the pile. His eyes darted in all directions, but no one was watching him. He stuffed the pistol into his pants and held the rifle at his side.

Slowly, at an even pace, Eddie Paragon walked to the edge of the camp. Then, with a final look toward Rec Pakken to make sure Baruk Kaah wasn't on to him, he walked into the forest and out of the camp.

65

President Jonathan Wells replaced the phone on its cradle. General Powell had called with the news: Quin Sebastian was on his way to Kentucky. At least that was going according to plan. Now he had to deal with the problem before him. He looked up, returning his attention to Ellen Conners, Director of the Delphi Council.

"John, I need you to sign that document," she said again, not letting up on her position. "For the Delphi Council to be effective, it must be allowed to recruit agents."

Wells sighed. "Ellen, the council is supposed to be a think tank. It's supposed to develop strategies to help us battle these invaders. For what possible reason does it need permission to raise a damn army?"

Conners gave him her best Madam Medusa look, the look that withered her opponents throughout her years in the Senate. John Wells was used to it. He smiled at her.

"Damn it, John, listen to me," she urged. "We are a think tank. I've gathered the best minds I could find from the political, military, and scientific communities. But we need the ability to place agents in the field. How can we move quickly if we have to wait for some other agency to provide us with manpower? Besides, if this situation lasts throughout the foreseeable future, we'll need people specially trained to deal with it. Can you send just any FBI or CIA agent into the conquered territory and expect them to function as they would here in Houston? My God, man, look what happened to Decker and his marines."

Wells listened to her words. They made sense, on the surface. But what was the intent behind them? And, even if Conners was sincere, what if someone else came to power? The Delphi Council and its special privileges could be abused. He fingered the document before him. "By Executive Order," it began. All it needed was his signature.

"John, we're wasting precious time," Conners said. "Every second we waste is another dead soldier or civilian. Every minute is another chunk of land lost to the invaders. I need agents to go in there and find out how they work — and why our technology doesn't."

Swayed by the necessity of the moment, Wells signed the document. He would worry about curbing the long-range ramifications of the Delphi Council later. Right now, he had to give Ellen Conners the authority and ability to carry out her mission.

He handed the signed paper to her. "Do what you

have to, Ellen. But don't make me regret this decision."

"You won't, John," she smiled. "Someday this decision will be remembered as the first step toward our victory."

She left then, off to put the new Executive Order into practice. Wells sipped his coffee. It was cold and bitter, but it settled his nerves. He had been putting his next decision off for a while, but now was the time to implement it. He reached for his phone.

"Carter," he said into the receiver. "Have the boys prepare Air Force One. I'm going to Twentynine Palms to see Decker."

66

Thratchen checked the pendant again, looking for any imperfections in the runes. It was a red, multi-faceted stone held by a gold chain. The stone sparkled when the light hit it, reflecting bright beams from its many faces. On each face, painstakingly carved by Thratchen's own hands, were runes of magic.

It had been a long time since Thratchen had called upon these arcane skills. While magic was not beyond the axiom levels of Tharkold, technology usually provided a faster, easier solution. But here, in Orrorsh, it was more prudent to use the tools available to him. Less chance of contradictions being formed that way. And, he discovered as he prepared the spell, he liked using sorcery. It added a new element to his already-extensive repertoire.

Satisfied that he was prepared, Thratchen stepped into a shadowed alcove to wait. It wasn't long before Scythak appeared at the end of the corridor, fresh from his audience with the Gaunt Man. Thratchen marveled at the weretiger's size. Even in man form, Scythak was huge. He stood over six-and-a-half-feet tall, with massive shoulders and powerful muscles. In tiger form, he was even larger. In either form, he towered over Thratchen. His size and strength did not frighten the Tharkoldan, though. It merely made him cautious.

Scythak drew closer, moving nearly silently for one so big. Moving like a cat. As he approached the alcove, Thratchen stepped out of the shadows and blocked the hunter's path. Scythak stopped when he saw Thratchen, regarding him from under heavy brows.

"I thought I smelled your stench, Thratchen," growled Scythak. "Get out of my way. I have a mission from the Gaunt Man, and I do not have time to deal with you."

The powerful man started forward again, but Thratchen held up his hand. "Before you go," Thratchen said, "I have something to aid you in your mission." He held up the pendant, letting it dangle from its chain. The pendant caught the light from the gas lamps in the corridor as it twirled lazily, reflecting it into Scythak's eyes. "Do you see it?"

"I see it," said Scythak, interested. "What is it?"

"It's a pendant of Orrorshan reality," Thratchen lied. "I know that you can retain your own reality, without any help from devices, but this mission is too important to risk that odd chance of disconnection. Besides, a little insurance couldn't hurt."

It was understood by those who regularly traveled through different realities that there was an inherent danger involved in the process. Even the strongest stormer could find himself "disconnected," cut off from his reality and set adrift in a wash of alien axioms. Thratchen hoped to play on that nagging concern, perhaps fanning it into outright fear.

The stone continued to reflect light into Scythak's eyes, shining indecipherable patterns across his line of vision. Satisfied that he had the weretiger's attention, Thratchen spoke the words of power. His breath caused the pendant to twirl faster, intensifying the reflected light with each rotation. And the magic flared.

"What is your mission?" Thratchen demanded.

"I am to travel by dimthread to Takta Ker, go down bridge to Baruk Kaah's realm in the western United States," Scythak said, his voice distant as the beams of light hypnotized him. "From there I must enter Core Earth reality and locate the stormer named Andrew Jackson Decker. I am to bring him and the stormer aiding him back here."

"Very good," said Thratchen, moving the pendant closer to the hunter's face. Scythak smiled like a child given candy. Thratchen spoke another word of power, then said, "Now listen to me very carefully. When you see Decker, you will kill him. You will not protect him or bring him back here. You will simply kill him, because if he remains alive you will find yourself disconnected, cut off from your own reality. Do you understand?"

The stone seemed to pulse with energy, its beams flashing directly into Scythak's eyes. "Yes, I understand," the hunter replied obediently.

"You will not remember that this is your true mission until you actually see Decker. Until then, you will do exactly as the Gaunt Man has told you. Only when you see Decker will you remember that you must kill him. For every moment that you delay, total disconnection will become more inevitable. You will become transformed to an alien reality. Do you understand?"

Another pulse of energy. "Yes, I understand."

"You will forget that we have spoken, that I have told you anything. All you remember is that I gave you a pendant of Orrorshan reality. Only when you see Decker will the fear flare within you. Then you must kill him. Do you understand?"

The pendant glowed from within. "Yes," Scythak said, "I understand."

The spell complete, Thratchen snatched up the pendant nimbly, cutting off the beams of light. Slowly, the hunter's vision cleared. Scythak stared at Thratchen like a man who has awakened to find something particularly odious in his bed. "If you have something for me, give it here," the weretiger growled.

Thratchen held out the pendant and Scythak grabbed it away. He slipped it over his head, letting the stone fall into the folds of his shirt. "Now get out of my way," Scythak warned. He moved off, down the corridor in the direction he had been going when Thratchen had stopped him. "I have no more time for the likes of you," Scythak called as he walked past. And then he was gone.

Thratchen stepped back into the shadows, smiling broadly. There was still a chance the spell might fail. But if it worked, the Gaunt Man would be deprived of Decker's strength just when he needed it most. Then, when the High Lord was frantically trying to improvise a new solution, Thratchen would strike. If all went well, he would be firmly in control of Orrorsh when Kurst arrived with the women stormers. Just in time for Thratchen to attach them to the machine for his own use.

Yes, Thratchen thought, his schemes were working out very well. Now if Kurst could only keep Mara and Tolwyn alive long enough to reach him, then everything would fall into place.

67

Kurst sat beside Tom O'Malley in the cockpit of the airplane, listening to the hum of the engine. Outside the window, the snow was a frenzy of white that made vision useless. It was like flying inside a snow drift.

"How can you see where you are flying, Tom O'Malley?" asked Kurst.

"I'm flying by instrumentation," Tom answered.

Kurst had no idea what that meant. He decided that further explanation was not necessary, however, just so long as the plane stayed in the air.

"We're over Timor now, Mr. Kurst," Tom explained. "My radar is picking up a major disturbance about three hundred kilometers in front of us. That must be the storm front."

"We'll have to pass through it to reach Borneo," Kurst said.

"We should hit the edge of it in about twenty-five minutes. Then the ride will get pretty rough."

Kurst let his thoughts wander, thinking about everything that had happened thus far. As he replayed scenes in his mind, he looked for anything he might have missed the first time. Any piece of stray information could possibly prove useful at some point. Then his thoughts turned to the upcoming climax in Orrorsh. Would Tolwyn and Mara put up a fight? Yes, he was certain. The others would fight as well. Especially Bryce, who had grown stronger than he or the others realized. But Kurst saw it. And a powerful holy man in Orrorsh could prove troublesome. Only Djil was an unknown quantity. Kurst had no clue as to what the shaman was capable of.

"There it is, Mr. Kurst," Tom said, snapping Kurst out of his pondering.

Before them was a huge wall of swirling cloud, driving sleet, and crackling lightning. It stretched to both sides and as far up as they could see. As they flew closer, great claps of thunder shook the plane violently. But Tom held it steady. He was a good pilot.

"Be prepared to experience some disturbing visions, Tom," Kurst warned. "Reality is not stable on the boundaries between two axiom sets. Ignore what you see and simply fly."

To his credit, Tom O'Malley did not question Kurst. He concentrated instead on holding the airplane steady, on keeping their course true. The wall of storm was on top of them now, its jagged stripes of lightning shining into the cockpit. The harsh light made Tom look corpselike, and Kurst felt a strange sensation of premonition come over him. The feeling saddened him, and he thought that odd.

The plane hit the wall then, jerking wildly as rain and wind engulfed it. Kurst held on to the panel in front of him, forcing his mind to remain calm. If he gave in to his instincts, he would change form. The wolf was not what he needed now — he needed the man.

Outside, rain splattered the windshield. But the rain was not water. It was thick, steaming blood. Kurst let his gaze rest on O'Malley. The pilot ignored the gore dripping down the window. He was fighting with the controls, pulling up on the stick in a valiant effort to keep their altitude. Lightning flashed in front of them, exploding through a nearby cloud. Where the jagged bolt touched, the cloud transformed into silvery batlike things that flew into the windshield as well. Soon they covered the glass, and visual flying was again hampered.

"I'm not picking up any navigational beacons anymore, Kurst," Tom yelled so that the hunter could hear him, raising his voice above the constant thunder that battered the plane. "And I can't see where we're going. All I can do is fly straight and hope there's nothing too big and heavy somewhere in front of us."

"Perhaps," Kurst called back, "it is better that you cannot see what occurs outside. I have known the shifting realities to drive men mad."

Tom didn't comment. He simply flew as best he knew how. And that was very good indeed. Then, as quickly as it had begun, they were out of the storm. Kurst could tell because the thunder had died off drastically, and the constant pelting of blood-red rain ceased, too. But more, Kurst felt his world's presence like a wash of warm water. Immediately the ever-present tension of holding his own reality in another cosm was gone, and he felt his body and mind relax. He closed his eyes and nearly growled with pleasure.

"We're not out of this yet, Mr. Kurst," Tom warned. "We must have been struck by a stray bolt of lightning. The left engine is on fire and we're losing fuel. I'm going to have to take us down."

Kurst tried to get their bearings by looking out the window. The bat-things and the steaming blood were evaporating within the set reality of Orrorsh, so his line of sight was better. "Can we make it to Borneo, Tom?" he asked.

"I don't know if we'll even have the option to try, Mr. Kurst," Tom said.

Then they were dropping, down through the clouds of black ash, down through the gently falling snow.

Down toward the sea.

68

The army that Baruk Kaah established on the border between the Living Land and Core Earth Sequoia National Forest was like many armies: it contained air elements and ground assault elements.

In other ways, it was very different. Its air element was a boiling cloud of blackness and lightning, where shapes of mad dogs and frothing horses could be seen by those that could stand to look into the heart of it. It also had flying reptiles and twirling starfish-shaped creatures that seemed to hover in the air. Its land groups were lizard men and huge dinosaurs, wild men and women, and terrible giant insects.

Baruk Kaah struggled to maintain order among his people, but it was difficult. The concepts of military units and strategy on a grand scale were alien to their world, and even the High Lord had trouble focusing on such thoughts when his Darkness Device was not aiding him.

He commanded the Wild Hunt to remain above his forces, ready to strike at any Earthers that proved too powerful for his spiritual magic. The gospog had arrived recently, and the gotaks were busy outfitting them with the dead weapons taken from the Earthers. His singers, those especially strong with the living magic of the land, chanted ceaselessly about him, weaving a song of speed and strength that would make them powerful in battle.

Baruk Kaah took a mighty breath and let it out slowly, savoring the live taste of the air and the promise of seasons to come on this new world. He had healed well after his defeat to the Core Earth hard point, and he felt stronger, more powerful than ever before. The setback his forces suffered when trying to create another dominant zone to the south was temporary at best. This time he would lead the charge himself. This time the land would become his. All he required was a little more time to gather the Jakatts and the gospog. Then they would surge forward, a living army to defeat the dead of Earth.

The High Lord noted the presence of the ravagon, the only one of the three originally sent to him by the Gaunt Man who still remained in his camp. But he could not see the Earth singer Eddie Paragon anywhere. A terrible feeling started to crawl up his knobby spine, making his body twitch in a combination of fear and rage.

"Ravagon," he called, "where is the singer Paragon?"

"I do not know, High Lord," the ravagon said. His words were subservient on the surface, but Baruk Kaah could hear the contempt that rippled beneath them. "I last saw him during our discussions with the Horn Master."

Anger blurred his motions, making it hard to read his desire. But a stalenger reached out its tentacles to communicate with the High Lord. The stalenger said nothing; it waited for Baruk Kaah to make his wishes known.

"Fly, stalenger," the High Lord commanded. "I want Paragon found. And then I want him brought back to me. He will pay for this affront to my generosity. He shall learn what life is — and the lesson will be very long, and filled with the most terrible sensations."

69

Eddie Paragon stopped to rest, leaning against a tall tree. He was tired, thirsty, hungry, and very sure he was lost. Why did he ever think he could find his way out of this forest? He was a rock'n'roll star, not Daniel Boone. He let his body drop heavily to the ground. If he was going to die out here, he might as well be as comfortable as possible.

God, he needed a shower! And a shave and a haircut, too. It had been a long time since he had enjoyed any of those ministrations. With little else to do and no desire to start walking again, Paragon decided to examine his weapons. Both were heavy, and he assumed they were loaded. But he didn't want to start taking things apart in fear of not being able to put them back together again. Also, he didn't want to accidentally shoot himself. That would be embarrassing, he imagined; to die by a self-inflicted gun shot wound after escaping from the High Lord of the lizard men. That would make a wonderful article in one of the check-out counter tabloids.

There was a loud crashing sound, and Eddie almost screamed when he heard it. He forced himself back to his feet and peered around the side of the tree. If it was Baruk Kaah, or the ravagon, or even the Horn Master, Eddie was determined to fight to the end. He had no illusions that the end would take very long to arrive, however.

He waited, straining to see into the shadowy forest. There was another crash, and then he could see leaves and bushes swaying as something pushed through them. Paragon raised the rifle, placing his finger around the trigger. He hoped it was as easy to use as it always looked on TV and in the movies. There was probably a step they never showed you, a secret that he wouldn't be able to figure out. Then he would have to use the rifle like a club. That would rush the end along that much faster, thank you very much. He pushed all thoughts from his mind, watching the rustling bushes ahead of him.

It exploded out of the foliage with a high-pitched squeal, startling Paragon. He dropped the rifle. But what emerged wasn't Baruk Kaah, or the ravagon, or the Horn Master. It was a small, dog-sized lizard that reminded Paragon of a giant armadillo. It was running very fast on its four legs, its armor plating bouncing up

Alan Jude Summa

and down with the effort. As the fear subsided, Eddie began to laugh.

"You're what scared me half to death?" he said to himself, retrieving the rifle from where it had fallen. "Eddie, you are just too nervous for your own good."

The roar that followed set off his frazzled nerves again, but he caught the rifle before it could fall.

"Shit!" he screamed. "What was that?"

Out of the forest, chasing after the giant armadillo, was a man-sized dinosaur that burst into sight running on two tri-toed legs. Its head was all jaws and teeth, and it bellowed loudly as it ran. Its long tail chased behind it, swaying back and forth.

Paragon raised the rifle and took aim, but then the dinosaur was gone, crashing through the woods in pursuit of the armadillo. He lowered the weapon and took a couple of deep breaths to settle himself.

"Eddie Paragon, you really must get a grip," he said.

Then he started walking again, moving in the direction he hoped led to the storm front.

And toward home.

70

"Let's go," James Monroe said, standing in the doorway. He was looking only at Julie Boot, suggesting they leave Andrew Jackson Decker to die.

Or what amounted to the same thing.

"What about Ace?" she asked, a trace of bitterness in her voice.

"There's nothing more we can do," Monroe replied stonily. "But there are other patients here who need us. It's time you got your priorities straight, Major."

"Don't you see?" she screamed angrily, regretting the anger instantly. She stopped, fought for calm. "Don't you see," she continued shakily, "he responded to me. However slight, it was a response. That has to mean something."

"He'll come out of it or he won't," Monroe said. "It's out of our hands, Julie. Let him go and come help those who really have a chance."

She almost gave in then, almost rose from her seat and walked with James Monroe out the door. But something in her screamed, "wrong wrong wrong!" Decker did have a chance, but he required her help. And he required it now.

"I'm not wrong, James," she said, tired. "Not this time. I've never felt so sure. We've got to help Ace and we've got to do it now."

"We have a responsibility to those who need us more. We don't have time for a lost cause." Monroe, disgusted with her, turned and left the doorway. She heard his footsteps move slowly through the hall, finally fading in the distance.

Julie put her feelings for Monroe aside, and tried to concentrate on the man before her. What had she done to make Decker respond? Had she truly done anything? Unsure, she took hold of his hand and squeezed it.

"Ace," she whispered, leaning close to him. "Ace, hear me. You must wake up. You must live."

And then she began to talk to Decker, telling him about herself and the situation at Twentynine Palms. She told him things she never told anyone before, carrying on a conversation as though he were listening to every word she said. She hoped he could hear her, that he would follow her voice back up to the surface. That he would open his eyes and talk back to her.

But even if he didn't, she would sit there and continue to talk to him. Because deep down, she knew that it was helping.

71

Andrew Jackson Decker stepped through another door in the unending dream of choices. He had been alone for some time now, not even interrupted by a visit from the Gaunt Man. The dream kept him busy, however, constantly moving from scene to scene as he made his choices. Most of his decisions involved natural disasters of some sort and how to avert them. So far, he had found the least destructive paths.

A few times he had experienced a weird sensation. He thought he heard a voice, calling to him from some great distance. But when he paused to listen for it, the voice slipped away. It reminded him of Vicky's voice, soft and full of love. He missed her so much. It wasn't fair that something as unpredictable as cancer had taken her from him. How could you fight something like that? In the end, he discovered you couldn't. You could only hope the hurt would not be too great as the disease ran its course.

Thinking about Vicky, he again heard the gentle voice. It seemed closer now, more urgent. He tried to focus on it, but it remained vague, insubstantial. If he had to make choices, then let him choose to find the voice!

"Vicky!" Decker called. "Where are you?"

Then he heard the voice, clearer, more distinct. It was beyond the doorway behind him, back the way he had come. Decker ran to the door. He reached for the knob. But before he could grip it, energy crackled from the knob and pushed him back.

"No!" he screamed. "This is my choice!"

He reached for it again, forcing his hand through the

glowing field of energy, ignoring the pain it caused. Again his fingers closed on the door knob. And the knob faded away.

"You won't make this easy, will you?" Decker said aloud.

He pounded on the door then, smashing his fists into the hard wood. But no matter how hard he hit it, the door refused to budge.

"You can't stop me, Gaunt Man!" Decker raged. "I will get through this door!"

"Then I will simply place another one before you," the Gaunt Man said, appearing behind Decker. "Your choices are before you. Nothing exists for you back there anymore."

"You're wrong, Gaunt Man," Decker said. "My life exists back there. My freedom. You can't keep me from getting that back."

"Oh, but I can," the Gaunt Man said, but his usual smile did not accompany the words. "Even now my agents move to eliminate the voice that calls to you. And without the voice to support you, you can only move forward."

"But listen, Gaunt Man. The voice is still there. And it's louder now, stronger." And Decker was right. He could hear the voice much clearer now. It wasn't Vicky's voice, he realized, and that saddened him. But it was someone who cared for him nonetheless. Someone who was trying to help him.

"Create as many doors as you want to, Gaunt Man," Decker said. "In the end, I'll just step through them all."

With that, Decker threw his body against the door. The wood splintered, broke, and Decker was through the door. He picked himself up and ran then, following the sound of the voice.

And behind him, he heard the Gaunt Man's shouts of rage.

72

In Victoria River Downs, in Australia's Northern Territory, a ravagon stood in a snow-covered air field. Around him huddled a pack of shaden, waiting obediently like hounds for their master. The midnight black shapes were a mass of tangled tendrils at the winged demon's feet. What they were doing in Core Earth was a mystery. He was just glad they had not been able to kill Kurst and his party. The Gaunt Man would not have liked that.

The ravagon had been dispatched by the Gaunt Man to intercept Kurst and his party. Apparently the hunter had fallen out of favor, or at least had done enough to warrant the Gaunt Man's distrust. It was the ravagon's assignment to "accompany" Kurst and his charges directly to Illmound Keep in Orrorsh realm. But he had arrived too late, for they had already been to this air field and gone.

The ravagon slashed out with one mighty talon and ripped one of the shaden in half. Its dying squeal filled the night air, rising up to the ravagon like sweet music. But the act did not completely quell his frustration. That required the deaths of a dozen more of the shaden. When he finished, the burning fluids that spilled from the dead creatures melted a wide patch of snow around him. He ordered the remaining few to disperse.

"You are close, Kurst," the ravagon said to himself. His great wings flapped loudly, then he pulled them around himself like a cloak. "It will not be long before I catch up with you. When that happens, I hope you show some sign of betrayal, some evidence that you have turned against the Gaunt Man. Because if you do, I will take great pleasure in killing you where you stand."

He spread his wings again, letting them billow in the cold breeze. Then he took to the air, flying in the direction his senses indicated, following Kurst's scent.

Flying toward Orrorsh.

73

"We're going down!" Tom shouted as Mara entered the cockpit.

"Hold on to something!" Kurst advised her as the airplane started to descend.

Seeing there was little she could do in the cockpit, Mara grabbed a window seat back in the cabin and strapped in. Outside, she could see flames trailing from the engine on the wing. That, she realized, was the cause of their problems.

She looked around at the others in the cabin. Bryce was silent, his head bent in prayer. Tolwyn sat up straight, every muscle in her body tensed as though ready to explode. Djil, stretched out comfortably across two seats, snored loudly. The dwarves were talking to themselves, suggesting ways to repair the damaged craft. Mara took in all of this with a detached calm as the plane continued to arc down in a long glide. Tom was doing what he could, but Mara estimated impact with sea level within twenty minutes — if the engine didn't blow up first.

The thought shocked her, reminding her of similar times on her world. The war between Kadandra and the Sims produced many instances where death was imminent and all but guaranteed. She had always made it through those instances. But many she cared about didn't. Their names and faces flashed before her eyes —

Kendal Alec-Four, Mikkos, Tong Tyen-Three. She remembered each loss with the clarity of a sensover-chip dream, but without the option of turning it off. Before the painful memories could overwhelm her, she let herself focus on the people she was with now. Tolwyn, Bryce, Djil, even Kurst; they were vivid images in her mind. As she pictured them more clearly, adding details such as mannerisms and styles of speech, she felt herself becoming closer to them. It was almost as if they were joining, becoming one, like Djil's knotted rope. Like the volunteers at the transference facility …

Mara snapped away from the thought like a nervous cat leaping at a sound. She glanced around and saw that both Tolwyn and Bryce were looking at her, and even Djil was awake and sitting up. What had just happened? she wondered. Did the others experience her sensation of joining? And did the feeling scare them as much as it scared her? She suddenly felt very alone.

Sometimes, she thought, it was better that way.

Mara checked her chronometer. It had been twenty-two minutes since she sat down. Tom had kept them in the air longer than she had estimated.

"We're going to hit! Brace yourselves!" Tom called from the cockpit.

Heartbeats of silence followed. She felt the landing gear drop and lock into place. Then the plane hit the ground, bounced, and hit again.

"Well, that wasn't too bad," Bryce said.

"Father, the wing is on fire and we could explode at any time," Tom explained as he emerged from the cockpit. "We have to get out of here now!"

Tom unlatched the hatch and threw it open. The night air was warmer here, and it smelled of burning fuel and charred metal. Mara waited her turn as the dwarves exited quickly, followed by Bryce and Tolwyn. Kurst was next, bounding through the opening and into the night. She hesitated at the doorway, checking to see that Djil was with her. He was right behind her, smiling.

He reached out and gently tapped her head with one of his long fingers. "Think about your feelings, Mara-Two," he said. "Think about the volunteers."

"How do you …?" she began, but he hushed her with a wave of his hand.

"Just think about it," he said again. "Those thoughts can help us, if you can sort them out."

"Move it, you two!" Tom called. "Get away from the plane now!"

Mara leaped from the plane, landing on a sandy beach. Had they made it to Borneo, or was this just one of the many islands that dotted the area? She had so much to think about, but right now there was no time. Together with Djil, she ran toward the rest of the group. They all hit the sand as the airplane exploded behind them, filling the night with fire and light.

74

Mara's vision cleared and she lifted herself from the ground. Beside her, Tolwyn rose, sword in hand, and stared toward the copse of trees at the edge of the beach. Djil, to her left, did likewise. In front of her, Father Bryce was being helped to his feet by Kurst, and all the dwarves lay scattered about like tenpins. But each one moved, and so did Tom.

"That explosion will attract attention," Kurst said. "Any number of horrors could appear, drawn to us like moths to a flame."

"You do know what happens to moths when they get too close to a flame?" Tolwyn asked.

Behind them, popping sounds burst from the wreckage of Tom's airplane as smaller explosions were set off. Mara cybernetically dropped an infrared lens into place within her left eye. She scanned the edge of the jungle for any sign of activity, but nothing registered.

"Which way, Kurst?" she asked the hunter.

He sniffed the air and cocked his head as though listening to the very breeze. "Good job, Tom," he said finally. "I believe you've landed us on Borneo. The town should be that way." He pointed into the jungle.

"How far?" Bryce asked.

"About a week's travel," Kurst replied, "once we find suitable transportation."

"Suitable transportation? Here?" Bryce yelled indignantly.

Kurst moved closer to the priest, leaning in so that their noses almost touched. Then he said, in a very low, menacing voice, "If you insist on shouting, then you will be left to deal with whatever shows up in response on your own. Do you understand me?"

"Begging your pardon, Mr. Kurst," Toolpin asked innocently, "but who put you in charge?"

Kurst whirled on the dwarf. "This is my land, my reality. I am the only one who can get you where you want to go. That puts me in charge."

"Then be on with it, Kurst," Tolwyn said in a tone that matched the hunter's. "Lead us."

75

Bryce checked his pack to make sure the Heart of Coyote was safe, then he followed the group into the jungle. He wondered why it was warmer here than it was in Australia, but he decided not to ask Kurst any more questions for a while.

Inside the jungle, the darkness was thicker, deeper. The flames from the wreckage barely broke through the thick growth, and as they moved further even that light faded. Bryce stumbled a few times, and had to hold on to the dwarf in front of him so that he didn't wander off the path — such as it was.

"Who am I holding on to?" Bryce asked softly.

"It's me," the dwarf said.

"Who?"

"Oh, sorry. It's me, Toolpin, Father Bryce."

Toolpin! Bryce sighed.

"And who are you holding on to, Toolpin?"

"To you, Father," Toolpin replied. "My, these questions are easy!"

Bryce halted, catching the dwarf so that he stopped as well. The priest had a bad feeling that he and Toolpin were no longer with the rest of the group. He hoped he was wrong, but he felt rather alone in the unnatural darkness.

"Toolpin, where are the others?"

"Why, I couldn't say, really. I assume they're around here somewhere."

Something moved nearby, and Bryce hesitantly called to the sound. "Kurst? Tolwyn? Are you there?"

There was no reply. Bryce hesitantly stepped forward, and Toolpin went with him, in the direction of the sound. That was a mistake, Bryce realized. But it was too late. The darkness moved to meet him, inky blackness that flowed around him, surrounded him. He heard Toolpin scream, but it was muffled by the solidifying darkness.

The priest felt the dark cling to his body, slithering across his arms and legs, through his hair and beard. It had the consistency of pudding, filling his eyes and mouth as it engulfed him. He was drowning in the night! Toolpin, still beside him, was struggling against the unseen muck. But why, he wondered, was the dwarf upset? The dark was warm and soft, almost comfortable. And it sang to him, lulling him to sleep. It was ...

"No!" a part of Bryce's mind screamed. "Do not succumb! Resist!" He had to shake off the numbing acceptance that filled his mind like the muck filled his mouth. He had to break free! He struggled, joining his efforts to Toolpin's, but it seemed hopeless. The stuff refused to let them go.

Then he felt a tug as something grabbed him from behind. There was another tug, much stronger, and he was pulled from the darkness. He spit black foam and wiped more of the stuff from his eyes as Tolwyn helped him out of the strange material. The dwarves held torches that provided light, and Bryce saw that he had been pulled from a mound of blackness nestled in the trees. It was a trap of some kind, like a spider's web spun from the night.

"My God," Bryce said, "Toolpin is still inside that thing."

76

Tolwyn pushed forward into the unnatural darkness after settling Bryce into Mara's care. Something from out of the dark mass called to her, but she resisted, sword questing in her hand as she cat-walked further into the solid night. The voice beseeched her to rest, to let the warm darkness surround her, comfort her. She had no time for comfort.

She forced her way through the muck, finally emerging in a cavelike area. She spit the stuff out of her mouth, wiped her eyes, and looked around. She could not quite see as it was still dark, but she could make out vague forms around her. A great shape loomed before her, and she sensed that this was the source of the darkness.

"Toolpin? Where are you?" she called.

There was no answer, save the voice of the blackness that spoke not in words but in emotions. Comfort, it intoned. Peace.

"I have no time for this!" she shouted.

She attacked then, her blade moving through the great shape. She sensed the being's amusement at her feeble swing. It raised itself up to strike back.

Kurst was beside her then, emerging from the solid darkness in his huge wolf form. The source of darkness hesitated, unsure what this new addition meant to the fray. Kurst, however, did not hesitate. He launched his wolf body at the shape and let his wolf claws slice through the blackness. A silent scream filled Tolwyn with fear and pain, but she realized that these were the creature's feelings and not hers. With this thought in mind, she was able to push down the emotions and move to join Kurst.

The shape grappled with the werewolf, forcing his claws down and away from their target. Tolwyn saw that where Kurst had cut away the solid night, a gleaming white skull rested. The skull glowed from within, hinting at its unnatural origin. The wolf sliced at the skull, his claws scraping across the white bone. Then the shape threw him down, easily pinning him to the ground.

But Tolwyn knew how to defeat the monster. Kurst had shown her the object to attack. She swung her weapon in a mighty arc, aiming for the white suspended clearly in the dark. The skull shattered elegantly beneath the striking blade.

The apparition collapsed in a heap of muck as the skull exploded. With a dying cry, the living night around them faded. Tolwyn, Kurst, and Toolpin were left beneath the jungle's trees, standing knee-deep in black foam.

"I used to like the night," Toolpin said weakly, then he dropped heavily to the ground.

77

Eddie Paragon never wanted to go to a baseball game again, let alone sing the National Anthem. He had come to this decision hours ago, as he plowed his way through the primeval forest that used to be a well-cared-for national park in California. The ball game had been the start of this nightmare he found himself in. If he survived, he vowed he would never again set foot in a stadium. Maybe he could even get the government to ban the game. It wasn't the National Pastime anymore; as far as Paragon was concerned, it was the National Threat.

He stumbled down a small hill, pushed his way through thorn bushes that seemed to delight in ripping at his flesh, and finally collapsed beneath one of the giant Sequoias. He was exhausted. Worse, he had no idea if he was closer to the edge of Baruk Kaah's territory, or if he had walked in circles and was even now approaching the High Lord's camp.

Leaning back, Eddie allowed his eyes to close. "Just for a little while," he told himself. "Just until I catch my breath."

It felt so good to rest. He listened to the forest sounds, realizing that he had never really heard them before. In his old life — which was about six weeks and a reality ago — he never had the time or inclination to walk beneath the trees of a massive forest. He could never sit still long enough to listen to the wind, or the chirping birds, or the rustling leaves. He had missed such simple pleasures. Now his life depended on him recognizing nature for what it was; both beautiful and dangerous.

Those were the thoughts going through Paragon's rapidly tiring mind when he heard another sound. It did not register as out of place initially, and had it started up only a few seconds later he probably would have been in a deep sleep. It took a few seconds more to remember where he had heard the sound before, but when the memory returned it awoke him instantly. The sound was that of air being sucked in, held, and let out. It was the sound a stalenger made when it drew in air with its mighty organic pump and let it out in short bursts. The action caused its starfish-shaped body to rise into the air and spin, riding its own wind currents in order to travel.

Paragon opened his eyes and looked to the sky. He didn't see a stalenger anywhere, and the sound was gone now, too. Maybe he had dreamed it, he thought. Maybe one simply passed by on its way somewhere else. A stalenger did not necessarily mean he was being pursued. It didn't mean anything.

He got up, brushing leaves from his clothing. It was time to move on, he decided. Time to see what was over the next hill. He hefted the rifle and took a step forward. That's when the attack came.

Long, thin tentacles snaked down from the branches of the tree above his head, whipping around Paragon. They felt like piano wire, cutting into his flesh as they struck. He looked up and saw the stalenger. It was anchored between two thick branches so that its tentacles could extend freely from the center of its body. Already the strong limbs were wrapping around Eddie's arms and legs and neck. He had to do something quickly, or else give up now and face whatever was in store for him back with Baruk Kaah.

He tried to raise the rifle in order to aim it, but a tentacle slashed out and pulled the weapon from Paragon's hands. Struggling to escape from the stalenger was futile, as more and more limbs whipped down toward him. But he was able to reach the pistol that was stuck in his waist band. The pistol was much easier to aim with one hand, which was all that Eddie still had available. He pointed the barrel toward the stalenger and squeezed the trigger four times.

The gun discharged four slugs. Two went wild, but two struck the stalenger. Hot lead sliced through its fragile body, and immediately the snaking limbs went limp. Paragon pulled himself out of the tentacles. He retrieved his rifle.

"Thank God that worked," he said. He was very aware of how loud the gun blasts had been in the relatively quiet forest. It was time to move out.

Paragon climbed over the next hill and paused. There, about a mile distant, was a raging wall of clouds and rain. He had made it at last. He had reached the storm front.

"Now," Paragon said, "all I have to do is make it through there."

Somehow, he thought again, he would get even with baseball for putting him through this torture. He began to plan his revenge as he walked toward the storm.

78

Corporal Hank West observed the wall of storm through a pair of high-powered binoculars. His orders were to keep watch on the storm (or at least as much of it as he could see from his position) and report anything out of the ordinary to his commanding officer via his radio. It was a boring job. But West had heard what happened in this area a few days back. Who would have believed the Sequoia National Forest would be a battle zone? He didn't want to get caught in a repeat performance.

The storm swirled angrily within the wall of cloud. It looked like it wanted to burst free, to spread its destructive power across the land. But it didn't change its position, at least never by more than a few yards. It was the most stable weather front West had ever heard of. He also heard that on the other side of the front was a different world.

Oh sure, it was still Earth. But it wasn't Earth, at least not the Earth he knew and loved. His Earth allowed for things like radios and TVs and Nintendo. On the other side there were none of those things anymore. They said his gun wouldn't even work over there. It was now a place for things from the past — things like dinosaurs and cavemen. West wanted none of that. He was definitely a modern man.

"Give me a Slurpee and Paula Abdul any day," he said aloud, laughing. But then he remembered that prehistoric movie with Daryl Hannah and he smiled. "Well, maybe the past wasn't all bad," he thought.

He lifted the binoculars back to his eyes and scanned the base of the storm. Still nothing.

"Wait a minute," he muttered. "What's that?"

Emerging from the storm was a figure ... a man. He was drenched, his clothes matted to him by the raging rain. He carried a rifle in his arms as he stumbled out of the storm. He took a few more steps, then fell to the ground.

West grabbed his radio. "Corporal West reporting,"

Jeff Menges

he said, trying to keep the excitement out of his voice. "Something has just stepped out of the storm. Repeat, something has stepped through."

"What is it, corporal?" came back the voice of his commanding officer.

"It's a man," West replied.

"Say again, corporal."

"It's a man, lieutenant," West repeated. "And I think he's one of ours."

79

The Gaunt Man stood before his Darkness Device, high within his tower at Illmound Keep. The black-stone heart that called itself Heketon vibrated with power, singing its will into the Gaunt Man's soul. He nodded, understanding what it wanted from him, but not understanding why.

"Why have you become concerned with such matters, Heketon?" the Gaunt Man asked. "All goes according to our plan. Your prophecy to me comes true with each passing hour."

The song changed, rebuking the High Lord with a painful rhythm.

"I forget myself, Heketon," the High Lord apologized. "I do not question the advice you give me."

He placed his hands upon the smooth, shiny stone. The power of the Darkness Device throbbed beneath his fingers, sending a surge of tingling energy up his arms. Then, with great effort and concentration, he joined his will to Heketon's. The Obsidian Heart pulsated, drawing power from the High Lord as it completed a magical circuit.

And then Heketon was gone, disappeared in a burst of arcane sorcery. The Gaunt Man found himself alone in the tower.

"I have placed you into hiding, as you advised me," the Gaunt Man said, speaking to the now-empty place once occupied by the Darkness Device. "What have you foreseen, Heketon? What is coming that you refuse to share with me?"

The Gaunt Man needed answers, but he could not get them from the Darkness Device. Though it was his to control, in many ways it controlled him. The Gaunt Man understood this, accepted this. But it was sometimes frustrating. He almost wished that Heketon did not have such a strong will of its own, but he left the thought unfinished lest the Darkness Device pick up the thread of it and become angry. He had enough to deal with right now, without an insulted Darkness Device as well.

He stepped over to the ornate mirror that rested against the wall. "Wicked," he said the word that activated the mirror, calling it by its name. "Reveal to me Scythak, the weretiger."

For a moment, the Gaunt Man was gazing on his own reflection. Then the image shifted and Scythak appeared. He was just stepping off the dimthread the Gaunt Man had provided him with. From the view behind him, which was mostly obscured by a thick mist, he must be in Takta Ker. Yes, there was the jungle bridge that led to the Living Land realm on Earth.

The High Lord laughed as Scythak looked around. He sensed he was being watched, but he did not know where the observer was. Good, the Gaunt Man thought, a little paranoia will keep the weretiger cautious.

As Scythak started to descend the jungle bridge, on his way to find Andrew Jackson Decker and bring him to Orrorsh, the Gaunt Man called up the image of his servant, Picard.

"Yes, master?" Picard asked when he sensed the High Lord's presence.

"Find Thratchen and send him to my tower," the High Lord commanded.

"As you wish," Picard replied, and his image faded.

Next the Gaunt Man ordered the mirror to seek out Kurst. For some reason, it was harder to observe the werewolf than it was Scythak. Perhaps something from the hunter's past that was not entirely obliterated remained as a source of interference. Perhaps it was the same thing that made him betray his master — if he had indeed done as Thratchen said. The Gaunt Man concentrated, and the form of his most-favored hunter appeared. But the scene was obstructed, not vivid.

He could barely make out the deep jungle that surrounded Kurst, or the large number of folk that stood by him. He recognized the blue-and-red patterned energy that marked many in the crowd as stormers. The scene, full of so many stormers, disturbed him for some unknown reason. They were only stormers, after all, albeit a rather large and uncommon gathering. The two women were there, and they carried an eternity shard with them. How rich! An added bonus to go along with his prize! And were those Ayslish dwarves? The Gaunt Man almost laughed out loud. How could such an entourage cause him distress?

"What stories will you tell me, Kurst?" he wondered. "How will you explain these odd companions to me?"

He reached out with his mind then, trying to locate Kurst's position by the examining the axioms around him. He gasped. Kurst was here, in Orrorsh. So close!

"How did he get so close without my knowledge?" the Gaunt Man asked. The mirror image offered no answer. Instead, it shifted and blurred, and Kurst disappeared from view.

"Why does that happen?" the High Lord raged. He reached into the mirror with his will, trying to recover the image of Kurst. But something else was there. It was another image, vague, less defined than even Kurst's was. He tentatively touched it, seeking to discover its identity. It was slippery, elusive. He tried again to grab hold of it, and for a moment it was his.

"Kane?" he said.

Then the image was gone, slipping away from him like sand through his fingers.

"You sent for me, master?" Thratchen asked from the doorway. How much had he observed, the Gaunt Man wondered. No matter. There was other business to attend to.

"Kanawa is apparently ready to drop his bridge," the Gaunt Man explained. "I need someone there to observe the process. Someone I trust. My own operations are nearing their critical junctures, so I am needed here. But someone must make sure that Kanawa does not attempt any actions that could jeopardize my carefully laid plans. You are that someone, Thratchen."

The Tharkoldan nodded. "Very well, High Lord. I will leave immediately."

The Gaunt Man smiled. "Yes," he said coyly, "you will."

Thratchen quivered, an almost imperceptible reaction. Was he afraid? The Gaunt Man hoped so.

"As you command," was all Thratchen said.

"True," mused the Gaunt Man. "I want you to go to this place called Japan and witness the invasion. I estimate that the storm will break upon the island nation within the next hour."

Thratchen's eyes went wide. "An hour? How can I

get there in time?"

"Simple," the Gaunt Man said, nodding at the mirror. "The power of the mirror is not limited to viewing. It is also a portal, although a fickle one at best. I can send things, living and unliving, through it — to whatever destination I choose. You shall travel that way."

Thratchen eyed the mystic device with evident displeasure. "But High Lord ..." he started uncomfortably.

"Is the eternally curious Thratchen afraid?" the Gaunt Man mocked. "Did you not travel to this world in similar fashion, without the aid of a dimthread? I admit the sorcery involved in the mirror is not as refined as the process your stormer invented, but it serves its purpose."

"But High Lord ..." Thratchen tried again, but the Gaunt Man cut him off.

"In fact," the Gaunt Man said, reaching forward and grasping Thratchen's shoulder in a crushing grip, lifting him into the air without effort, "some of the minions I sent through the mirror actually survived the trip. Do you remember my early experiments sending advance scouts to other cosms without dimthreads? This method is vastly superior to that costly venture."

The Gaunt Man spoke arcane words and pushed Thratchen into the mirror. The High Lord's hand plunged into the silvery coldness, and Thratchen let out a brief cry. He pulled back his hand. Thratchen was gone, on his way to Japan.

With any luck, he would arrive in one piece. And with all his parts intact and in the correct positions.

80

Dr. James Monroe found Coyote at the large window overlooking the compound, holding the ever-present gray cat on his lap. Monroe put on his doctor-to-patient face and walked up to the teen.

"How's it going, Coyote?" he asked in a tone that suggested that he and the teen were old friends.

Coyote looked up and smiled. "Okay, I guess." The cat looked up as well, but its eyes were not as trusting.

"Good," Monroe said, ignoring the cat. "I'm glad to see you guys made it here all right. I was really worried about you after you left Philadelphia." He even sounded like he meant it.

"Oh yeah? It did get pretty hairy a few times, but we made it through. Except for Rick Alder. And Decker."

Rick Alder? He was the cop, wasn't he? Monroe asked himself. What happened to him, he wondered. He had to find out more. Especially, he needed to know what happened to Tolwyn.

"Look, have you eaten?" Monroe asked.

"No, not yet."

"Come on, then. Lunch is on me."

Coyote smiled, gently placing the cat on the window sill. "If you toss in desert, I'll follow you anywhere."

"You got it," Monroe shot back. "But you have to promise to tell me all about your trip across country."

"You got it," Coyote laughed.

Monroe laughed too, and deep inside he was thrilled. He couldn't get the image of Tolwyn's emerald eyes out of his mind. Coyote could fill in the blanks in the amazing woman's story. After all, he had a right to know what happened to her. He did help bring her back from the dead.

"So," the doctor said as the two walked toward the stairwell. "How was Tolwyn when you saw her last?"

As Coyote began to tell his story, Monroe risked a glance back at the cat. It was standing where Coyote had left it, its suspicious gaze locked on the doctor. He was very glad when the door closed and he could no longer see the cat's eyes.

81

Scythak did not particularly enjoy traveling by dimthread, but a perversity in his nature reminded him that Kurst hated it even more, and so he made the pretense to himself of reveling in the sensation. Then the trip was over. Scythak had arrived in Takta Ker, the cosm of the edeinos. He was at the bridge of living jungle that connected this world to Earth. He was that much closer to completing his mission. There was a faint moonglow, lighting the deep mist that covered everything. For a moment, the great weretiger had a feeling that he was being watched. But the feeling faded as quickly as it had come.

"The Gaunt Man," he muttered. He had often felt his master's eyes upon him as he went about his work. He knew that such observation bothered his smaller rival. If Kurst did not like it, then to Scythak it was an honor to be cherished.

The world around him pressed against him, trying to impose its laws of reality upon him. He roared with laughter. There was no way the primitive axioms could eliminate his own laws. He withstood the wash easily. Things in his own world were darker, more innately connected to the realms of magic and the unliving. Here in Takta Ker that connection felt tenuous and unreal. How could the edeinos exist without magic and technology? The thought of losing his connection with Orrorsh upset him. He fingered the pendant around his neck, remembering Thratchen's words.

"It is a pendant of Orrorshan reality," Thratchen had

told him. "In case the impossible occurs and you become disconnected."

Just remembering its presence helped him. He let his thoughts return to the mission at hand, and Scythak started down the jungle bridge.

As he walked the living path, he considered paying a visit to Baruk Kaah. But he dismissed the thought quickly. He had nothing to say to the High Lord, and no time to engage in protocol. He had to find Decker. He had to protect the runes and the stormer who was able to interrupt their work.

And he had to —

(kill, kill, kill)

— to bring them both back to Orrorsh.

Scythak was sure there was something he was forgetting, but he could not remember it. Oh well, he thought, it would come to him in time.

He barely noticed that the pendant was pulsing in his hand.

82

Mara thankfully dropped to the ground when Father Bryce announced a rest stop. Kurst did not appear pleased, but he offered no protests. The others merely flopped down without a word, their weariness a silent agreement to the priest's suggestion. Tolwyn, who seemed the least affected (other than Kurst) by the exertion, stepped over to Bryce and crouched next to him, a soft smile on her lips. They exchanged quiet words and laughs, then she nodded and stood, stretching the kinks of the journey out of her limbs.

"Why is it so hot here," Mara asked as she wiped sweat from her forehead.

"It is as the Gaunt Man wills it," Kurst replied. His

voice sounded strange, forced. It was as though he were fighting some inner battle, a battle that became more evident the longer they stayed in this realm.

What hold does the Gaunt Man have over you, Kurst? What is your connection in all this? But she could not ask him that, so she tried to think of other things.

Kurst was beside her then, leaning close to whisper in her ear. "Do not alarm the others, but follow me."

He got up and moved nearly silently into the jungle. She looked around quickly. The dwarves were lounging. Tom and Bryce were on their backs, eyes closed. Tolwyn was beside a small pool, splashing water on her face. Djil was sitting quietly, examining his knotted rope. So Mara did as Kurst asked, following him into the overgrowth.

He motioned for her to be silent and directed her gaze into the clearing below them. On a road that looked more like a path, an enclosed carriage waited idly by, its team of horses snorting impatiently. The carriage had a thrown a wheel. Two men dressed in Victorian garb were examining the wheel where it lay, trying to determine how they were going to reattach it to the carriage.

"Our transportation," Kurst whispered. Then he started toward the men. Even in human form, Kurst reminded her of a predator stalking prey. She wondered what he thought of her, then realized it didn't matter. She was very much like Kurst, thanks to the Sims; a warrior, a hunter. Part of her like that aspect of herself. Another part hated it, even feared it.

But she was almost as good at it as he was, and both men dropped without so much as a cry of surprise.

"Go back and get the dwarves," Kurst told her. "They should be able to get the wheel back on the carriage. Then we can ride the rest of the way in comfort."

Mara sheathed her claws and headed back to the others. She wondered what it would be like to ride in a carriage. That was even more primitive than Tom's plane! "Giga-rad!" she whispered excitedly.

83

"Father?"

The voice startled Bryce for an instant, sounding so young and vulnerable. He had fallen asleep in the carriage as it traveled over the bumpy road. Kurst and Mara had found it, but they didn't explain why it was abandoned. True, it had a busted wheel, but the dwarves fixed that in no time. They really seemed to have a knack for mechanical things.

He blinked, clearing the sleep from his eyes. Mara was talking to him. She was seated across from him, on the opposite bench. Djil and two dwarves were sitting beside her; Tom and three more were crammed in beside him. Kurst and Tolwyn were up front, driving the horses. The other dwarves were on the roof, keeping watch.

For a moment Bryce found it difficult to gain his voice. Finally he said, "What's up?" and his voice sounded terribly hoarse to his ears.

She didn't say anything. She just stared at him with her big eyes. Mara was a mess, he thought. Her face was puffy from lack of sleep. Her hair was frazzled and matted with sweat. My God, he thought, she is only a girl! Why do we keep forgetting that?

"You know," Bryce said, trying to find the words he knew Mara needed to hear, "I miss my friends terribly. Sometimes I wonder what I'm doing here when I should be back in New York with them." His voice became softer as he spoke, gentle, rolling. He felt a pang of truth in his own words that sent a surge of tears to his eyes. "I miss them ..."

"I was just thinking the same thing," Mara mumbled.

"It must be worse for you," he said, keeping his voice low so as not to wake the others. "I'm far from home, but I sometimes find it hard to imagine how much farther you are."

"It's not so bad," she said, too quickly. "I'm really no different from you."

He laughed. "I guess not. We just have to go in very different directions to get home. I'm really glad you're here, Mara." He paused for a moment, treading carefully as always. "The others, even Tom O'Malley, are very alien to me. You're the only one who I feel as if I know."

"You know Tolwyn," she said, and the words were like a blow even though they were said with no malice.

"I first met Tolwyn," he said carefully, "when I was giving Last Rites to a dead woman. Then, somehow, Tolwyn was there, inside that body. I don't think I've ever lost the wonder of that moment. I thought I had performed a miracle. I hadn't at all, but I still sometimes think of her as Wendy Miller, sometimes see her as a dying woman whom I saved, rather than as the other-worldly fighting woman that she really is. It's difficult. At least with you I know who you are."

"I wish I looked more ... like her ... more normal." Mara was blinking quickly. "Instead ... instead of like a machine ..."

"You don't look like a machine," Bryce shot back. His words were final, certain. "You look like a young woman. Tell me what it was like, growing up with such intelligence. I was a very mediocre student myself."

"It's useless!" she spat. "Useless! Sometimes it's like a thing in my brain, driving me on to *do* things, when all

I really want is to run and dance. And then the war and all, and all my friends fighting the invaders." She looked up at him, completely lost. "It's not fair! Some of what I am is because of the chipware, and I don't know how much is programmed and how much is me."

"No," he said softly, looking back at her steadily. "It's not fair. You know, it's very hard for me, having met you and Tolwyn and Kurst and the dwarves. You're all from someplace else! Sometimes I wonder if God's love is for people from other worlds as well."

"I doubt it," Mara said miserably.

He ignored her remark. "But then I realize that it must be, that God is on those other worlds, too, loving everyone in every one of those other places, because He is strong enough and loving enough to do so."

"But what does that mean, Father Bryce?" The question came from Djil, who was watching him from the other side of the carriage.

"It means that we're all in this together, and that as long as we remember that and care for each other as we care for ourselves, then we can beat this thing."

Bryce leaned his head back, contemplating his words. They sounded strong, certain. But, he wondered, how much of it did he really believe?

84

There was one moment when Thratchen felt that something had gone wrong: the plunge into the mirror was simply a strange sensation, as of passing through the surface of a silvery pond. It was not uncomfortable, it was not shocking — it did not seem dangerous.

Then the coldness came.

It was not the cold of a cube of ice, or even of a howling winter storm: it was the cold of the depths of space, instantaneous, compacting, freezing all motion into a single instant of time. Thratchen would have screamed, but he was incapable of moving his mouth, of drawing breath, of reacting to the nearness of death in any cogent way.

Then it was over and he was through, falling briefly before hitting the ground. Thratchen howled his rage at the Gaunt Man's action. But at least he had survived the jaunt. He took a moment to survey his surroundings. He was in a building of some kind, a modern office building in Osaka, Japan. A nearby window showed that a storm covered the city, its dark clouds rolling across the sky. He leaned close to the window, trying to see how far up the building reached, but the top disappeared into the dark clouds. Thratchen let his sensors examine the axioms of the area. It was still Core Earth, but the stelae for Kanawa's reality had been prepped and were waiting for the arrival of the bridge.

Thratchen moved through the corridor, opening door after door as he searched for some clue as to why the Gaunt Man had dropped him here. Then he found it, beyond one of the inner doors.

He stood on a stairway, overlooking a vast chamber that filled the center of the building. The chamber's ceiling was a glass skylight, and through the open partition he could see the boiling clouds. The floor was over thirty stories below him, probably extending beneath ground level. It appeared that the final invasion was not going to be a public affair. That made sense, Thratchen thought. Kanawa always liked to manipulate his realm from behind the scenes.

Then light fell from out of the clouds, dropping through the skylight and into the building like an arcing rainbow. The light was a maelstrom bridge in its purest form, not wrapped in the trappings of its High Lord's reality. Thratchen respected that. It told him that Kanawa was very sure of himself; he needed no illusions to remind him of his reality.

He felt the surge of axioms as they washed down the bridge and into the realm. He could feel the tech levels rising, could sense the changes occurring all around him. But Thratchen remained unaffected by it all, standing within a bubble of his own reality.

Thratchen watched for a time as Kanawa's agents descended. There were few warriors. Most were scientists, technicians, and other thinkers. Kanawa ran a different sort of invasion, but Thratchen could see nothing that should cause the Gaunt Man to worry. He turned to go, when a presence filled his senses.

Descending the bridge of light was an Oriental man dressed in a dark suit. Dark glasses hid his eyes from view. He carried a metal briefcase. A scar sliced vertically across his right cheek. Behind him were two heavily-armored guards — the famed samurai of Marketplace. The man could only be Kanawa, for he definitely reeked of a High Lord's power.

Kanawa stopped his descent and looked directly at Thratchen. The samurai leveled their weapons at him, as well. He was deeply disturbed that they had become aware of him so easily.

"What do you want here, son of Tharkold?" Kanawa demanded in a very business-like tone. Even though the distance of nearly half a city block separated them, Thratchen found that he could hear the High Lord easily.

"Son of Tharkold no longer, High Lord," Thratchen replied, shouting so his own words could be heard. "I bring you the greetings of the Gaunt Man, who welcomes

The Dark Realm

Francis Mao

you to Earth. He thanks you for your timely arrival."

"A deal is a deal," Kanawa said. "But I have work to do. If you will excuse me ...?" The High Lord continued down the bridge, dismissing Thratchen without so much as a second glance.

There was no more to be learned here, Thratchen decided. He left the huge chamber and sought an exit out of the building.

85

Scythak ran. It was a steady run, loping without effort. This was what he loved. This was joy! The ground scrolled away in flashes of green and tan, and even the roughness of the stones beneath his pads was an affirmation of life and of the hunt. He had shifted to his weretiger form once he descended into the Living Land realm, and now he was nearing the storm front that marked the separation between the primitive reality and Core Earth.

He had traveled such areas before, and the maddening fluctuations in reality did not bother him. He shifted back into his man form just before emerging from the storm. He stepped from the wall of cloud and crouched, sniffing the air. He immediately became aware of the man approaching him. The man was a soldier, carrying weapons and instruments of Earth's higher technology. But such items did not frighten the weretiger. There were much worse things in Orrorsh. With a sigh, Scythak rose and walked slowly toward the soldier, senses as alert as possible.

"Another one!" the soldier called. "You're the second guy to step out of there this week!"

Scythak said nothing. He just watched as the soldier walked closer.

"I'm Corporal West," the soldier said. "Are you hurt? There's another transport getting ready to leave for Twentynine Palms and I bet we could get you on that if we hurried."

Twentynine Palms? Scythak wasn't sure what that was, but he felt it was closer to Decker

(kill, kill, kill)

and that was where he had to go.

"Yes," Scythak finally said, testing the words and language the Gaunt Man had given him. "I would like to go to Twentynine Palms."

86

Sebastian Quin stepped off the transport in Frankfort, Kentucky. Here was the relocation center where he would gather information before starting his trip into the Zone of Silence. He would spend a few days, perhaps as long as a week, talking to the refugees who had made the trip out of that mysterious area. He would learn everything they could tell them, then he would organize the truth from the memories and make his plans. He grinned like a boy. It actually felt good to have a mission again, especially one that didn't involve overthrowing a small government.

He shouldered his pack, letting the weight of his gear settle on his back. Then he went in search of people willing to tell their stories. With any luck, he might even run into someone who had come all the way from New York City.

As he started to walk away, the pilot called to him.

"Are you really sure this is where you want to get off?" the pilot asked. "You know, most people get on here to go somewhere else."

"I'm not most people," Quin replied, and walked

toward the main building of the relocation center.

87

Vice President Dennis Quartermain stormed into General Clay Powell's office in Houston, Texas.

"I want some answers, Clay," Quartermain demanded.

"Have you tried an encyclopedia?" Powell replied flippantly.

"Cut the crap and listen to me, you military stooge," Quartermain yelled. "I want to know where President Wells is, and I want you to tell me what's going on with that Quin Sebastian guy. Don't try to deny it, I figured out who he was after my brief meeting with him. Why is the President meeting with two-bit mercenaries?"

"Listen, Dennis," Powell said, not in the least bit bothered by Quartermain's forcefulness. "I am not at liberty to discuss these matters with you at this time."

"I'm the Vice President, damn it! You have to keep me informed!"

Before Powell could say anything, his intercom sounded. "Air Force One is enroute to Twentynine Palms, General," said his secretary's voice over the system.

"Thank you, Betty," he said, pressing the button so that she could hear him. "Look, Quartermain ..." he started, but the Vice President cut him off.

"Never mind, Clay," Quartermain smiled. "I'll just come back when you aren't quite so busy."

The Vice President turned and left Powell's office. Thanks to the secretary's screw up, he had some of the information he needed. He had much to discuss with Ellen Conners, and there wasn't much time.

88

Thratchen flew from Kanawa's office building, only to land a short distance outside of Osaka, in a wonderful garden beside a small stream. Something had drawn him here, and he decided to stop and see what that was before returning to Orrorsh. Next to the garden was a courtyard, surrounded by a collection of buildings centered around a great structure set atop a stone foundation. The great structure was made of wood and stone, vaulting to the sky with fluted roofs stacked one atop the other. Ornate carvings and designs decorated it, each vying with another for attention. A flight of broad steps led up to a great door which stood slightly ajar, and from within a smell of smoke and the sound of voices wafted.

Thratchen stretched out with his senses, both natural and technological, and finally realized what had attracted him to this spot. Kanawa's axioms did not penetrate to the grounds around this holy structure. The area had resisted Kanawa's influence completely.

Slowly, mulling different possibilities, he ascended the flight of steps. Forgetting his desire to return to Orrorsh, forgetting any possible danger, forgetting everything except his unquenchable thirst for knowledge, he pushed open the door.

Although it appeared multi-storied from outside, there was only one floor within. There were great pillars everywhere, and a lofty ceiling was suspended high above him. Screens hung between the pillars partitioned the space, and it was obvious that the entire structure was a temple of some kind.

He made his way around the screens, trying to find the center of the temple — and the source of power that protected it from Kanawa's reality. He wondered where the worshippers were as he continued through the temple. He could hear their singing, a low chant that made him somewhat uncomfortable, but he saw no evidence of their presence. He pushed aside a final screen, more out of frustration than any need, and there was the temple's core.

It was a simple shrine, marked by a red archway. Through the archway, atop a low platform, was the statue of a stylized lion carved from a blue and red stone.

Thratchen stepped gingerly toward the statue, gasping at the power emanating from it. It was an eternity shard, literally bursting with the energy he and the raiders craved. He reached to touch the statue, and immediately the chanting stopped.

Eyes were upon him, and Thratchen whirled. Standing there were six men in white robes, their heads shaved bald. They were monks of this temple, Thratchen was certain, all of indeterminable age and smelling of stormer.

"Why have you come to our temple, demon from another world?" the first monk asked.

"You have something I seek," Thratchen said. The six regarded him calmly, unthreatening and unthreatened. "Tell me about this hard point. What is its significance?"

There was silence, save for the crackle of a fire somewhere nearby, behind one of the many screens.

"Do not test me," Thratchen warned the silent monks. "Why is this place special? Answer me! You have no concept of who or what I am!"

"We are quite aware of what you are," a second monk replied. "And we are aware of the terrible change that has come over our land. But our temple resists the change, and so do we." He began to hum a tuneless note, repeating it over and over.

"You are aware — fully aware — of the invasion of

your world?" Thratchen said, amazed. "That is very interesting. Tell me, what is it you feel?"

"Wrongness," said another, and then he too began to chant. The sound was almost numbing.

Thratchen shook his head, put one hand to his ear. What were they doing to him? How were they doing it? The third and fourth monk joined in the chant, and their voices were as one that rose and rose and fell and rose in steady rhythm. Thratchen started to sweat. They were invoking their religion to protect themselves from him! What did the holy men of Orrorsh call it? Ward enemy, he believed. How rich! Did any one of these pitiful monks think they could match his power? How absurd!

He might have struck them all down then, in the moment before the last two began to add their voices to the chant, but he was curious. Besides, he was confident that he had nothing to fear from their premature abilities.

The first monk had the aura of protection around himself, while the others seemed to be concentrating on some other kind of effect. Thratchen was intrigued. He moved toward the first monk, easily pushing aside the ward. He chuckled as the flimsy thing started to collapse. But then the ward reestablished itself, forcing Thratchen back and sending numbing pain through his body.

How was that possible? It was as if ...

Thratchen paused, taken aback by his own thoughts. Could it be? Had these stormers learned to share the possibility energy that their bodies stored? He remembered the transference facility on Kadandra and his blood ran cold. What Mara's people had accomplished with technology, these simple monks had done with nothing more than their own wills.

They were preparing another ward, and Thratchen felt his fear rise. These stormers could hurt him! Perhaps even destroy him if they got lucky. No! Not when he was so close to the answers he sought. He backed away, stepping around the eternity shard. He could almost see the energy leap from one monk to another as they concentrated.

"How are you doing that?" Thratchen raged. "How is that possible?"

"The idol showed us how to shift our inner strength among ourselves," the first monk said. "It told us how to cooperate before it stopped singing."

Singing? What was the monk talking about? But then Thratchen understood. The constant murmur, the background noise that filled this planet with sound to those sensitive enough to hear it, had died away. It wasn't completely silent, but it had been seriously stifled since the arrival of Kanawa. That meant the planet no longer had the power to repel the invaders.

It suddenly made sense to Thratchen. He had discovered the secret of Apeiros' children. Through cooperation and creativity, they could accomplish the impossible—including this strange group power. Those stormers with affinity for the Nameless One had no capacity for cooperation, as evidenced by the problems happening all through the Earth invasion. He had to try one more attack so that his built-in computers could record the results. If he survived, he would be able to study the recording later.

He rushed forward, charging through the ward to reach the monks. It began to buckle, collapsing under the strength of his own faith. But then the energy shift occurred again, and the monk focusing his faith into the ward received a burst of power. Thratchen was thrown back, the pain almost causing him to black out. This ability was dangerous!

His experiment completed, Thratchen ran from the temple before the monks could focus their combined powers into some other form of attack. Outside, he let the cool air revive him. Still, it would take time for the pain to subside. He spread his wings, taking to the sky. If the recorder worked, he had the secrets he needed — all he had to do was decipher what he was watching.

But there was something else of importance that this episode had taught him. The Gaunt Man's methods were doomed to failure. He had simulated this group power effect with his machine, but he was missing the key element. The stormers he attached to it were not cooperating. They were being forced. Eventually that would destroy the project, of that Thratchen was certain.

That was the knowledge that Thratchen would wield against his master. That was the secret that would elevate him to the status of High Lord —

— and then make him the Torg.

89

Tolwyn sat beside Kurst, admiring his handling of the team of horses. Finally, she thought, they were riding within a normal carriage. It was a vehicle she understood, drawn by horses she could see. It required no magic to work and did not lift them high into the air. It traveled as carriages were meant to — along the ground at a moderate speed. Although, she mused, they would get to their destination faster if they had one of Alder's magic vans.

This was their third day of travel, and they seemed no closer to their goal, even though Kurst assured them they were making progress. She tried to get the hunter to tell her about Uthorion, but he pleaded ignorance and returned his concentration to the horses. At one point during their trek, she saw Kurst stiffen and look from side to side. She asked him what was the matter. All he said was, "the Gaunt Man," but afterward she noticed that he was more alert than before.

As the day wore on, a half-remembered marching tune came to her lips. She struggled with the words for awhile, fighting to recall the entire song. When she finally had it all in her mind, Tolwyn started to sing.

Her voice was clear and strong. Modestly, she thought it might even be considered good. Kurst looked at her strangely at first, but then he went back to watching the road. Braxon and Praktix, the two dwarves currently on guard duty atop the carriage roof, laughed at the sound. Then, before Tolwyn could become too self-conscious, the dwarves joined her in song. They seemed to know the words better than she did, and when the dwarves within the carriage picked up on the second verse, the carriage literally rocked with the sound.

They traveled in this fashion for a few hours, singing Ayslish marching songs, dwarven ballads — Bryce even taught them the words to an Earth song he called "Burning Down the House." Even Kurst lost some of his aloofness as the songs lifted them out of the tiresome doldrums they had been sinking into. All was well, and they felt like nothing could stop them.

Until Tolwyn screamed.

Kurst pulled on the reins, bringing the horses to a halt. "What is it, Tolwyn? Are we under attack?" Kurst asked quickly.

"No, I do not believe so," Tolwyn said in a ragged voice. "Not physically, anyway."

"Then what is it?" he asked impatiently.

"The song is gone," Tolwyn said, hunting for the right words to convey her distress. "It has been there since I awoke in Philadelphia, and when it just cut off …" She hesitated, seeing that Kurst did not understand. He thought she meant the marching songs, not the deeper song that came from her dreams. She leaned over the side of the carriage and called down. "Christopher Bryce, come out here. And bring the stone."

The priest emerged from the carriage carrying his pack. "Do you feel it too?" he asked. "Or rather, do you sense that something is missing?" he clarified.

"Yes," was all she said, for a terrible fear gripped her.

Bryce removed a wrapped object from his pack. He carefully unfolded the cloth, revealing the blue and red stone shaped like a human heart.

"Ever since I arrived on this world, I have heard the song," Tolwyn explained. "This world was so full of life, so rich in possibilities! That was what the song was. But it was also through that song that the world called for my help. It has been with me through everything that has happened, a constant companion. Until a moment ago when the song stopped."

"No, Tolwyn, it hasn't stopped," Bryce smiled with relief and raised the stone toward her. "You can still hear it if you listen closely. It's gotten much lower, less perceptible, but it's still there."

Kurst nodded, finally understanding what they were talking about. "Another realm must have attached itself," he said. "When enough of them have attached to Earth, then the planet will weaken."

"How many different realities are supposedly involved in this invasion?" Bryce asked.

"There were supposed to be seven," Kurst replied. "But I believe one of the invading realms was beaten back before it could connect."

"I'm sorry that your world has lost its song," Praktix

said to Bryce.

"It hasn't lost it," the priest declared. "It's only resting its voice until the time is right to sing the next chorus. And when that time comes, then all of these High Lords will see just what —"

Praktix's cry cut off Bryce's speech. "Halt!" she called out suddenly, her hand moving quickly to the battle spike at her side.

Tolwyn was up in an instant, her own sword drawn and ready.

"Something's wrong," Praktix chimed.

"Most definitely," added Braxon.

"Explain yourselves," Kurst roared, tired of these guessing games.

"There's a very odd disturbance in the ground ahead," said Praktix as she leaped from the carriage. "I've never felt anything like it."

Praktix started forward at a trot as Tolwyn watched. All seemed clear. If it was an ambush, it was incredibly subtle and incredibly small. Then dread washed over her in cold prickles. The skin on the crown of her head tightened and a subtle shiver ran down her spine. "Praktix!" she cried, leaping from the carriage herself.

Too late.

A black fissure appeared in the path ahead, hissing open with a gout of dust and the smell of rotting meat. A sharp purple shape erupted from the hole, huge and writhing, a wormlike mass of lashing tentacles and chewing jaws.

Praktix was unbalanced by the breaking ground. She flailed wildly, trying to keep her footing. But the monster kept rising out of the earth, shaking the ground as its unending mass swelled forth. With little else to do, the dwarf fell against the giant worm and dug into its body with her battle spike.

The worm's howl was an ugly sound, and its bucking tore up more of the earth around them. Kurst fought to keep the horses under control while desperately seeking safer ground for the carriage. Neither he nor the others in the carriage would be able to help. Only Tolwyn, Braxon, and Bryce were clear and in range to aid Praktix.

Hundreds of glistening eyes swiveled to find the source of irritation, fixing on Praktix where she hung on for dear life. The worm raised itself even higher, slashing toward the dwarf with the tangle of tentacles that dripped from its head. The wriggling mass rained a violent storm upon Praktix, striking and pulling away in a wash of blood.

Tolwyn saw all of this on the move, taking it in as she rushed to the dwarf's aid. Braxon was beside her, keeping up with her long strides through sheer force of will.

Praktix endured another lashing from the abrasive tentacles, then released her grip on the spike. Tolwyn heard Braxon cry out as Praktix fell. The worm writhed and pulsed obscenely above them all, and Tolwyn felt the bile rise in her throat. She sought an opening, a weakness to strike at. But the creature was too huge. What could her blows do to one such as that?

Bryce pushed his way between Tolwyn and Braxon, placing restraining hands upon them both. "We must leave," he pleaded. "We can't hope to defeat this creature!"

She barely acknowledged him as she searched for Praktix. The dwarf lay unmoving at the base of the beast, crumpled upon the broken ground next to the steaming fissure. A fury built inside her.

"This is not right, Christopher," she said. "Praktix ..."

"We must help my sister," Braxon shouted as tears

streamed down his face. "Lead us, paladin," he pleaded to Tolwyn. "Show us how to kill the beast."

"No," Bryce tried to reason with the dwarf, "we've got to leave now."

"Leave?" Pluppa asked outraged. "We can't leave! Praktix might still be alive!"

"Could be!" called Gutterby, swinging his battle spike.

Tolwyn saw that they entire group had gathered around them: the dwarves, Kurst, Mara, Djil and Tom. The horses and carriage must be out of danger, she thought absently.

Bryce looked around dubiously. "What can we do against that?"

"It would take every drop of energy in my weapon just to get the thing's attention," Mara yelled above the rumbling ground.

"We must get to Praktix. We must at least try," Pluppa said.

The other dwarves added, "Ho!"

There was silence for a moment, then Bryce snapped out, "All right. But what do we do?"

Mara strode forward, clutching Tolwyn's arm. "Provide me with a distraction," she said seriously. "I have the fastest reflexes. I'll go in there and get her out."

"Fastest, eh?" growled Kurst, and even as he spoke his arm flashed out toward Mara's face. Her own hand was as fast and she grasped the hunter's wrist before he could touch her. His other hand shot out, but she caught that as well. Mara grinned.

"We'll both go," he conceded.

Without another word, the dwarves began trotting forward in single file, moving around to the worm's other side. A tremor ran through the beast's body from front to back as it moved to follow their motion. Mara and Kurst walked catlike, in the opposite direction, waiting for the proper moment to make their attempt.

Bryce held Tolwyn's shoulder. "Stay in reserve," he suggested.

Tom agreed. "They look like they know what they're doing."

Djil simply watched the spectacle that was about to unfold without saying a word.

"What can the dwarves do to distract it?" Tolwyn asked, uneasy about staying out of the fray.

No one answered her, but she saw the dwarf named Grim step forward. He pulled a small amount of pitch from a pouch on his belt. With a wave of his hand, he spoke words that Tolwyn recognized as magical in nature. Then he lit the pitch, blew on it once to fan the flame to life, pulled a small piece from the burning mass, and heaved the larger portion with all his might at the looming worm.

The other dwarves covered their eyes and ducked in a single motion that looked to have come with long years of practice. Tolwyn watched, amazed, as Grim seemed to guide the flaming ball by mimicking its motion with the small piece in his hand. It flew at the worm, striking into the mass of tentacles at the beast's head the same moment Grim struck his open palm with the smaller piece. There was a simultaneous explosion of fire where the ball hit, and a cry of pain from Grim.

"Ouch!" he shouted. "I always burn my finger when I use that spell!"

Mara and Kurst darted in with rapid, precise strides at the moment of impact. They hefted the fallen dwarf and started back toward Tolwyn. The worm, meanwhile, its upper body engulfed in fire, began to fall toward the ground. It smashed into the jungle with a loud crash, its coiled body flailing in death throes.

"That was some distraction," Mara gasped as she gently lowered Praktix to the soft grass. Braxon pushed his way through the crowd to reach his sister.

"Distraction?" Grim said in embarrassment. "I thought you said destruction!"

90

Bryce stood aside as the dwarves and Mara leaned over Praktix's still form. He knew some first aid techniques, but Mara was definitely better suited to treat the dwarf's wounds. He turned to the aborigine standing beside him, hoping to strike up a conversation and learn more about the man. But Djil was looking blankly into the distance, as though he was seeing something far away. His hands, meanwhile, had clutched around the fifth knot on his rope.

"What is it?" Bryce asked, beginning to take such events as commonplace among this group.

"Decker," Djil said softly. "He needs help."

"Of course," Bryce said impatiently. "That's why we're here."

But Djil didn't stay to listen to what Bryce said. He was walking down the path. Bryce ran over to him.

"What are you doing?" the priest asked.

"Going to the Dream Time," Djil replied, and then he disappeared into the thick foliage.

91

Julie Boot hesitated. She remembered what happened when Monroe had tried to remove the staves from Decker's chest. She didn't want to be subjected to something like that. But she felt that if she touched the staves … what? That Decker would open his eyes and sit up? That was ridiculous. But what if …?

She grasped the staves.

And suddenly Julie was no longer in Decker's room. She wasn't even in the hospital anymore. She was … *somewhere else*. She was on a sandy beach, beside an ocean of red

(blood)

water that constantly splashed against the shore. Dozens of doors stood along the beach, held upright even though there were no walls to support them. Where was she? How had she gotten here. It was like some crazy

(nightmare)

dream come to life. Had she gone insane? Or had she touched the staves and been killed by the same force of energy that almost fried Monroe? All she knew was that she didn't like this place. But something here needed her. She started toward the doors.

"So, Decker has help," a voice said, startling her. "Maybe I made this trip for nothing."

Julie looked around, spinning wildly at the sound. A short black man was standing a few yards down the beach. He was impossibly old, with a tangle of stark white hair atop his head, and a matching white beard hanging from his chin. She felt no malice in this man, no threat.

"Decker?" Julie asked. "You know Decker?"

The black man nodded. "We have to help him. He's reached the final door, but he can't get it to open. The Gaunt Man's a tough one. Very strong."

Julie spun around frantically. "Which door? There are so many of them!"

"Look again, woman," the black man smiled. "Things

in the Dream Time aren't always what they seem."

He was right. When she looked again there was only one door. She approached it cautiously, carefully reaching out to touch it. The door buckled out and she pulled her hand back. She turned again to the black man.

"Decker bangs on the door, but it will not open," he said. "He needs your support to finish his journey."

Julie swallowed hard, watching the door shake as something on the other side pounded into it. What if the black man was wrong? she asked herself. What if that isn't Ace on the other side of the door? What if it's

(*a monster*)

something else? She shook the thoughts away and grasped the door knob with both hands. Using all her strength, Julie pulled.

The door swung open with no effort, and the sudden release when she was expecting resistance caused her to lose her balance and fall. A form fell from the open doorway, landing in the sand beside her.

"Ace?" she asked. The form, clearly a man lying face-down in the sand, offered no response. But a bellowing cry of rage emerged from the doorway. The beach literally shook with the sound of it.

"Be on your way, woman," the black man said leaning over her. He closed her eyelids with his fingers. "Be on your way."

And Julie was back in the hospital, her hands releasing the glowing staves in Decker's chest.

"Weird," she said aloud.

"Who are you?" The voice was rough, scratchy. It sounded like Dr. Monroe, but it came from the man lying on the bed. It came from Decker.

"Ace?" she inquired, not caring that excitement made her voice sound higher.

"I haven't been called that in a long time," the man on the bed said. "But I am Andrew Decker."

92

James Monroe watched the sentimental scene from the hallway, refusing to enter his brother's room. They were all in there: Coyote, Rat, Tal Tu — even Julie and the damn cat. They were all laughing and congratulating Andrew Jackson Decker on his miraculous recovery. How typical! His brother the wonder kid comes out of a coma and they want to give him a medal! The whole scene made him want to throw up.

Worse of all was the look Julie was giving Ace. It was the look of a woman in love, not the look of a nurse to her patient. How do you do it, Ace? How do you make them fall for you even when you're flat on your back unconscious? Monroe felt the jealousy rise within him, and he welcomed it. It was warm and thick, something to hang onto that was all his.

He noticed that the staves were still embedded in his brother's chest. He wondered if they hurt him. Monroe smiled wickedly. He hoped they hurt like hell.

He looked once more at Julie Boot, remembering the few fantastic nights they had together. Part of him wept for the loss he knew had already occurred, even if she didn't realize it yet. But another part of him was glad to be rid of the bitch. She was just in his way, trying to block out his memories of Tolwyn of House Tancred. Coyote had told him all about the woman warrior and her travels across the country. He couldn't believe that he had missed her by only a few days. But he would find her again. She was his destiny. That's why he had brought her back to life, so that the two of them could be together forever. That's why fate led him here.

With a final glance at Julie Boot, and a sneer at his brother, Monroe turned and walked toward the stairs. He had a quest now, a mission in life. His brother's return was his signal to get on with it.

So Dr. James Monroe, once of the famed Deckers of Pennsylvania, began the next portion of his life. And all he took with him was his hate for his brother, and his obsession with a woman who had come back from the dead.

93

Andrew Jackson Decker looked up at the faces around him. The teens were there, young Rat and Coyote. The edeinos named Tal Tu was there, holding his gray cat in scaly hands. And the nurse, Major Julie Boot, who had been with him when he awakened, sat in the chair beside his bed. He felt he owed her something, but he didn't know why.

He glanced at himself, examining the staves that jutted from his chest. They didn't hurt, but there was a draining sensation associated with them that seemed to sap his strength.

"So the others have moved on?" Decker asked.

"Yeah, they went to Australia," Coyote offered. "They said they had to get to Orrorsh so they could save you."

"Did they take the Heart of Coyote with them?"

"Yes," Rat chimed in. "Father Bryce is carrying it."

"Good, they might need it," Decker said, thinking of his own confrontations with the Gaunt Man. But already those memories were fading with each waking moment, dissolving like dreams in the light of day.

"I'm glad to see you're better, Ace my boy," said a friendly voice from the doorway.

Decker recognized it immediately. President John

Wells was standing there, surrounded by a few security types.

"Well, are you going to invite me in?"

"Of course, Mr. President," Decker smiled.

"What did I tell you about formality, congressman?"

Decker laughed, especially when he saw the looks on Rat and Coyote's faces. He thought that laughing might hurt, but it actually made him feel better, stronger. Julie, too, seemed stunned to see the President of the United States in her hospital. Decker quickly introduced everyone, and Wells seemed genuinely pleased to meet them.

But then he became serious. "We need to talk, Ace."

Decker nodded. "Could you give us some time alone?" he asked, and his visitors exited.

Wells motioned for the security men to wait outside, and they reluctantly closed the door behind them.

"So tell me, Ace," the President began, "what in the world is going on?"

Where should he begin? Decker tried to sort out everything that he had experienced over the past few weeks. Finally he decided that the best place to start was at the beginning.

"Sit down, John," Decker urged. "This may take a while."

94

Bryce and the others set up camp in the clearing where Kurst had secured the horses. They had a small fire going, and Praktix was covered in blankets beside it. Mara was still with her, doing what she could to ease the dwarf's pain. The priest sipped hot coffee and watched as the other dwarves patrolled the perimeters of their camp site. They were extremely military in their mannerisms and, after a brief inspection, Tolwyn had declared that the dwarves would sound the alarm before anything got within twenty meters of the camp.

That's why it came as such a surprise to him when Djil walked out of the jungle and into the circle of light cast by the fire. Kurst, sitting beside the priest, quietly said, "Do not blame the dwarves, Bryce. The aborigine walks where he wants. He is like the jungle itself, moving with it instead of through it."

Bryce didn't understand Kurst's words, but he gathered that the hunter was impressed by the shaman. Djil sat by the fire. He had discarded the furs he wore when they arrived in Orrorsh realm, for the night was warmer here. Sitting there, illuminated by the flickering flames and free of the bulky furs, Bryce could see how skinny the aborigine was. Nothing but flesh and bones.

"My name is Djilangulyip," the shaman said in a sing-song voice. "I've seen a lot of things as shaman to my people. Tonight I want to tell you about some of them."

He looked slowly about, from face to face, and Bryce admired his style. Djil was a master storyteller.

"Decker is better," he continued. "I walked his dreams and watched as he broke free of that nasty fellow. The Gaunt Man, Kurst calls him. Anyway, Decker's still in danger, still has the evil magic upon him, but at least he's awake now."

"We're glad to hear that. But why did you call us here?" Bryce asked. "Why did you enter Tolwyn's dreams — however you accomplished that — and urge her to come to this place?"

"I didn't call you here, I just guided you."

"Doesn't that amount to the same thing?"

Djil shook his head. "The Earth called to its children,

preacher-man. But the children have lost their ability to hear. But I heard, and I don't mind saying that I was frightened by the sound. Imagine what it must take to scare something as big and powerful as this old world! But scared or not, I was also responsible, so I cast about in the Dream Time to find others who heard. That's how I found the sword-woman. That's how I found all of you."

Bryce began to ask another question, but Djil spoke first. "Hold your questions for a while longer, preacher-man. Let me tell you a story first. I saw it in the Dream Time, and I think it may answer some of what you want to ask."

"The story begins a long time ago, so long ago that time had no meaning," Djil began. "Let us see this place where there was no time. There was no space, no space at all. There was only the nothing, and the nothing was all alone."

"The Void," Kurst corrected. "In Orrorsh, the legends call it the Void. It existed in the Place, in the Time of Nothing."

"Who's telling this story?" Gutterby asked angrily.

"I will! I will!" Toolpin offered.

"No, it is Djil's story," Kurst said. "I apologize for interrupting."

Djil smiled, showing the hole where a tooth had once been. "It is everyone's story, a part of the Dream Time. But I will tell it now. The nothing was alone, empty. Then one day (although days had no meaning) the nothing met the everything."

"Eternity," Kurst explained, then fell silent when Djil and the dwarves gave him fierce looks.

"The nothing and the everything were different in every way," Djil continued. "Where the nothing was empty, the everything was full. They met, touching in a whirlpool of energy. The nothing finally found something to fill it, but to do so meant destroying each piece of the everything as it came in contact with it. The everything, meanwhile, had found something to help it free the stuff that would build worlds. If only the crumbs weren't devoured as they burst free."

"The Maelstrom of creation," Kurst clarified.

"Will you shut up!" the dwarves yelled as one. Bryce smiled. They really did like stories, he thought.

"Well, two of the crumbs were strong crumbs," Djil said. "They were able to survive the raging whirlpool — excuse me, Maelstrom. These crumbs were live things, great spirits fallen from the mouths of greater spirits, and one was the Nameless One. He was like the nothing, empty, needing every kind of sensation to fill him. He reveled in destruction and chaos. The other child, Apeiros, saw the good in all and was full of hope. She loved freedom and creating things — making the impossible possible."

Everyone looked at Kurst. He looked back, and everyone waited expectantly. "Those are the names my legends use," he declared.

Djil resumed without missing a beat. "Don't think good and bad where these two are concerned. Those concepts have no meaning to beings one step removed from the primal forces. They simply were; reflections of the nothing and the everything that spawned them. Apeiros set possibilities free by making them real — things of color and shape and sound and idea; creation was her power. In this way other, lesser things were able to survive the Maelstrom. But when the Nameless One (who Apeiros named because he could not summon the creativity to name himself) saw the bits of creation, he gobbled them up. So Apeiros had to set more possibilities free. And they were both surprised, because neither one knew how to do what the other had done: Apeiros had never thought about destroying things before, and the Nameless One had never thought about making things before. So they both learned something.

"And in the learning came the problem. The Nameless One was furious that Apeiros could do something he couldn't. So the war began. It was a war of creation against destruction, of two equal forces trapped in a conflict that could last forever — just like the Maelstrom that raged above them. The Nameless One, maybe learning just a bit from Apeiros, eventually came up with a solution. He cheated. He called to the nothing for help.

"He opened up the door to the nothing, and let the nothing in to eat the morsels Apeiros made. To a great spirit like the nothing, even Apeiros' power was hardly a moment's problem. So it looked like the Nameless One would win after all.

"But Apeiros was smart, too. She created something — but not just another thing to be destroyed. She created a whole new place, a new space that wasn't the same nothing space she and the Nameless One lived in. Oh, she had the help of the everything, but sometimes everybody needs some help. Together, Apeiros and the everything left to live in the new place, leaving the Nameless One alone with the nothing. And the nothing was still hungry.

"Now the Nameless One was in a terrible fix. If it didn't find things for the nothing to eat, the nothing would eat him! Try as he might, though, the Nameless One couldn't find where Apeiros and the everything had gone. But he could sense them. And he sensed that somehow Apeiros had released all of the everything so that whole universes were springing into being.

"The Nameless One, using what possibilities remained floating around him and what little he had learned from Apeiros, fashioned bundles of power and threw them in all directions. These bundles were full of destructive urges, and they had intelligence, too. They flew and flew, finally landing on worlds where people could find them. People like Kurst's Gaunt Man. And when enough of these bundles cause enough destruction, then the Nameless One will come running, hoping to finally catch Apeiros or the everything."

"And where the Nameless One goes, can the Void be far behind?" Kurst finished. Then he added, "Frightening stuff — if you believe it."

Djil pointed at the Heart of Coyote, which Bryce discovered resting in his hands. He must have taken it out of the pack during the story, but for the life of him he couldn't remember doing so.

"Belief is a funny thing, Kurst," the shaman said. "But do you know what that silly blue and red stone is? It's belief made solid. It's a piece of the everything."

95

James Monroe walked across the tarmac toward the motor pool on the far side of the compound. He needed to find transportation to one of the big cities. San Bernadino, maybe. Or even Los Angeles. Then he could get on with his quest. Excitement coursed through his body; with each step he was closer to reaching Tolwyn.

He heard the approaching helicopter before he saw it. The low, steady beat of the spinning rotor blades built slowly at first, getting louder until the craft finally appeared over the buildings across the compound.

Monroe watched as it rocked back and forth erratically, dropping its blades dangerously close to one of the buildings as it tilted to one side.

"What's wrong with that pilot?" he muttered. "He can't fly worth a damn."

The helicopter set down roughly, landing with an audible crash that bent the undercarriage. Before Monroe could decide whether the pilot was crazy, reckless, or in trouble, he saw a splash of red splatter across the inside of the windshield.

"Good God!" he screamed in surprise, and started off at a run toward the helicopter.

Monroe made his way around to the door of the large transport. Each window he passed was marred by dripping red splattered upon the inside of the glass. He reached the door, but found that it was already swinging open. The doctor stepped back, and something inside him screamed "run away!" He just stood there, however. This moment was important. He knew it was! And if he survived, there would be power as a reward for his bravery.

The door completed its swing, revealing the dark opening into the belly of the chopper. Monroe swallowed, trying to ignore the cold chill running down his spine. A form appeared in the darkness. At first it was indistinct, nothing more than a huge shadow moving within the deeper shadows. Then it stepped into the diffused light of the ash-filled day, and Monroe gasped.

The man that emerged from the helicopter was close to seven feet tall and as wide as two men. He had a wild look about him, crazy eyes that reminded Monroe of the gray cat's eyes.

A hunter's eyes.

He held his hands at his sides, bent like claws. Red

covered those large hands, staining them, painting them all the way up to his elbows. The doctor identified the liquid immediately. He had seen enough of it over the years. It was blood. And worse, the bright crimson also stained the man's lips and mouth. The man stepped closer, and it took every ounce of willpower Monroe could muster to keep himself from bolting like a rabbit before a wolf.

"You smell like Decker," the blood-covered man said. The stink that emerged from his mouth caused Monroe to gag. "But you're not him. Not exactly. But you're from his litter, aren't you little man?"

Monroe nodded, suddenly angry that this person knew his secret. He forgot the bloody windows, forgot the man's size. All he remembered was the anger he felt toward his brother and Julie Boot, and he let it mix with this new anger. Then he charged the larger man, wanting only to pound on him, to cause him pain.

The blood-covered man laughed. It was a wicked sound. He caught Monroe around the neck with his large, blood-covered hands, and lifted the doctor with no effort. Monroe's feet dangled a good half a foot off the ground.

"Should I kill you, little man?" the larger man asked. "Should I show you what I did to the soldiers in the flying carriage?" The large man studied him with his cat-like eyes. "Or should I let you go?"

Something was happening to Monroe, something strange. He felt it deep inside himself, a feeling like static building before the lightning comes. It was the power! But he had no idea what to do with it.

The large man sniffed. "You're a stormer," he laughed. "Or at least you're about to be. If you make your choice." An evil grin twisted his blood-smeared lips. "Let me help you. You can try to destroy me, which will make you a stormer but end your pitiful life. Or you can side with me, agree to help me. And perhaps I'll let you live."

Monroe could feel the static bouncing within him, around him. So much power! There could even be enough to smash this arrogant psychotic, if he could figure out what to do with the power. At the thought, endless possibilities began to flash across his mind. He saw countless ways to defeat the large man, countless ways to free himself and escape. He just had to grasp one of them as they appeared and wield it like he wielded scalpels in the operating room. But there was another option open to him.

"What," Monroe forced the word through his constricted throat. The larger man loosened his grip ever so slightly. "What do you want from me?" the doctor finished.

"I want your brother. I want Andrew Decker."

Monroe couldn't believe it. That was his choice? Either fight this monster of a man, or direct him to the brother he hated? That was no choice at all.

"I'll show you where he is," Monroe said, smiling at the thought.

He laughed as the lightning crackled inside him.

96

The Gaunt Man turned away from the mirror, faint wisps of mist still rising from it like a dying fire. Scythak was close to Decker now. All the man-tiger had to do was capture Decker and bring him to Orrorsh, where the Gaunt Man could reestablish full control of the stormer. Once attached directly to the machine, there would be no way for Decker to escape before he completed the task appointed to him.

He had to finish removing all the possibilities of the Gaunt Man's failure. That was most important as the Gaunt Man reached the crucial stages of his plan.

Even so, the runes were still implanted, still doing their work. The machine still ran, draining Decker's possibilities, draining the others. But without Decker or another of similar strength, there was no one to sort the possibilities. For all his power, that was one of the things the Gaunt Man could not do. To him, the energy was all the same. There was no difference that he could see. Why could some stormers see them? He knew the explanation that was simplified as the legend of the Nameless One and Apeiros, but he never really believed in the legend. It was always a story to him, nothing more. If the Nameless One and Apeiros ever existed, they were nothing more than memories now. And soon even those memories would be replaced by his own elevation to godhood. Soon he would be Torg in more than just name. Soon he would have the power as well.

He turned back to the mirror and searched for Thratchen. He found the cyber-demon easily, for Thratchen was even now landing in the courtyard of Illmound Keep. Good. He would be here when Kurst and the others arrived. The Gaunt Man waved a hand over the mirror, and his own image returned to the chilled surface.

The Gaunt Man collapsed heavily into his throne of bones to think. He went over his plan in his mind, looking for any flaws. After countless centuries of study, he had determined the ingredients necessary to elevate himself to Torg. The process required a phenomenal amount of possibility energy available in one place — more than any world he had ever conquered could contain. But legends spoke of a world that literally sparkled with the energy. After more centuries of searching throughout the cosmverse he found the world of legend; he found Earth. But there was no way he could attach his realm to the planet. The world was just too strong for a single High Lord to take. He needed help. He needed other Possibility Raiders.

Six realities were now attached to this possibility-rich world — more than enough to keep the power surges from repelling them. Already each High Lord was busy establishing areas of power and influence, busy stripping power directly from the succulent sheep that inhabited this world. Let them take what they wanted, he thought. There would still be more than enough for his purposes.

The second part of his plan was proceeding well. His sorting machine was using stormers to sort desirable possibilities from undesirable ones, forming a pattern on which to build the reality he so desired — a reality where a mortal being can be reborn as the Torg.

The third portion of the plan required an incredible amount of physical energy. This energy (which was even now being sucked from the planet by his infernal machine, as evidenced by the slowing of the planet's spin) would be fired through the possibility pattern created by the first machine, burning along the latticework of the almost-real and perhaps-true to make the possible real.

He had only recently come up with the idea to use Decker to sort a specific type of possibility in addition to the pattern he desired. He had set the congressman to work showing him the paths that led to the Earth actually surviving the entire process. It would not be good if the planet and its people (the fuel he needed, after all) died before he had a chance to make his possibility pattern a reality.

Damn the stormer who helped Decker resist him! Now there was the possibility of failure, however small. He needed Decker to finish his work. He needed to know that no possibility of failure still existed.

The Gaunt Man stood, picked up his cane, and left the tower room, heading for the stairs that led to the cellars.

To the sorting machine.

97

Decker doubled over with pain. Suddenly the staves were active again, and the constant draining sensation he felt increased twelve-fold. His vision swam, and he heard the voice from his dreams

(nightmares)

shout, "Choose! Choose!" The doors were there, beckoning him to throw one open as opposed to another.

"Go to hell!" he gritted through clenched teeth.

"Ace? What is it? Ace?" Julie said, startling him.

He thought he was alone in his room. The President had gone off to the rooms made available to him to get some rest after their long discussion, and Decker had decided to give standing up a shot. Now he wasn't sure about the wisdom of his decision.

Julie put down the tray of food she was carrying and rushed to his side. She supported his weight, helping him back onto the bed. Her touch was like water to the fire of pain that raged through him. Her concern made his vision clear, made the crackling light of the staves dim.

"I think I can fight him," Decker said. "I think I can force him out of my mind. Especially when you're near. You seem to add strength to me. And I need strength right now."

"You need to get back into bed," she scolded.

"No," Decker said, sitting up. "I need a shower. Then I need to meet with the President. He's set up a meeting with a bunch of the military types to assess our situation."

"What is our situation, Ace?" Julie asked quietly, suddenly no longer the self-assured officer but a frightened, uncertain human being.

"Bad, but not impossible," he said softly, giving her a smile. Decker took her hand then, holding it the way she had held his when he came out of his long sleep. For the moment, that was enough for both of them.

98

"He's in that building," Monroe said, pointing toward the hospital. "Room 436."

"There are too many soldiers around," Scythak decided.

Monroe thought the large man's name was strange when he first heard it, but he didn't say anything. He noticed that this Scythak was quick to anger, and he didn't want to be on the receiving end of a violent outburst. After all, he could still see the blood drying on the large man's hands.

"I think they've noticed your handiwork," Monroe commented, gesturing toward the helicopter they had left back on the tarmac.

"Yes," Scythak breathed heavily, "maybe that bit of fun was an indiscretion. Nothing to be done about it now, though." He studied the hospital and the soldiers all around it with his cat eyes. For long moments neither man spoke. Then Scythak said, "We need a place to hide. It has to be nearby, in sight of the hospital. If I make a move now to capture

(*kill, kill, kill*)

Decker, he might get hurt in the resulting battle. I

need to wait until the time is right."

Monroe knew he was missing something, especially when Scythak's hand went to the pendant he wore around his neck. The large man fingered the stone that hung from the gold chain without realizing it. Monroe doubted the man even remembered he wore such jewelry. It certainly didn't seem to be his style. But the doctor didn't say anything about the pendant. Instead he thought about a place to hide out.

"Come on," Monroe said at last. "I think I know a perfect place."

99

"Ashes to ashes, dust to dust, amen," said Father Christopher Bryce over the funeral pyre. Praktix did not survive the night, even though Mara had done everything she could. The dwarf had internal injuries, Mara had explained, she had lost too much blood. Bryce was sick with the words he spoke. They had become a recording over the last few weeks, an endless chant that he said with more and more detachment. No, that wasn't true. Each death still hurt. Some more than others. He watched Braxon put the torch to his sister's remains. This death hurt a lot.

Tolwyn and the dwarves sang a hymn to Dunad then, to the warrior god of Aysle who even the pragmatic dwarves respected. The others remained silent through it all, even Kurst (who constantly raised his nose to the wind throughout the ceremony), until the pyre blazed brightly. Then Tolwyn spoke in her soldier tone.

"We must move on now," she said. "Our goal is nearby. We must not let this sadness deter us — or others will suffer these fates, over and over again. It is for life that we go on." Bryce smiled. She would have made a fine preacher.

The dwarves moved over to Mara, helped her rise. The girl was still upset with herself. She was having a tough time excepting this loss. Bryce pressed his lips together. He had counselled doctors who had lost patients before. And he had counselled young people who had lost friends. It was the combination of the two that was difficult for him to comprehend. He contented himself with walking nearby, smiling at her when he could catch her gaze, trying to envelop her with his caring.

They all climbed into the carriage; Kurst and Tolwyn behind the horses, Triad and Toolpin on top, the rest inside. They rode in silence for a time, and Bryce tried to find words to comfort them all. But nothing came to his lips but a frown. He heard the music but didn't pay much attention at first. It was a catchy, old-fashioned tune, like the songs on a player piano, and he hummed along with the sound. When the scenery outside the carriage window suddenly changed, it took him a while to notice it. But there it was — a town!

"Hey!" he shouted, banging on the roof of the carriage. "Hey, stop! Let's take a look around."

The carriage was moving slowly along the cobbled path, and Bryce had no trouble leaping down from the cab. He was standing in what appeared to be a town right out of Victorian England, right down to the low fog that filled the streets. He heard Kurst call for the horses to stop, so he walked toward the tavern across the way.

A strange smell reached Bryce's nose, but he put it out of his mind as he walked. He had to see who was playing such fine music! He had to dance just once to its bouncy tune. The door to the tavern was open, and the light pouring out was warm and bright. It would be good to have some real food for a change, and maybe they could find a few real beds. A good meal and a good night's sleep was just what they all needed right now. He was forty steps from the door, and the music pulled him along.

Thirty steps. He could see people now, or at least shapes, twirling and laughing in the light beyond the doorway.

Twenty steps. He could smell ale and sizzling sausage wafting out of the establishment. Someone inside called for a serving girl, and Bryce smiled.

Fifteen steps. A woman appeared at the door, framed by the golden light. He couldn't see her features because of the way she was silhouetted, but she had a round, pleasant shape that reminded him of home.

Ten steps. A strong hand grabbed Bryce's arm and spun him around. It was Kurst, and he was looking at the priest with hard eyes.

"Get back in the carriage," Kurst ordered.

"What is wrong with you. Kurst?" Bryce yelled. "This is a town. Do you know what that means? It means hot food and warm beds. It means a touch of civilization out here in the jungle."

"It means more than you know, priest," Kurst said. "If you enter that place I cannot help you. You will belong to them, and we will go on without you."

Bryce looked for the humor, the joke, in Kurst's eyes. There was none. "What are you babbling about?"

"The Gaunt Man surrounds himself with places that are between this world and the next. Way stations, you might call them. This is one of those places."

Bryce smelled the sausage, and his mouth watered. He tried to pull free of Kurst's grasp, but the hunter was too strong.

"Everything here is dead, Bryce. Those inside cannot move on. They are stuck, trapped in time. If you enter, you will be trapped as well. Take a deep breath, Bryce. What do you smell?"

Bryce breathed in the air, and suddenly he understood what Kurst was saying. Beneath the aroma of sausage and ale was another smell. A dark smell. It was the smell of dust and decay, or things long dead. The priest wanted desperately to be ill.

"No time," Kurst said. He dragged the priest back to the carriage.

"Not even one dance?" Bryce asked before Kurst closed the carriage door.

"It is not as exciting as it appears," Kurst said. "The dead are a very boring lot."

The smell was stronger now, making Bryce gag. "Then let's leave them to this place and be on with our journey."

The hunter nodded, closed the door. Soon the carriage was past the town, but the smell stayed with them for a very long time.

100

At oh-eight-hundred Special Operative Lance Odell was dressed as an intern, sorting laundry in a corridor six doors from the room the meeting was to be held in. Outside, the long day was finally coming to an end, and twilight was settling over Twentynine Palms. Odell folded another bed sheet, keeping one eye on the closed door.

Three minutes later, people started to arrive. First came four soldiers. Two stationed themselves in the corridor; two disappeared into the room. Odell smiled at the ones in the corridor. They ignored him. He folded another sheet.

At five minutes past, Colonel McCall and an aide arrived. Behind them were Lieutenant Charles Covent (recently at the battle front but now recovering from wounds sustained while fighting the enemy) and the civilian, Eddie Paragon. Paragon had arrived on the base with a wild story of having been with the leader of the dinosaurs since the invasion started in New York. It sickened Odell to see someone so obviously against the discipline that marked military life included in such an important meeting.

At six minutes past, Congressman Andrew Jackson Decker entered the room. With him were Major Julie Boot and the edeinos visitor, Tal Tu. That was another transgression that Odell couldn't understand. Let's just invite the enemy to our war conference! These were the kinds of decisions the Delphi Council was going to correct. That's why Lance Odell was first on line to become one of the Council's operatives — one of the Spartans. He even loved the code-name.

Finally, at seven minutes past, President John Wells and his security detail arrived. The door closed with a resounding slam. Odell folded the last of his sheets, then wheeled the laundry cart past the soldiers stationed at the door and onto the elevator at the opposite end of the corridor. He couldn't wait to report his findings to Quartermain. For a moment he considered trying to get some details as to the specifics of the meeting, but then dismissed that as too dangerous. Besides, Quartermain would be interested in knowing the names of the people in that meeting.

Odell was sure that the Vice President would be as disturbed by the mixing of civilians, the enemy, the army and the President as he was.

101

The carriage stopped and Bryce came awake with a start. He had been sleeping, lulled by the steady rock as they traveled along the path. He noticed that the smell of the way station was still with them, but then decided that this smell was fresher, closer. It was a foul death-smell, reminiscent of rotting garbage and carrion.

"What is that?" Bryce exclaimed as he stepped from the carriage.

"Fields," was all Kurst said. "We've got to be careful, now. There might be soldiers or other creatures about."

There was a field of sorts to their right. Bryce could see it in the faint light of the approaching dawn. But full day would be long in coming. Still, the promise of light after the extended night was a welcome sign. The smell, however, was like something that had been under the sun for far, far too long.

"Dear sweet God," Bryce exclaimed as his nostrils were assaulted. Mara moaned beside him

"It's the field," Kurst said again. "A large open area. We have to go around."

Bryce stared at the huge clearing, perhaps two hundred yards square. It was not a natural clearing, for trees were stacked at the corners, dragged from where they had been felled, and the land itself was neatly plowed in even rows of crops.

As the priest watched, plants began to burst from the ground. But the plants were man-shaped, a disgusting synthesis of twisting roots, rotting flesh, and packed soil. Some of the plants opened vine-covered mouths, screaming their arrival out of the earth. In the holes they emerged from, the priest could see the remains of human bodies, which seemed to serve as either seed or fertilizer for the terrible plants. From the number of rows, many

The Dark Realm

people died to create this field.

"Gospog," Kurst explained.

"This is an abomination," Tolwyn whispered.

"Maybe," said Kurst. "We can't stop here, though. There are too many Caretakers about, and probably the Others as well."

"We must destroy this place," said Tolwyn.

Kurst looked at her a moment, as if wondering whether to reply or not. Apparently he decided against it, and turned to go.

"It must be destroyed," Tolwyn repeated, feeling at the edge of her sword with a roughened thumb. "This is an offense to all things."

Kurst turned on her. "Is it?" he asked, his voice cold, chilling. "And let us give thanks that this is the only offense to all things that has ever existed or ever will exist, so that destroying it will cleanse the world of evil and save all lives for all times to come! Are you mad? We are attempting to enter the castle of the Gaunt Man in order to destroy the machine that is destroying Decker. And you want to alert him to our presence by wrecking some minor tool of his in a fit of ... of what?"

"This is no minor thing. Look at that field! There must be ten thousand of those things ready to ripen! An army of horror, and we could destroy it now! You find it surprising I wish to destroy it? I find it surprising you do not."

"No," said Mara, ignoring both of them. She was standing forward, almost at the edge of the clearing, gazing out at the field. She turned back to look at the others.

"No," said Mara again, and Kurst and Tolwyn both forgot the momentary feud watching her. "I remember this, from my own world. They make armies, armies to crush the opposition in unending advances. Ten thousand of these are more dangerous than twice their number of real soldiers, because no one cares if they die — not even themselves. I had friends killed by gospog." She turned and strode from the cover of the trees, clutching at her right shoulder as she walked.

"No!" hissed Kurst, leaping for her, but Mara was suddenly moving too fast for even his lightning reflexes. Mara was running now, shouting at the top of her lungs, screaming almost as she ran, heading into a field of despair. The Caretakers saw her immediately, and some raised their guns, hesitating at the sight of a girl screaming and running through their field.

Kurst, still hidden, flexed his hands open and closed. "What should I do?" he asked Bryce, real pain on his face. Bryce was surprised at that look.

But it was too late for Bryce's reply. Mara pointed her laser and fired. Where the beam touched, there was a burst of flame. The Caretakers screamed and moved to stop her, but they were too far away. Bryce looked around and saw Djil toss a flaming torch into the field. Grim worked his magic and another ball of fire rolled out of his hand and engulfed a section of the field.

Bryce stared at Tolwyn uncertainly. "This could be a mistake," he suggested.

Tolwyn nodded. "Yes. And it could be for the best."

Bryce, Tolwyn, and Kurst stood by and watched as the others helped Mara start the fire, spreading it like an ax across the whole field. There were shallow screams on the air now, and an even more horrible smell as the plant-things burned. The Caretakers, now trying to put out the fire, ignored Mara and the others.

The air was filled with smoke and ash and the terrible smell, as flames crackled from the entire field, roaring in sheets up and down, fed by the light wind. Mara stood still, eyes watering, staring at what she had done.

They all stared in fascination at the wall of flame, and Bryce thought he could see faces and bodies writhing in the flames, their screams mere echoes above the fire's roar. Even Kurst seemed fascinated.

"Nothing to be done now but continue on," Kurst said. "If the Gaunt Man didn't know we were coming, he does now."

Bryce turned once more to watch the flames, to see their crackling glow mingle with the brightening sky. It was a signal fire, he thought, an affirmation that the Gaunt Man was not unopposed. He hoped it was more than just a futile gesture.

102

Kurst whipped the horses, forcing them to run as fast as they could. He had to get them away from the gospog field. They were probably going to be caught anyway, but time and distance might work in their favor. It would take those that came to investigate a little while to figure out exactly what had happened. Unless Thratchen came to investigate. Or even the Gaunt Man himself. Then they would be discovered before another step could be taken.

He knew he should be angry. Not only had they endangered their mission, they had also struck out at the realm Kurst owed his allegiance to. But he wasn't angry. He almost felt good watching the damnable fields burn. He needed to think about that. Every sense was extended, alert, looking for signs of pursuit. He saw none.

He thought about the upcoming meeting with the Gaunt Man. How would that go? Would he turn Mara and Tolwyn over to him? Would he help dispatch the others? He was so sure when this mission began. Now different emotions warred inside him. He snarled in frustration.

"We need to find a place to rest before we reach the Gaunt Man," Tolwyn said from her place beside him. "Otherwise we will be no good as fighters."

Kurst pursed his lips. Did she really expect to fight the Gaunt Man? He knew the answer to that. And he knew that he had to continue the illusion that that was what they were going to do. He slowed the horses, and turned into a small clearing beside the path.

"This will be a brief stop," he announced. "We are close to our goal, and there will be scouts looking for the cause of the blaze."

He dropped to the ground and leaned against a tree. He would not sleep, he told himself. He only needed a short rest. He thought of Decker, lying on his back with the rune staves sucking at his life force. Then he closed his eyes.

And there was darkness.

103

Tolwyn watched as Kurst's eyes closed and his breathing became regular. She smiled. Even the great hunter needed sleep. She checked on the dwarves, making sure that two of them were standing guard. Then she laid down on the hard ground and closed her eyes as well.

Tolwyn slept. And dreamed.

There were people all around, clustered about her, breathing over her shoulder, staring and muttering, and most were also crying out for something. Something they wanted her to do, but their words were obscure and meaningless, and only their need came through. There was something she had to do, but she had no idea what it was.

And she knew that if she failed to do it, she would die.

Tolwyn of House Tancred looked down, saw her sandaled feet stark against the sand of the arena. Her sword was clutched tightly in both hands — no shields in the arena — and sweat trickled down her arms and onto the pommel, threatening to loosen her grip. From across the way, barely visible through the tremendous light of the sun overhead, a door was opening. It rumbled up into the stonework, and from within she heard a fearful roar that sent ripples up and down her spine. Fighting terror, she strove to think rationally, knowing that in the arena, fear would be her undoing. What advantages could she press?

Perhaps her opponent (man or beast) would be blinded by the change from dark to light! With a gulp of hope, she ran forward, kicking up sand as she went.

The going was slow, the sand loose, her sandals ill-fitting. But she had no time to stop and untie them, only to try to kick them off. It did not work. The sandals hung onto her feet as though there was glue on the thongs. Then she saw her opponent, and coldness clutched at her chest.

It was a great green ogre, all scales and rough, bumpy skin, and it roared as it stepped into the sun, shaking the stands with its power. A huge club was clutched in its right fist, and Tolwyn's heart sank. She had seen this monstrosity before, destroying other opponents in the arena! She was next, and the damn sandals were annoying her. She looked up and the ogre was upon her, his huge club upraised. He smashed down then, the club whistling through the air, and she felt the impact on her shoulder as she desperately dove aside, the heavy wood cracking bone and tearing flesh so that she screamed with the pain.

Tolwyn awoke with a start.

"It was just a nightmare," Christopher Bryce told her. He was sitting near her, drinking from a canteen.

"Not just a nightmare," said Djil, striding from the bush into their little clearing. "I was taking a very short walk in the Dream Time, and I saw the things that chase Tolwyn. This is a land of living nightmares. You're still unwhole, sword woman, and it's dangerous to dream in these parts if you're not whole."

If Bryce shared her frustration, he hid it well. "What can be done?" he asked the aborigine, real concern in his voice. She smiled at that.

"We must walk together, sword woman," Djil replied, addressing Tolwyn. "I can help you break through the wall that binds your memories. You must be whole for the confrontations to come. But only if you want to be."

She nodded.

"There is danger."

"I am ready."

104

Tolwyn and Djil walked in the Dream Time, across a field ripe with blue and red crys flowers. He held her hand, leading her to the things she could not remember.

He led her past dark paths until they reached the caverns that were her own, and there he left her, standing at the dark mouth, with the ocean roaring into rocks far beneath her. She heard the cry of a gull overhead.

"When you find what you are looking for," he called, "you will know it. At the other end lies understanding.

I will wait for you there. Dream well!"

Before she had a chance to reply, Djil was gone. She must do this on her own, or she would never be whole again.

Tolwyn entered the cave.

She remembered the last stand of the Knight Protectors on the battlements of Lady Ardinay's castle. She remembered her last discussion with the Lady, before the Carredon arrived. Before she leaped to fight it. They stood together on the rampart, the other five Knight Protectors around them, and they spoke loudly to each other to make themselves heard above the clash of arms and the shrieks of war.

"Remember the land, Tolwyn," Ardinay said, brushing her fingers gently across Tolwyn's brow. "The land is important, it is what makes Aysle so special."

The Lady was radiant, standing proudly beside her knights as Uthorion's forces pressed forward. Tolwyn loved this woman who was their leader, loved her with all her heart as she loved the land.

"Dunad," Pella Ardinay said, "show us the way to banish these things of darkness. Show us how to preserve the land." A glowing ball appeared in the Lady's hands. It was bright and warm, and it felt very good to Tolwyn. The Lady handed it to her. "This is the land, Tolwyn," she explained. "Dunad has helped me gather it. Place it in your heart and remember it always."

The ball drifted into the warrior's hands, then expanded to fill her with the image of Aysle. "I have done all that I can, my warrior," Ardinay said. "Now you must do what you can."

Below them, the Carredon arrived, and Uthorion was atop its back. "I will do what I must, Lady," Tolwyn declared. Then she leaped over the rampart to face the evil dragon.

"Remember the land," Ardinay called once more. "And die well, my cherished knight." The she disappeared as well, off to face the vile Uthorion who had entered her castle.

Tolwyn emerged from the cave, and Djilangulyip stood waiting for her.

"I know now, Djil," she said. "Something has happened to Aysle, something terrible. It is as the dwarves said. The light has been dulled by the darkness of Uthorion. But I remember the light."

She faced Djil, who regarded her silently. "I can make everyone remember, and the darkness will lift." Djil nodded his understanding.

"But I must discover what caused Pella Ardinay to change," Tolwyn added. "From what the dwarves have said, she still lives, even after all these centuries. That is not possible for a human. And it is not possible for the Lady to have become evil."

"Anything is possible, sword woman," Djil said. "Have you got everything you came for?"

Tolwyn smiled grimly. "I know who I am, and I remember the land."

"Then let us go back."

Tolwyn of House Tancred awoke. She saw Christopher Bryce staring down at her with concern, and she smiled.

"Are you all right?" he asked.

"I am," she replied.

105

Andrew Decker and Julie Boot stood by the window

of his room, looking out over the compound. He was lost in thought, going over the details of the meeting. McCall and Covent were good men, fine soldiers. He trusted them. He wasn't sure about the rock singer, Eddie Paragon, though. For goodness sake, the man didn't even like baseball! But he had provided them with important information about the leader of the invaders — Baruk Kaah. Tal Tu had confirmed the information, and even admitted that the singer knew more about the High Lord than he did.

But some of Paragon's news was disturbing. The Wild Hunt sounded very dangerous. And gospog, whatever they turned out to be, gave the edeinos an advantage the United States hadn't planned on. It gave them the ability to use our own weapons against us.

Already Covent and Paragon were on their way to the front. They took Tal Tu with them. Decker was getting ready to follow them, to help in any way he could. He didn't want to bring Julie along, didn't want to expose her to danger. But another part of him wanted her beside him. He had to think about that.

"I'm going with you," she said at last.

"Excuse me?"

"You heard me, Ace," she said. "You need me. And I hate to let patients get out of my care before they're fully healed."

"But …"

"That's an order, congressman," she said, taking his hand. He couldn't think of an argument to dissuade her. And he didn't want to.

106

Kurst directed the carriage into a town which seemed to have sprung up within the jungle. Bryce was struck by the way it reminded him of the earlier town, but this one was more solid, less dreamlike than the other. Also, with the sun beginning to rise somewhere beyond the ash cover over head, images had become more substantial. It was disconcerting to see the jungle pressing in on the Victorian town, and the shadow of a volcano rising over the town was even stranger. You don't see those kind of sights in England, but the town appeared to have been lifted whole cloth out of a London neighborhood from around the turn of the century.

"This is it," Kurst said, very softly. "Salisbury Manor is here. But you should know its real name. Call it Illmound Keep."

There were people everywhere, and horses, and hansom cabs, and wagons. They moved about as though nothing was wrong, as though it was absolutely natural for them to be here on Borneo. Kurst pointed, and Bryce followed his finger to the center of town. There a great walled estate loomed. And beside it was a bridge that shot up into the sky. It was an odd-colored structure, and it moved as Bryce looked at it. Then the priest saw why — the bridge was made of human bodies, and they appeared to still be alive.

"That is the Maelstrom bridge," Kurst explained as they piled out of the carriage. "It leads to Orrorsh cosm. Be wary here, for things are not always as they appear."

They followed Kurst down a side street, moving naturally to avoid suspicious gazes. Bryce noticed someone standing in a doorway. Out of the corner of his eye, the figure appeared to be a corpse, covered with dried blood and partially rotted. But when he looked directly at the figure, it was a simple shopkeeper gazing into the street. Bryce hurried after the others.

From every street, Bryce could look up and see the

The Dark Realm

Alan Jude Summa

Gaunt Man's estate. It was vaulted with many towers, and darkness clung to it like schools of feeding shark. The windows were dark and forbidding, and the stonework gave him a sense of intense cold. Grave cold. Looking across the vast face of the structure, Bryce felt a sense of danger, and of fear.

He was afraid of the Gaunt Man.

But before he could dwell on that, something happening up ahead called his attention. A group of young roughs were blocking the street. Kurst had spoken to them, but they made no attempt to move aside.

"I say again, move away," Kurst commanded in his most threatening tone.

The leader of the roughs laughed. "This is our street, human," he said in a heavily-accented voice. It reminded Bryce of Cockney, but not quite. "You're going to have to leave a few of the little ones if you want safe passage."

"And if we don't?" Kurst asked.

"Then we'll take you all!" the leader shouted as he began to change. He shifted, much the way Kurst did, growing thick hair as his features became more wolflike. He was a werewolf, but was nowhere near as impressive looking or as large as Kurst became when he shifted. The other roughs changed as well, turning into rat men who chattered in expectation of a kill.

"A werewolf leading wererats?" Kurst actually laughed, and Bryce decided he liked him better when he didn't. "Well, let's see who has the sharper claws."

Kurst did his shifting act then, growing larger, more powerful. His demonic wolf shape towered over the roughs, and the other werecreatures shrank back.

"We have no quarrel with you, dire wolf," the werewolf rough said. Bryce heard the fear in his voice. "We did not know that these were yours."

The werecreatures disappeared then, fading into the shadows that lined the street. When they were gone, Kurst shifted back to human form.

"What was that all about?" Bryce asked. "What's a dire wolf?"

"Apparently, I am," Kurst replied, shaken by the encounter. "There are things about my past that, like Tolwyn, I don't remember. This must be one of those things."

107

They were such infinitely useless fools, all of them! The Gaunt Man cursed low and often as the view in the mirror phased in and out until he thought his head would burst with the throbbing colors and the searing flashes of light. Damn all stormers to the depths of darkness anyway! And especially damn the fact that they existed in droves on the very worlds best for plundering.

Thinking of the plunderable power brought calm, and with the calm the Gaunt Man's mental control over the rituals necessary to enact the mirror became more solid. The view cleared, and he was looking at the outside of his own castle, the open courtyard that none might pass without permission.

He had moved the mirror into the basement so that he could view distant happenings while he worked to re-establish the machine's link to Decker. He saw the burning gospog field, and the scene filled him with rage. And now he watched as Kurst led a large band of others through the maze of spirits that patrolled the grounds.

"You relentless sneak!" he breathed in a voice twisted with inhuman pain and hate that would have slain a normal human to hear it. "What changes have been wrought in you, Kurst?" For a moment, he considered raising a general alarm, summoning warriors from the very stones of Illmound Keep to engage and overwhelm and annihilate the intruders. But if this were just Kurst's way of bringing them to him, then he would be a fool to risk upsetting that plan. Best to let the hunter run his course.

Again he turned to the mirror to watch as Kurst spoke a word that had been taught to him in strictest confidence, setting to rest the bones of seven warriors that otherwise would have risen up to tear at the flesh of any mortals so foolish as to cross the keep's grounds. The graves remained quiet, then, and Kurst led the group onward, past the runes painted on the lower entrance that should have sounded an alarm but did not as the hunter gestured in the prescribed fashion. The Gaunt Man realized at that moment that if the gospog field had not been burned, alerting him, they might have entered the keep in complete secrecy. His fleshless fingers clenched and unclenched.

"Oh, they will die," the Gaunt Man whispered, "with the possibilities torn from their souls without preparation. They will scream as they die, and I shall be there, laughing at them all the while, driving runes into each and every one of them and sending them into my machine."

But Kurst was a bit of disquiet in an otherwise obvious course of action. To smash these overconfident stormers was all the Gaunt Man wished. But what of Kurst? If he proved to have betrayed him, what course was available? Kurst was a valuable investment, not easily discarded just because a flaw had shown itself. Far better to spend some time with the machine, re-educating, eradicating, remolding. If it was a painful process for Kurst, so be it.

The ungrateful lout certainly deserved much pain for his betrayal. The Gaunt Man smiled and left the mirror, passing a hand over its coldness so that the image of Kurst's face was frozen on the surface.

The machine was at the other end of the massive chamber, fully a hundred yards away. The Gaunt Man, eager to bring the stormers under control, crossed the room, speaking words of power as he moved. He did not run, but walked easy with loose-limbed strides.

The machine rose in power as its sounds rose in pitch, and all seemed to be functioning perfectly. He touched the flat plate, intoned his wishes out loud to better form them in his mind, then crossed quickly back to the mirror to witness the effects of what he had done.

Darkness wrapped him like a cloak as the machine screamed the scream of a tortured soul. The Gaunt Man laughed at what he now saw.

108

Kurst moved cautiously, sight and smell at wolf-level, ears arched forward like a wolf, looking for signs of danger. Behind him, Tolwyn moved almost as quietly, her sword held forward and up in her hand, her eyes bird-bright as she flicked her head back and forth. Bryce was behind her, trying to walk silently and failing miserably. Kurst glided through the darkness. The corridor was damp and smelled of things that grew in the deep places of the earth.

Behind Bryce, the dwarves moved in steady single file, a fighting unit far more dangerous than they looked. All held their battle spikes at ready, carefully avoiding clanging the metal against the stones of the wall. Behind them, Tom followed. Kurst could hear nothing of either Djil or Mara.

Something like a blue light danced before his eyes then, and he stopped, a low growling emerging from his throat. An attack? His hands came up, wolf-paws and extended silvery claws.

"What?" Tolwyn whispered, but he did not reply.

It passed, a feeling of dread and chill that had come upon him with the flash of light. His eyes cleared and he again saw only the dank corridor stretching before him, the shadows unmoving, a stairway on the left leading up, and cross-corridors further ahead.

"It was nothing," he whispered, turning to let Tolwyn see his lips that he might speak more softly. "I think those stairs are what we want. Let me scout ahead just for a moment." Before she could reply, he turned and was gone.

A feeling of freedom came over him as he moved up the stairs, a sense of space and release of pressure: all those others around him were a danger, a hindrance. He was Kurst, and he worked best when he was alone.

He padded up the steps one-by-one, feeling for deadfalls or alarms, remembering in his bones the layout of the keep. This stair rose to nearly the top level, then across two rooms to a little-used access stair. Yes. It was his fate, his ultimate goal. He would leave the others here — they would find the way, they were clever and resourceful — and he would go, on his own, to the Gaunt Man's tower.

He stood a better chance alone, for if he did meet any of the guards or servants, they would know him and let him pass. And he could arrange a diversion for the others, if they were not stealthy enough. And when he reached the tower, he would find the stairs that led down to the cellars and the machine. He would find a way to destroy the machine by himself, and then find the others and escape. Would they all be able to survive the Gaunt Man's wrath? If he were quick enough, perhaps. Perhaps the damage to the machine could be subtly done ... enough! No need for thinking — he knew what he had to do, and how best to do it.

Slowly, step by step, Kurst wound his way higher and higher into the castle of his master. His footsteps were barely audible as he moved; the loudest sound he made was a low growl that came constantly from his throat, like the rumbling of the far distant machine.

109

Lance Odell watched as President Wells and Decker met for the last time. Air Force One was outside, waiting to carry the President back to Houston. Boot and McCall were a respectful distance from the two men, giving them as much privacy as they could. Only one of Well's security men was nearby. Odell, dressed as a soldier and standing guard at the door, quickly memorized every person's position. Then he made his move.

He stepped up to Decker, smiling and reaching out to shake the congressman's hand. Decker was taken aback by the approach, off balance. That was just what Odell wanted. He took the congressman's hand, then shifted his weight quickly, placing himself behind Decker and holding his arm behind him in a crushing grip. With his other hand, Odell produced an automatic pistol.

The security guard moved to intercept Odell, throwing his body between the gun and the President. He took two shots as Odell fired, dying before he hit the floor. Decker tried to free himself, or at least to knock off Odell's aim. But the Spartan was strong. He easily held the weakened congressman in check.

"This is for America, Mr. President," Odell yelled.

"Do what you think you must, young man," Wells said calmly. "Just don't kill anyone else."

His next two shots caught John Wells in the head. Decker screamed and lashed out at the sight of his friend falling, actually pulling free of Odell. Not wanting to take any chances, Odell whipped the pistol across Decker's head, knocking the congressman to the ground. He saw McCall and Boot moving toward the President, saw the other security men racing in from outside. Odell slipped out the opposite door, then into the air shaft he had scouted earlier.

They would look for him, but they wouldn't catch him. All he had to do now was make a call to Quartermain and have him send in the Spartans.

Just like they planned.

110

The Gaunt Man watched Kurst progress upward, drawing ever closer to the stairs that would then lead him down into the bowels of the keep. He could see the glowing blue and red sparks as they detached themselves from the hunter's body and floated upward to the mirror's surface. He laughed each time this occurred, for it was clear that Kurst was in pain and yet had no idea what was happening to him. Satisfied that Kurst would soon be taken care of, he moved away from the mirror, pulling something brown and twisted from a pocket of his garment. He held the dried thing in his palm and whispered a few words of power. The thing burst into flame

Smoke billowed from it, a thousand times the volume that could have been expected, writhing unnaturally away from the Gaunt Man. It was a mist of madness that billowed like fog, puffing around corners, boiling down stairways and through doors. It was a gray mist that obscured vision although it was transparent. It carried death, and it filled the manor.

"Fly, spirits of the mist," the Gaunt Man ordered. "Deal with the intruders. But do not kill the women. Save them for me."

111

"We cannot wait any longer," Tolwyn declared. "If he has been hurt, he needs our help. If he has betrayed us ..." She did not have to finish the statement.

Bryce frowned. "I just want to get on with this. Lead on."

Tolwyn moved with catlike grace and caution, wincing at the noise Bryce made behind her. The dwarves moved well, and Mara and Djil were ghosts behind them. But Tom had feet of stone. Ah well, not much to be done about it.

She found the stairs Kurst had taken, started up them one slow step at a time. There were side passages almost immediately, and he could have taken any one. Trying to find him looked hopeless, but the offshoot passages were small, and smelled musty with age. It did not seem likely he had gone that way.

She bent low over the next stair, staring at it through the gloom. Was that a footprint, marked with claws at the tips of the toes? It was hard to tell if she was imagining it or not, but it looked like his tracks, and they were moving up. She followed, hunching over every step, still seeing faint prints. Were they really there? She sighed and continued.

It was foolish to have let him leave the group — he was their only guide! Even if he was trustworthy, if he was killed they would have to stumble around in the dark, just like they were doing now.

She did not notice the writing on the archway through which she passed, or the way the letters glowed and the corridor shifted.

Seconds later her subconscious realized that something was wrong: silence followed her. The rustle of the dwarves, the scrunch of Bryce's shoes — the sounds were gone. She whirled, sword ready.

And she found herself alone. Alone in the Gaunt Man's keep.

A faint mist grew up around her, so slow that at first she did not notice. But she did see the chamber come into being, its high vaulted ceiling suddenly rising above her, a descending stair dropping away across the wide, carpet-covered floor. There was no other egress. Fearful of what might have happened to the others, she started forward.

The carpet beneath her feet squished as she walked, and for a moment she imagined that she had stepped on something alive. She walked further, and the squishing continued, only now it was accompanied by tiny screams of pain. With her sword she caused a breeze that forced the mist to part momentarily so that she could see the carpet better. But the rug was no longer a swirl of bright colors. It was a mat of maggots, wriggling and sliding one over the other in a dance of bodies.

The maggots continued their wriggling dance, piling atop each other. The carpet of worms gathered its members from the far corner of the room, creating a mound in the center of the floor between Tolwyn and the stairs down. Soon it was a mound the same height as she was, shaped like some mountain in miniature. Tolwyn put one foot in front of her in the direction of the stairs, and the mound moved!

Two appendages like legs formed out of the mound, made of intertwined worms and swirling mist. Then two maggot arms formed from its side, reaching for her. Instinctively she swung her sword, and a spray of maggot juice blinded her as the metal slapped into the piled insects. She staggered, gasping and spitting, and teetered on the brink of nothingness. With a yell of surprise, she tumbled down the steps which somehow appeared beneath her feet. Jarring pain shot through her as she bounced down several steps, coming to a halt at a small landing. She hunched, dazed, her sword lost in the tumble. For long moments her body would not respond to desperate mental commands, and she feared broken bones or worse. But slowly the disorientation faded, and Tolwyn rose up, staring up into the mist. The maggot-beast was still coming. It was almost on top of her, reaching out. There was no time to turn and run.

Rather than stand in its grip and let it crush her slowly, Tolwyn summoned her strength and rushed forward. She smashed into the maggots, as if diving into a pile of leaves. Her arms flailed, tearing at the soft larvas, a yell of battle spilling from her throat. Caught off guard, the beast feel back. It lost its balance and toppled, coming apart as it fell. Maggots splashed everywhere, but the beast had lost consistency for the moment. She found her sword a few steps further down, retrieving it as the worms and mist began to come back together. She decided not to wait for that to occur.

Tolwyn raced down into the bowels of the keep.

112

Bryce tried to remain as close to Tolwyn as possible, but it was hard because he didn't want to bump into her, especially not while she was holding that sword. In these close confines, touched unexpectedly, she could take his head off before realizing who he was.

As for himself, he held nothing more than his pack, which contained the Heart of Coyote. It had helped them defeat the Carredon. Would it work against the Gaunt Man? He thought about that. Wasn't this Heart an eternity shard? Wasn't that what the invaders were after? Maybe it wasn't such a good idea to bring it along, he thought, but it was too late now. He shivered in the darkness.

He paused, trying to see Tolwyn in the gathering mist up the stairs. Had she gotten that far ahead of him? "Tolwyn?" he called. "Where are you?" There was no answer. Tolwyn had vanished into the gloom. He turned to find Mara and the others, but they had disappeared as well.

"Mara? Djil?" he called at random. "Braxon? Pluppa?" There was silence.

"Here," a voice whispered, but it was not a voice he knew. It froze him to hear it, the breathy, echoing hiss. A chill tingled up his back, and Bryce knew he was about to face death.

"Dear Lord," he gasped. "Give me stre —" He cut off the prayer, shocked into silence by the image rising from the mist.

A great skull, twice the size of a man's, floated in the air before him. Its eyes bored into his, a red glow deep in the skull. The jaw moved and he heard the whispered "here," again. The skull elongated and then returned to normal shape, as though viewed under water. Bryce took a step back, rubbing at his eyes. He wanted to turn and run, but the foulness of what was before him pinned his feet in place.

"What do you want?" he quavered.

"Christopher Bryce," it whispered, and he didn't know if it was calling to him or answering his question.

"Begone," he said, very softly, then louder and with more conviction, "Begone!" Something of his old feelings, his old training, took him then. It was a feeling of outrage at things blasphemous and inhuman. This certainly was both of those. The situation was almost ludicrous! He fumbled for his cross as he met the glare of the specter before him.

"Yes, match my gaze," the vision panted. "Look deep and submit to me. You cannot win." Coldness surrounded its words, and the world was suddenly icy. Bryce tried to look away then, but could not.

"Christopher Bryce," it said. "Come here."

He took one step forward, incapable of any other movement, as the great jaws began to open. He managed to bring his cross up in front of him. Then, as if under water, he slowly straightened his arm, touching the skull with his cross.

There was no flash of light or clap of thunder, nor any scream of dismay. The spectral being simply vanished, soundless, and Bryce stumbled back as a tugging pressure was suddenly released. He drew a shuddering breath, aware again of the darkness, the dank smell, and the slick feel of the stones beneath his feet.

He found a stairwell leading down.

113

Mara saw nothing, heard nothing, smelled nothing. Yet she knew something was very wrong. Her left hand was throbbing.

As part of the process of building microchips, it was very important to keep a clean atmosphere. Normally, finger to thumb set up the static charge that kept out random dust particles and such, but in an atmosphere particularly dense with impurities, the built-in alarm system would make her hand throb, just like it was doing now.

What impurities?

Unfortunately, she was not equipped for gas analysis, nor for extended pure breathing. She did have a tube in her arm connected to a five-minute supply of air, but that was usually reserved for potential drowning. Was now a good time to use it?

"Tom," she whispered, "the air is bad here. Pass it on."

"How interesting," came a voice next to her and she jumped, already focusing and aiming her weapon. But recognition shocked her, held her from firing.

"Thratchen?" she asked.

"You remember me! How flattering!" the cyber-demon exclaimed. "Put away your weapon. I will not harm you."

"But you're a Sim!" she shot back, remembering the battles she was involved in on Kadandra.

"Yes, and you're a Kadandran. So what? At first I did want to kill you, I must admit. I wanted to make you pay for your discoveries. You actually helped your people repel a Possibility Raid. But now I realize I was wrong. I should thank you for putting me onto my path of destiny."

Mara made no reply.

"Really," Thratchen continued. "I only came here to tell you that the air is filled with a mist that is full of spirits. Bad air, as it were. But you've already figured that out. Quite remarkable."

"Spirits?" Mara asked, looking around.

"Yes, spirits. Mischievous entities more inclined to

frighten than harm," Thratchen explained. "But they can be dangerous. Be wary."

Then Thratchen was gone, disappearing into the mist.

She touched the wall, resting her hand while she calmed herself. The wall was wet, sticky. She pulled her hand back, and it came away wet with blood. Mara looked at her hand, thinking of all the people who died on Kadandra because of her findings. Blood began to drip from the wall, now, running down in bright red streams. She thought of this world, of Earth, also doomed because of her curiosity, her obsessive quest for knowledge. The blood poured down the wall.

"Illmound Keep is a house of illusions," Thratchen called out of the mist. "Nothing within these walls are as they seem."

"Why are you telling me this?" Mara screamed. "Why are you helping me?"

Thratchen's laugh chilled her. "I am not merely helping you, girl. I am helping myself."

The wall itself changed as she turned her head to the side. From the corner of her eye she saw that it was not wood and stone that gave the wall its shape, but flesh and bone. And the flesh bled.

Mara raised her laser and fired a burst of searing light at the wall, cutting a gouge in the living tissue. The keep rocked with the sound of pain, and Mara lost her footing, splashing into the blood that pooled on the floor. Crawling, she discovered a staircase leading down. For an instant, she imagined she was walking into the keep's stomach, but she dismissed the image.

She told herself it was the mist spirits, trying to frighten her. They were doing a good job.

She started down the stairs.

114

Djilangulyip walked slowly down the corridor, gliding as quietly as possible across the strange surface. As last in line, he turned his back and looked the way they had come almost as often as he walked forward. It was during one such turn that he first saw the movement. It came from far back down the corridor they had traversed, a figure leaping from alcove to alcove as it approached.

"Mara, child," he whispered to the young woman in front of him. "We have followers." He ran quickly back down the corridor, looking for a convenient side passage to use for an ambush. When he found one he ducked in and looked back: the figure was getting nearer, doing its best to remain hidden. He turned again, but there was no sign of Mara or any of the others.

Had she assumed he meant for her to run? No time for second guessing now. The figure was moving with visible speed, suddenly filling the corridor with its great size. Djil stepped out to meet it.

"And what manner of creature are you?" the shaman asked congenially.

The winged monster halted, genuinely surprised by the little man's action. He tilted his head curiously, and answered the question put before him.

"I am a ravagon," the winged monster said. "I seek Kurst and his companions, to bring them before the Gaunt Man."

Djil thought for a moment, then let his hand slip from the war boomerang he was readying to throw. "I am one of Kurst's companions," he declared. "You may take me to the Gaunt Man."

The ravagon tilted his head to the other side and folded his wings around himself like a cloak. This stormer was definitely behaving strangely.

"Very well, stormer," the ravagon said finally. "Come with me."

115

Kurst stumbled forward, his legs responding only sporadically. He had to pause every few moments as the waves of pain rippled through him.

"What is happening to me?" he cried.

But he knew what the problem was. He had seen it happen a hundred times before, to those he hunted and brought to the Gaunt Man. It was the machine. It was ripping possibilities from him, tearing them away before they could be fully realized. He remembered that this was done to him a long time ago, before he was Kurst, before he was the Gaunt Man's hunter. It was when he was —

The pain hit him again. It was awful, slashing through his memories like his claws slashed through flesh. How could the Gaunt Man be doing this? There were no rune staves within his chest, no suction-cup wire devices connecting him to the machine. He fought the pain and actually managed to stand up straight. He searched the long corridor for some sign, some evidence of what the Gaunt Man was doing to him. He was in the deep cellar, in the last hallway before the iron-studded door to the Gaunt Man's workshop. Could it just be his proximity to —

The walls flared with energy and blue-red sparkles burst from Kurst's body. He howled with pain, shifting to wolf form out of habit. The wolf form was stronger, more powerful than Kurst's human shape. Perhaps it could withstand this punishment better than he.

He continued down the corridor, walking on two

powerful, fur-covered legs, his eyes searching walls, floor and ceiling for some clue he might have missed. The flare erupted again, and lightning arced from wall to wall in a web of crackling energy. Through the resulting pain, Kurst found understanding. It was the walls!

Carved into the walls, inscribed so carefully, so cleverly that they were almost impossible to see, were dozens of runes. The lightning bounced from rune to rune, forming an intricate latticework that mimicked the pattern over the sorting machine.

"Never life," Kurst read on a dozen runes. "Never death," he read on a dozen more.

Kurst ignored the pain, moving on when lesser beings would have collapsed long ago. He fought every step of the way, holding on to what was his with a fierce tenacity that was way beyond his endurance. His own name became lost in the rain of lightning and the swirl of blue-red sparkles, but he fought on.

He reached the iron-studded door.

The workshop. He knew the word, the name, but was no longer capable of attaching specific meaning to it. It was a huge room, and at one end was an amazing conglomeration of tubes and wires, glowing and humming now with incredible power. At the other end was the Gaunt Man. He was surprised he remembered that name.

Kurst nodded his head drunkenly, trying to recall what he remembered. He knew the Gaunt Man. He had a mission with that one, a confrontation. But he could not — something in his mind held him back. What had he meant to do with the Gaunt Man? He saw the other, bone thin and frighteningly tall, standing over a large metal plate set up on a bronze framework. A skeletal hand lost in a leather gauntlet held one of the glowing balls of blue-red sparkles, and as Kurst watched, the fist closed. The sparkles trickled from between the fingers and fell onto the plate, disappearing into the metal. Kurst screamed.

"Welcome, Kurst," said the Gaunt Man to the man-wolf. "So good of you to come. I've removed that disgusting sociability you'd picked up somewhere. You really had no need for it. Now come here."

The command was spoken as part of normal conversation, yet it whipped forth with an audible crack. Kurst took two steps forward, then he stopped. He fought against the words, the order. Then he remembered ... the machine! He had come to destroy ... couldn't be done ... no possibility — what? He lurched forward and fell to his knees, gasping for breath.

"I am. Not. Your. Slave." The words came out of his clenched teeth like bullets, one at a time. Kurst discovered that he meant those words.

The Gaunt Man's laughter was terrible to hear. He stepped toward Kurst, advancing with slow deliberation.

"I'll rip away these feelings Kurst," he said forcefully, anger blazing in his emaciated face. "There will be no possibility of such behavior left anywhere in you. Then I'll turn you on those stormers you brought here and listen to your howls as you slay them and drink their blood." Another flash of blue-red burst out of Kurst's chest, and the werewolf whimpered with the pain. He fell forward onto his clawed hands and fur-covered knees, then onto his side where he lay gasping. The sparkles floated gently into the Gaunt Man's hand. He closed his fist, and more crushing pain assaulted the werewolf.

"You cannot defy me now, Kurst," the Gaunt Man

explained triumphantly. "There is nothing left of you."

Kurst wept.

116

Scythak watched as the compound suddenly became alive with activity. Something had happened in the hospital, over in the area where all the soldiers and vehicles waited for someone to emerge from the building. Perhaps the activity was for the best. He could strike during the confusion and be on his way before they even noticed him.

"It's time," Scythak said to Dr. James Monroe.

"Time?" Monroe asked. "Are you going after Decker now?"

"Yes," Scythak replied, letting his hand shift into the tiger's claw. "And here is your reward for betraying your litter."

The claw slashed out, tearing a great, bloody hole in Monroe's throat. The doctor, eyes wide in surprise, tried to ask another question. But the words never reached his mouth; they simply bubbled out of the gaping wound in his neck, spilling more blood down the front of his shirt.

Monroe died. Then he fell to the ground.

"Stormer," Scythak spat, padding off toward the hospital.

Toward Decker.

117

Decker, numbed by the violent death of his friend and president, sat in the hall outside where the body lay. He couldn't think, couldn't weep. He could only see the pistol rise up, the bullets explode from the chamber in slow motion, the blood. He saw it over and over again, and he watched for something he could have done differently. But all he saw was —

Blackness. It burst across his senses, blocking out everything else except the now-throbbing pain in his chest. A door swung open in the blackness before he could focus his thoughts, revealing a huge latticework pattern of glowing light. But the pattern wasn't complete yet. It still needed things added to it, removed from it. He pulled away an extraneous angle, ripping it from the pattern, and laughter filled his mind. It was a familiar sound. The Gaunt Man's sound.

"Ace, are you all right?" Julie asked, and the pattern and blackness fell apart like dandelions in the wind.

"Yeah, I think so," Decker said, but he knew it wasn't true. There was something about the pattern he had interfered with, something familiar.

"Kurst." The name appeared in his mind with blinding clarity. Somehow, the pattern was tied to Kurst.

"Julie, you have to help me," Decker said.

"Of course," she replied, but she looked confused.

"Next time the blackness comes upon me, let me go to it."

"What? Have you gone crazy? You want to go back to that awful beach? No way!"

"There's something happening," Decker explained as best he could. "It involves Kurst, and I think I was just used to hurt him. But if I go back, I think that I can help him."

"Maybe you're thinking too much, mister," Julie said angrily.

"Please, just be ready to pull me back after —"

The blackness was all around him again, washing over him like a breaking wave. Then the pattern appeared, and this time Decker studied it more carefully. He saw that it was actually two patterns. The dimmer pattern was an almost-uniform latticework that had rough edges and pleasing breaks from the whole that were a touch sporadic. The second pattern, the one that overlaid the first, was rigid and unyielding. There was no creativity inherent in the design, no flashes of brilliance. It was merely functional, defining its place with well-ruled lines and right angles. That was the pattern the Gaunt Man wanted him to force the other pattern — Kurst's pattern — to conform to.

"Choose," came the voice of the Gaunt Man.

Decker began his work, pointing out possible paths of deviance from the ordered pattern so that the Gaunt Man could tear them away. Decker hated himself more and more with each possibility the Gaunt Man slashed, but he knew that his plan was Kurst's only hope. For while he showed the Gaunt Man all of the minor deviances, he held back the bright glow in the center of Kurst's latticework.

Decker touched the glowing light, and waves of honor and nobility rippled through him. This was Kurst's greatest possibility, the destiny that life had originally set for him. But the Gaunt Man had changed all that. But maybe not as completely as he had hoped.

"Choose," the Gaunt Man said again.

"Done," Decker answered, pulling his hand back from the light that looked like all the other lights to the Gaunt Man. And then the blackness faded —

— and Decker was in the hallway, sitting on the bench beside Julie.

"I didn't know how long to wait, but you were gone so long and …" Julie stammered.

"It's all right," Decker told her. "You did good."

"Too good, if you ask me," growled a voice nearby.

Decker looked up to see an enormous man that he

first took to be Kurst in his man-wolf form. But then he saw that the man was larger than Kurst — even in his wolf form. He was fully seven feet tall, massively built, with thick forearms that bent unnaturally at the elbow and ended in curled claws. His face was huge, framed by black and gold-stripped hair that covered his entire body. Like Kurst, this man was a shapeshifter. But unlike Kurst, he was a man-tiger instead of a man-wolf.

"You're Decker," the man-tiger growled through sharp teeth. "I can smell it. I'm here to —"

The man-tiger paused, and Decker saw something flash briefly around the creature's neck. Then he finished his thought.

"I'm here to kill you."

Decker moved then, grasping the pistol from the holster at Julie's side while he shoved her away. He spun to fire, but the man-tiger was already in mid-leap. All Decker could do was roll out of the way as the massive body passed over him. Before he could get fully to his feet, the man-tiger was upon him, all claws and pointed teeth. Somehow, Decker managed to position the pistol so its barrel was pressed against the werebeast's stomach. He squeezed off four shots, and the creature fell back, crashing to the ground.

Julie was holding him then, asking if he was all right, asking what that creature was. He put an arm around her.

"Ace!" she cried, pointing. He turned to follow her finger.

The man-tiger was rising from the floor, his face a snarl of hate and death.

118

Kurst felt wet tears drying on his face, but he could

not remember crying. He tried to get his bearings, but it was as if he was waking in an unfamiliar place. He lazily opened one eye and saw the sorting machine across the room. For a moment he saw himself suspended within the grid of energy above it, but then he saw that it was only a series of blue-red sparkles and not him. He moved his eyes, and there was the Gaunt Man, standing in front of his ornate mirror. What was the mirror doing down here? Kurst wondered.

The Gaunt Man was watching something in the mirror. Kurst looked up, the effort to crane his neck taking all the energy he had. His eyes fixed on the mirror, and he saw Scythak moving stealthily through a building of some sort. Good old Scythak, hunting as usual! Kurst smiled a tiny smile, continued to stare at the surface of the mirror.

The Gaunt Man turned away, looking back at Kurst. "Awake?" he asked. "Good. We must re-educate you now. Scythak is about to secure Decker, and when he does I'll begin. I have already used Decker to do a little sorting, but it is so much more effective when he is not up and about."

The Gaunt Man moved forward, blocking Kurst's view of the mirror momentarily. He sat down next to the man-wolf, touched Kurst's wrists.

"The first phase is complete," he said. "You cannot act against me. Unfortunately, since I was in a hurry, I made it too difficult for you to act at all. We'll remedy that soon enough."

He looked back toward the mirror, turning as he did so, allowing Kurst to see its surface as well. He saw that Scythak was in the hospital where they left Decker, standing before a woman — she looked familiar — and a man. The man was Andrew Jackson Decker.

Kurst watched as Scythak leaped to attack and a warm spot suddenly flared within his heart. What was that? The Gaunt Man gasped in surprise at the scene and turned back to Kurst.

"Upsetting," the Gaunt Man murmured. "Scythak seems to have gone berserk."

Kurst quickly closed his eyes, waiting. The warm spot was a dazzling shower of blue and red sparks in the darkness behind his eyelids. It was the presence and commitment of Tolwyn. It was the faith of Father Bryce. It was the determination and humor of Mara. It was even the friendship of Decker. But more, it was him — not Kurst, not the Gaunt Man's created hunting machine, but him. Dire wolf.

Dire wolf.

What had the street rough meant by that? What did it have to do with who he really was?

He felt the Gaunt Man shift position, felt the touch of a dry finger on his face. There was a sense of *nearness*.

Kurst struck.

One blow was all he had time for. The Gaunt Man's reflexive counter blow was devastating, hurling the man-wolf, howling, halfway across the chamber. He slammed against the wall, dropped, but the pain of the blow was half that of the pain in his hand where his claw had broken through the Gaunt Man's skin. That claw was now burned and twisted as if by acid. His whole hand throbbed with agony.

That agony was only half that of hearing the Gaunt Man scream.

It was the death-cry of a hundred souls, a hurricane wind; it was vibrating harmonics, an earthquake, and the sheer terror of an animal about to die. It was volcanoes erupting. It was all those things and more, indescribable and deadly to hear. Kurst moaned and held his ears, trying to block out the noise.

The Gaunt Man clutched his hands to his face, his eye. Bright white light spilled from between his fingers like blood. The light and the noise made Kurst black out.

It was for a moment only, but when he awoke there was silence. He raised his head, furred paws still cupped over animal-shaped ears, looking about the room. The Gaunt Man still stood where he had been, silent now, unmoving, staring at Kurst through one eye. The other, through splayed fingers, spilled forth blinding light like a miniature sun. They regarded each other silently, and Kurst could feel the tangible hate billowing toward him, like heat, threatening to crisp him where he stood.

"You dare much, my slave," said the Gaunt Man. There was no sign of pain in his voice now. "You think to slay me with a blow? See what you have wrought!" He pulled his hands from his face, and light flooded from the eye, bathing the werewolf in its burning starkness. Kurst howled and stumbled back, trying to escape the bright light, the heat, the hatred.

Through squinting eyes he saw the dim form of the Gaunt Man approaching, slowly and inexorably. Nowhere to run! Kurst licked dry lips, crouched, arms extended. Kurst had no choice now but to fight. Perhaps he could wound the Gaunt Man again.

"Come to me," Kurst said loudly.

The Gaunt Man stopped, his face twisting. "Bravado! How becoming!" He spat, and where the spittle landed on the stone there was a hiss of steam. "I'll flay the skin from your flesh, Kurst, and use your skull to hold the ashes of your body!"

"No," said another voice, a strong feminine voice that

echoed in the vast chamber. "Your reign is over, vile one."

The Gaunt Man whirled, and Kurst could see again. Tolwyn was standing in the doorway, sword upraised. The pilot Tom and the dwarves clustered behind her, their weapons ready as well. The Gaunt Man moved one step, but Tolwyn whirled with blinding speed. She threw her sword, twirling it through the air. It crashed into the wires and the tubes, shattering crystals and panels on the great machine. Flames jetted up from the blow, blackening and twisting the sword. But the damage was done. Fire quickly spread across the massive machine.

"You bitch!" cried the Gaunt Man, voice like thunder. He raised up one hand. "You'll pay for your audacity!"

Kurst sensed the buildings of a summoning, and he dove at the Gaunt Man. He heard his own yell as he was slammed away from the High Lord by the physical power of the building spell. But he knew he had disturbed the casting, because its power dissipated through his body.

The werewolf slumped to the floor, unconscious.

119

The weretiger was still alive! Decker clutched Julie's arm and started running down the hallway. He had to put space between them and the monster. They were almost to the end of the corridor when they heard a door open somewhere behind them. Decker looked back. The weretiger was on its feet, following them despite four bullets in the gut. Between them stood two soldiers who just emerged from a room off the hall.

The tiger loomed over the two men, who looked small and insignificant compared to the creature. Both men seemed stunned, unsure of what was happening. But they carried automatic rifles.

"Shoot it!" Decker screamed. "Kill the monster!"

One of the men responded, swinging his rifle from his shoulder and leveling at the beast. Before he could squeeze off a burst, the tiger drove his claws into the other soldier. Decker saw the sharp talons emerge from the man's back with a spray of blood.

Then the first soldier fired a burst of bullets that knocked the man-tiger into the wall. The soldier, his gun still pointed at the beast, turned to address Decker.

"What in God's name was that thing, congressman?" the soldier called. "Sweet Jesus, look what it did to Riley!"

Decker didn't have time to answer the man, for the tiger was pushing itself off the wall. It swiped its claws with such power that the soldier's head flew from his body, bouncing along the corridor floor like some crazy-shaped basketball. Then it grinned at Decker, showing its white teeth.

"Come on," Decker said to Julie, pulling her through the nearest door. He closed it, locked it, and ran on.

They only made it through two more doors when they heard the explosion of wood behind them.

120

Sorrow filled Tolwyn; she hated to use the sword like that, hated to lose it to the flames. But she had no choice. The machine had to be destroyed. She turned to watch the five dwarves hurl their battle spikes in a deadly volley of metal. The iron stakes hummed through the air and struck the Gaunt Man full on. But he was a High Lord, and High Lords were not so easily killed.

Tolwyn saw two of the weapons actually penetrate

the Gaunt Man's pale skin, but the wounds did not bleed; they glowed instead. The other three spikes rattled harmlessly off the High Lord to clatter to the ground. Tolwyn realized that, even if she still had her sword, she would be hard-pressed to think of what to do with it.

The Gaunt Man bent down as she watched, picked up one spike, and hurled it back at the cluster of dwarves. Gutterby howled, clutching at his arm where the point now protruded from his shoulder. The Gaunt Man laughed.

"We cannot attack him directly with any hope of winning," Tolwyn said to the dwarves. "Maybe we can hurt him in other ways." She pointed at the now-flaming machine. "Grim," she called.

The sixth dwarf stepped out of the shadows, a ball of flaming pitch in his hands. He let the ball fly, directing its course with the magic he possessed.

But the Gaunt Man was not without magic of his own. He opened his hand and the ball of pitch changed direction. It spun in the air, turning away from the machine, and leaped into the Gaunt Man's hand. He closed his fist.

Grim, amazed at the sight, wasted no time however. He tapped the piece of burning pitch he retained into his palm, setting off the spell.

"Ouch!" Grim cried out.

The Gaunt Man was engulfed in an explosion of flame.

"Quickly, Grim," Tolwyn ordered, "toss another fire ball at the machine."

Grim shrugged. "That was my last ball of pitch. It will take me time to prepare another spell."

"We have no time!" she exclaimed. "Dismantle the machine any way you can!"

The dwarves nodded and moved to do her bidding.

Tolwyn circled away from them, eye on the Gaunt Man. As she watched, he stepped out of the flames. She contemplated grappling with him to buy the dwarves some time when Bryce, Mara and Tom entered the room. A moment later, a ravagon walked in, carrying Djil under one arm.

The Gaunt Man looked around at the strange gathering and laughed loudly. Then he became serious. "This has been very amusing, but now it's over," he said evenly, addressing Tolwyn. "Call the dwarves away from the machine, stormer."

Time stood still as the Gaunt Man and Tolwyn faced each other. She studied his fragile-looking form, examining it the way she would any foe. But the weakness was a sham, for blinding power spilled from the wounds Kurst had inflicted upon him. There were only two options available to Tolwyn, really. She could flee, turning away from this enemy. Or she could continue to fight, even if it meant her death. She made her decision and strode forward.

"Decker," called a weak voice. They all turned as Kurst said the word and struggled to his feet. He was in man form again, working his way to an ornate mirror leaning against one wall.

"Kurst, be careful," Tolwyn warned.

"Decker," the hunter managed again. "I saw him in the mirror. Scythak is after him, trying to kill him. I can go to him, save him. The mirror is a pathway. I have seen the Gaunt Man use it as such. I've even traveled its cold tunnel. Now I must do so again. If I don't reach him in time, we've come all this way for nothing."

The Gaunt Man stood in the center of the room, watching them all. His calm was unnerving. Then everything happened at once. There was a snapping sound from the machine, a sound like glass breaking, and the Gaunt Man whirled toward it. The ravagon dropped Djil, who appeared to be unharmed, and rushed to his master's side as they headed across the vast chamber. Tolwyn let them go, grudgingly leaving the dwarves to their own fate as she moved to the mirror.

Bryce and Mara had gone to Kurst, supporting him with their bodies and their strength. They were next to the mirror, watching as the image of Decker ran through dark rooms. She could feel his fear. Something was chasing him. Something terrible.

"We must do something," Tolwyn said, pointing to the mirror. "Can this be used as a weapon?"

"Not by us," Kurst said, a little strength back in his voice. "I've got to —"

Kurst stopped abruptly. Standing before them was a demonic form, winged and horned, with metallic legs that ended in wicked claws. It grinned at them, and mocked them with a bow.

"Thratchen!" Mara exclaimed.

"There's not much time," the demon said to Mara. "If you want to save your friend, you'll have to show me something." The demon reached down, touched the mirror with one extended claw. He swung the claw into the silver glass, sending cracks rippling across its mirrored surface.

"This path is closed to you, Kurst," Thratchen said. "But there is still a way to reach Decker. Mara knows the way. It's how she got to Earth."

Kurst whirled on the girl, grabbed her by the shoulders as strength returned to him. "How do we save Decker?" he asked harshly.

Tolwyn watched as Thratchen stepped back, and she

heard the sounds of battle somewhere off near the machine. What was going on here? What kinds of games were being played by these beings of power?

Djil came up behind Mara then, muttering, "Remember your friends."

"But I don't have the equipment!" Mara wailed. "I don't have a transference cylinder! There's nothing to focus our energy through."

"We have this," Bryce said, pulling the Heart of Coyote from his pack.

Mara took the stone that Bryce offered, but her thoughts were to the volunteers that made her transference cylinder work. She thought of Djil's knots, and how this group was so much like those knots, coming together to accomplish the impossible. Then she saw the possibility of how she could save Decker.

"Christopher, come here, take my hand," Mara said. "Tolwyn, take my other hand."

Djil and Kurst joined hands as well, and the five formed a circle. Thratchen watched, enraptured. Mara ignored him completely.

Tolwyn stopped for one moment, ready to issue counter commands. Then a strange thing happened, and she bit back her words. All her life she had been a commander. She relied on her judgment, her training, her authority. But now things seemed different. She did not hold command over these people. She was still Tolwyn, still capable and trustworthy, but these people were her equals. They formed a group, and that provided them with the means to do almost anything.

Mara was in their minds then, joining with them on a deeper level than just holding hands. They all heard the Heart of Coyote singing its song of endless possibilities, and they all found the voice to join in.

Using this power, freely shifted among the group, Mara opened a gate to Decker. A dark hole formed in the middle of their ring. It was the blackness of night, and a warm breeze swept into the chamber as from another place. Tolwyn heard a woman's scream echo out of the darkness. Kurst heard it too and he started forward, into the gate.

Tolwyn moved quickly to interpose herself between him and the strange gate that had opened at Mara's command, but he was fast. His arm shot out, grasping her wrist, and he held her still. They stared into each other's eyes.

"You are wounded," Tolwyn said.

"It doesn't matter," Kurst replied. "You've got your memories back, now I need the chance to get mine. Besides, Decker is my friend."

His eyes bored into hers. He looked strong enough to fight, and something moreflashed between them; an understanding. Tolwyn backed away. "Go," she said, and he entered the gate and disappeared.

"How amazing," Thratchen marveled. "You actually did it! And I've recorded it all!"

121

Kurst stepped into the open gate —

It was not like the one time he had been sent through the mirror by the Gaunt Man. That time was cold, like leaping into ice water. And there had been intense pain. This time there was none of that.

This time there was the warmth of companionship, and the joy of many minds acting as one. It was ...exhilirating!

— and stepped out into a dark corridor. He was back at Twentynine Palms. What an amazing ability! But he had no time to contemplate what had happened. He had to reach Decker before Scythak did. The human could not survive against the man-tiger.

He raced down the corridor, through smashed doors and shattered walls, over torn bodies. None of those he ran past were Decker. They were soldiers, and Kurst was saddened by their deaths, but he did not stop to mourn them. He raced to save his friend. Finally, he leaped into a large room.

The room was crowded with rows of metal shelves and racks. Cabinets lined one wall. Kurst recognized the smell of oil, and large crates and barrels were piled everywhere. The weretiger had chased Decker into a supply room — or Decker had led the monster here. Scythak spun at Kurst's intrusion, growling with madness. Kurst saw that Decker was backed into a corner, the nurse Julie Boot huddled beside him. Decker had a pistol in his hands, its smoking barrel aimed at the weretiger.

"Put your weapon down, Decker," Kurst called. "It cannot kill Scythak."

The man-tiger cocked his head at the sound of his name, and his eyes cleared. "Leave this place, Kurst," Scythak ordered. "This is my kill."

Kurst shook his head. "The killing has ended."

"Perhaps, little hunter," Scythak sneered, "but not until I have eaten your heart and washed down the taste with your blood!"

Kurst let the shift take hold of him, feeling it reshape his body. He grew larger, but not as large as Scythak, and the wolf was there to meet the challenge of the tiger. He bounded on clawed feet, closing the distance between them with a mighty leap. Kurst locked his powerful jaws on Scythak's shoulder and bit deeply into the muscles. Unlike Decker's weapon, Kurst's claws and teeth could kill Scythak. To accentuate the point, Scythak screamed.

But the weretiger was the stronger of the two, bigger and more massive. Kurst's advantages were in speed and cunning. This room allowed for none of that. Scythak's claws ripped into Kurst's back, pulling him off of the torn shoulder.

The werewolf rolled out of the tiger's grip, coming to his feet some distance away. The tiger's jaws gaped open, saliva dripping freely from the tooth-filled maw. The two opponents locked eyes, and a recognition of impending violence joined them in a hunting dance. But which was hunter, which prey?

Human instincts screamed for Kurst to bolt in the face of this larger adversary. But the wolf stood his ground, his senses filled with the excitement to come. The tiger feinted to the right, and immediately Kurst saw that it was a trick. Scythak leaped then, sending his massive form at Kurst.

The werewolf dropped to the floor, under the larger body and raking talons, and struck upward with his own claws. Scythak roared as blood flowed. But the tiger was not finished. Scythak twisted in the air, striking Kurst in the back with a foreleg hit like a hammer blow. The wolf slid across the hard floor, smashing into a metal rack. The entire unit, full of items that Kurst could not identify, tipped wildly. With another swipe of a claw, Scythak brought the rack down upon the wolf.

Metal crashed all around him as Kurst tried to twist out of the way. But he could not gather his legs fast enough. The unit landed with a bang, smashing into his shoulder and then coming to rest at an angle across his back. Dazed, Kurst saw that the rack was held in place by a metal barrel, precariously balanced over him. That was all that saved him from the full impact of its crushing weight. The wolf had no idea whether the metal rack could kill him, but he knew the pain would not be pleasant. No matter, for while he was not crushed, the rack had pinned his large form, trapping him beneath it.

"How appropriate," Scythak growled. "The wolf has been caught in a trap. Stay there, Kurst. I'll be back for you after I finish with Decker and the woman."

122

Mara held the Heart of Coyote in her hands, listening to its song. The others were still in a loose circle around her: Tolwyn, Bryce, Djil. Thratchen had stepped back into the shadows he had come from, disappearing after he watched Mara call the gate. That's what he wanted! But she had no time to contemplate that now.

"I must help Tom and the dwarves," Tolwyn said, preparing to head toward the burning machine far across the vast chamber.

"Please wait," Mara said. "I know how to defeat the Gaunt Man."

Mara felt them all look at her, felt their eyes. Even Thratchen was interested, staring out from his unseen hiding place.

"It's like Djil's story," she continued. "We'll give him the Heart."

"Give him the power he craves? How will that stop him, Mara?" Bryce asked.

"He can't handle it like this," she said holding up the solid blue-red stone. "He has to distill it or something, that's why he uses the machines. In its raw form, this will destroy him."

Djil smiled, understanding dawning as his lips parted and his teeth gleamed forth like the sun. "The

Maelstrom," he said.

"The Maelstrom," Mara agreed.

A scream bounced through the chamber. One of the dwarves was injured — or worse.

"We must come together again, rebuild the gate," Mara explained quickly. She snapped a chip into one of the slots beneath her ear.

"What are you talking about?" Bryce asked again as he took her hand.

"The Gaunt Man is full of energy. But it's a destructive energy, a dark energy. It's the energy of the nothing — what Kurst called the Void. This is a piece of the everything, of Eternity," Mara said, holding the stone for all to see. "If the nothing and the everything come together, it will create a Maelstrom, just like in the story."

"But nothing was able to survive in the Maelstrom except the Nameless One and Apeiros," Bryce finished.

"Exactly," Mara said.

123

Kurst pushed at the metal rack with all his might, but he could not budge it. Not only was it extremely heavy, but he could gain no leverage because of the way he was pinned. Think! he screamed to himself. There must be a way out of this! Perhaps in human form he would be able to slip under the rack.

He shifted, letting his body shrink back to its human shape. But he was still pinned. He needed to be even smaller, to become something else.

That was ridiculous! How could he be something else? He was what he was, no more, no less.

But what if?

The thought took hold of him, refusing to let go.

How had Mara formed the gate?

He thought about that. She had gotten creative with stormer energy. *And we gave her our energy freely.* That was important. The Gaunt Man had been very careful never to give stormers any freedom. They had no choices beyond those he had specific control over.

If he could change into one form, shouldn't he be able to change into another?

Deep within him, a blue-red glow grew brighter.

Yes, he decided, he could become something else. All he had to do was let his form shift freely, without restriction. He concentrated, feeling the possibilities rise within him. Then he let them out.

And Kurst became a true wolf, the size of a large dog. The wolf slipped out from beneath the metal rack and scampered onto all fours. It was strange and exhilarating! He knew this form! But he didn't remember much more than that. He tested the form, finding that it knew how to walk on four legs even if he didn't.

Kurst, now truly a wolf, sought out the tiger.

He found the the other hunter and his prey outside. The scents were even stronger in this form, and Kurst could practically see by sniffing the air. Decker was firing shots from his gun as Julie worked to start a jeep. Scythak kept moving, shrugging off the slugs even though they obviously caused him pain.

Four legs pumped furiously, four padded claws scraped the tarmac. Then the wolf leaped, ripping at Scythak's leg with vicious teeth. The tiger kicked him, making air explode from his lungs, forcing him to release the leg that he was gnawing on.

"You've learned a new trick, Kurst," Scythak said. "I'm not impressed."

The wolf, smaller now, more animal, looked up at the

monstrous tiger that walked like a man. He could not stand against Scythak in his other form, how could he battle him like this?

"What other tricks can you do, dog?" Scythak laughed. "Can you roll over? Can you lay down and die?"

Kurst snapped, clamping his powerful jaws around Scythak's wide neck. He bit deeply, tasting the sweet blood as it gushed forth. Then he was flying through the air, again thrown from his prey by the stronger hunter.

He shifted back to man-wolf form, standing on two legs, throwing his head back to howl a challenge. The tiger was coming for him. He waited, an idea forming in his mind.

What did Scythak have over Kurst? He had strength and endurance. In a claw-to-claw battle, the outcome was obvious. Kurst would die beneath Scythak's teeth, unless he could figure out a way to compensate for the weretiger's size. He had been able to change into a small, normal wolf. He could transform into a giant man-wolf. But neither of those could match the weretiger pound for pound. He needed to find another possibility.

Scythak bounded closer, forgetting his mission concerning Decker as the blood lust for Kurst clouded his vision with red. He barely seemed to notice his torn leg, his bloody throat and shoulder. He had only pain to give; there was none for him to spare on himself.

The form of the bear came to Kurst's mind. The bear was larger than the tiger, stronger. It was not faster, not as cunning. But if it could land its blows, the tiger would fall beneath them. But what did Kurst know of the bear? He knew —

The pattern that the Gaunt Man placed within him splintered, letting out a few select memories as he forced his mind to think. They were not all of his memories, or even his most important ones. But they were the ones he needed now.

He remembered the bear.

Scythak closed the distance quickly, raising his huge claws to strike at the man-wolf. Kurst leaped to meet him, letting his body shift as he flew through the air. The man-wolf grew larger, wider. His hair became thicker, his weight denser. Werewolf had started the jump, werebear had ended it, crashing into Scythak with unbelievable force. The bear form knocked the tiger down, pinning him beneath his massive weight.

Kurst brought one powerful clawed paw down, crushing Scythak's right arm. The weretiger screamed.

"Get off of me, stormer!" Scythak cried, trying to push the bear away. He could not.

"Not stormer," Kurst said through the bear's muzzle, relishing the new-found power. "I am a storm knight." Then he brought his clawed paw down again, splattering the weretiger's blood upon the tarmac. Scythak died, still certain he was going to win.

124

Mara saw the Gaunt Man and his ravagon, standing before the flaming wreck of his machine. The dwarves had done an admirable job dismantling portions of the machine, but now they were huddled back near the wall. Tom was with them. Two more of their number were on the ground, bent in awkward, unnatural ways. It was time for the killing to end.

She let her built-in computer calculate the distance between her and the Gaunt Man. This had to be precisely done. That was why she was leaving a good deal of the job to her computer. That's what it was there for.

"Okay, let's form the circle again," Mara said, leading

the group as far away from the Gaunt Man as she could. They were against the wall of the massive chamber, far from the flames that ate at the machine.

"We're missing Kurst," Bryce commented. "Can we do this without him?"

"We must," Tolwyn replied.

The others nodded their agreement.

Mara let her mind fill with the feelings of the others. They were her group, her teammates, her friends. They shared their experiences freely. They shared their lives. They even shared the blue and red energy that blazed so brightly before her cybernetic eye. And out of that power, Mara formed the possibility of stepping through a gate over here, then stepping out of one next to the Gaunt Man way over there. She added the possibility that the gate would remain open for a few milliseconds — long enough for her to do what she had to and step back. Yes, Mara thought. It was all possible.

Then, with the power supplied by the others, Mara made the possible real. A gate opened in front of her, a portal to somewhere else. She entered it, the Heart of Coyote held out before her, and —

— she was halfway across the room, standing before the Gaunt Man. Her left leg was thrust back, for support. Her right was nearly touching the Gaunt Man's left foot. Her right arm was spread out for balance. Her left hand touching fingertips to the Gaunt Man's chest, as high as she could reach — thrusting into the light that spilled from his wounds. That was the hand that held the piece of the everything. She let it go, for when the everything met the nothing, then came the Maelstrom!

Mara stepped back, reacting with computer precision in the instant that the Maelstrom raged into being. The gate, still open by the power of the storm knights' minds, took her back in the blink of an eye. But Mara screamed. She had miscalculated, her fingertips a centimeter too far forward. Her hand was destroyed by the Maelstrom, and even though it was only mechanical, it was also cybernetic. As metal and plastic wired synapses ceased to be, pain fired through Mara's arm and into her brain. It was worse than losing a real hand, because this metal appendage was totally controlled by conscious thought. She fell to her knees in the center of the circle, between Bryce, Djilangulyip, and Tolwyn.

Somewhere else, she heard a whirling wind of destruction and a pitiful cry. But she could only stare at the severed metal where her left hand used to be. And at the tiny shard of blue stone with red swirls that dropped to the floor beside her.

125

Father Christopher Bryce added his mind to the ritual they were performing for the second time today. Mara, holding the Heart of Coyote, was the focus, but they all added the strength. And the gate opened. He saw Mara, clutching the heart-shaped stone in one hand, step forward and vanish! In the blink of an eye, without visibly crossing the intervening space, she was standing before the Gaunt Man, way across the chamber. Then she stepped back, in another blink, and she was among them again, on her knees. The hand that touched the Gaunt Man was gone, seared away, and the priest felt the young woman's pain as if it were his own.

Falling to the floor beside her, dropping out of the very air that Mara stepped through, was a small shard of blue and red stone. It was all that remained of the Heart of Coyote. Bryce reached down, lifted the stone to his chest. The song was gone, but at least a piece of the stone remained. He slipped it into his pocket.

Then the explosion occurred.

Bryce flew through the air, crashing into the wall near the iron-studded door. Djil and Tolwyn landed nearby, thrown by the force unleashed in the chamber. Mara was further to his left, near the cracked mirror. In the heart of the chamber a storm raged. It was localized, swirling around the still-visible Heart of Coyote. It filled floor to ceiling, stretching out seven feet to each side. It was a storm of blackness, closing in upon the glowing blue and crimson rock. It touched the ravagon and tore the demon apart without hesitation. It touched the machine, and what remained of the device was consumed within the Maelstrom.

But what of the Gaunt Man?

Within the swirling storm that billowed up from the glowing ball, Bryce could see the Gaunt Man. He was being battered by the mix of nothing and everything, caught within an endless cycle of destruction and creation. But he was holding himself together, using every bit of concentration he could muster to keep his body from being torn apart. Every so often a piece of his body did detach, but the Gaunt Man quickly caught it and replaced it, ignoring the obvious pain. Once he exploded entirely, but he reformed with considerable effort in the center of the storm. Bryce was nearly sick, but as he remembered what had come before, his jaw firmed. It seemed fit punishment for the High Lord.

The infinite storm went on, howling, and some of that howl was the rushing wind and the little flicks of blue or red lightning. And some of that howl was the infinite pain of the Gaunt Man, forever dying, forever being reborn.

Tom O'Malley appeared from out of the darkness on

the other side of the storm, giving the area of localized destruction a wide berth. Beside him were Pluppa and Grim, Toolpin and Gutterby. Neither Braxon nor Triad were with them, and that saddened the priest.

"Let's get out of this place," Bryce said when Tom and the others drew near.

No one disagreed.

126

At the same instant that the Maelstrom formed around the Gaunt Man, when the forces of creation and destruction met and consumed the sorting machine, Andrew Jackson Decker collapsed.

He had been watching the fight of the werecreatures, totally amazed by Kurst's ability to become not only a regular-looking wolf and a massive, demonic man-wolf, but also to shift into a huge werebear. It was the werebear that finally destroyed the weretiger. As the bear's claws (which looked disturbingly like human fingers) raised to deliver their killing blow, Decker doubled over in pain.

Something was happening! The staves in his chest grew exceedingly hotter, burning his flesh. He was engulfed in darkness, eventually regaining vision along the shore of the blood-red beach. The doors were there, stretched out before him in endless, haphazard rows. Above the doors, hanging low in the sky, was the pattern that he had been creating earlier. It was the pattern of the Gaunt Man's victory, the pattern that left no room for failures or defeats. But the Gaunt Man never was able to imbue that pattern with reality and, as Decker watched, the latticework crumbled, falling to the sand without a sound.

The doors began to tip, then, falling like dominoes

before an unseen wind. When the doors had all been knocked down, Decker saw the Gaunt Man standing in their place. He looked at Decker with a hateful gaze. Then he opened his mouth to scream. But before any sound could emerge, the Gaunt Man exploded into a thousand shards of light.

The blackness returned, then faded ...

Decker was looking up from the ground. Julie was standing over him, and Kurst. They helped him up.

"The runes are gone, Decker," Kurst said matter-of-factly. "The others must have succeeded. The machine is destroyed."

"Oh thank God," Julie said, throwing her arms around the congressman. He didn't resist.

Decker held on to Julie, squeezing her tightly. He let all of the fear and pain wash out of him as his tears mingled with hers. They kissed, and Decker thought that there could be no better medicine for the recent pain.

When their lips reluctantly parted, he looked at Kurst, standing nearby in man form. Decker reached out, taking the hunter's hand. The three remained that way for a time, then Decker remembered the current situation.

"I'm glad you're here, Kurst, however you managed it," Decker said. "I could use your help with another matter. I'm on my way to the front lines to help them turn back Baruk Kaah's forces."

Kurst nodded, but he didn't say whether he agreed with the plan or not.

"But first, I have to go say good-by to someone," Decker said, gently removing Julie's arms from around himself. "If you'll excuse me, I'll be right back."

Decker and Colonel McCall stood over the bed that

held the body of President Jonathan Wells. Neither man spoke. They just stood, silently, paying their final respects to the man who had led the country through these opening weeks of the invasion.

After a time, McCall left quietly, leaving Decker alone with the man who started him on the road that led to this place.

"I'm sorry, John," Decker said. "I should have stopped the gunman. I failed you."

He bent his head, letting the tears flow freely down his cheeks.

"I promise you I'll do whatever I can to stop these invaders," he said. "And then I'll try to find out who killed you. And why."

Decker said a prayer over his friend. For Wells, the bad times were over. He was finally at peace. But as for Decker and the others? The congressman had no clue. But he had a feeling.

And the feeling told him that the days were going to get worse before they got any better.

127

Tolwyn led the group up the stairs, seeking a way out of the hellish place called Illmound Keep. She quickly checked off the companions still with her, remembering each one with fondness and a touch of sadness.

Djil, the black man from her dreams, was right behind her. Christopher Bryce followed after that, helping the wounded Mara, lending her his support. Tom and the dwarves held up the rear. Only Pluppa, Gutterby, Grim, and Toolpin remained of the company of seven. She grieved for their losses.

The house itself had changed as they made their way out of the dungeons. No longer were the walls of wood and stone. Now they were of flesh and bone, and blood dripped from the walls in dizzying designs of crimson. But nothing barred their way, and soon they were out of the mound of flesh that once appeared as a fine manor house. Kurst had told them that nothing was as it seemed, so maybe this was the keep's true form. She ignored it and hurried on.

She stopped what few servants they came upon, asking where she might find Uthorion. But none of them answered her, and her rage built. Finally, just before they reached the place where they had left the horses and carriage, the winged demon named Thratchen stepped into their path.

"No more fighting, Tolwyn," the demon said, holding his hands open before her. "You have all performed in a spectacular fashion. Much better than I had hoped. What you did to the Gaunt Man ... why, the idea never crossed my mind! Now I will help you one last time, and then we will be done with each other."

Tolwyn looked for some sign of deception, for some hint of trap. She found none.

"Speak, Thratchen, then move out of our way," she said.

"Of course," the demon smiled. "I just wanted to inform you that Uthorion is no longer in Orrorsh. He hasn't been for a number of centuries now."

Tolwyn lunged, grabbing the demon by his leather shirt. "Where is he, Thratchen! Tell me or I swear ..."

"Please," he said, brushing her off of him. "I was getting around to it. You'll find the one called Uthorion in Aysle."

"Aysle?" Tolwyn said, letting the revelation batter her.

"Yes, Aysle," the demon repeated. "So take your

Francis Mao

company and begone from this realm. From my realm!"

Thratchen bowed, then flew back toward Illmound Keep.

128

Number 3327 sat in his very comfortable black chair, at his very functional black-and-chrome desk, carefully arranging various-sized metal ball bearings atop a magnetic disk. Behind him, a bank of dark television monitors sprang to life.

"Number 3327, did you feel the disturbance?" asked the image that appeared on the upper-left monitor.

"What was it? Has something gone wrong?" blurted the face on the middle monitor.

"I believe that the disturbance comes from Orrorsh," said the image on the lower-right screen.

"Yes, the Gaunt Man must be up to something again," added the face on the lower-middle screen.

"What do you think, Number 3327?" asked the image on the middle-left screen.

"You know what I think," said Number 3327, rocking back in his chair. "Now leave me," he ordered, and the screens went dark.

He lifted one of the metal balls gently, holding it between his thumb and forefinger. It was a perfect sphere, yet there were a million imperfections that could be revealed under the gaze of a microsensor. Number 3327 hated imperfections. He dropped the ball back onto the magnetic sculpture, then slid the entire toy — balls, disk, and all, into the garbage slot on the edge of his desk. The sonic disruptors evaporated it instantly.

Number 3327 pressed the intercom switch.

"Yes, Kanawa-sama?" asked an unseen secretary.

"Send in Nagoya," he ordered, deciding to dispense

with the conventions of courtesy today.

"Right away, Kanawa-sama," the secretary answered.

Number 3327 leaned back in his chair. What had happened in Orrorsh realm? he wondered. What had the Gaunt Man done that sent ripples through the realities, even as far away as his own realm? He checked the computer monitor on the desk, calling up information on the planet's spin. It was still slowing down, approximately three weeks away from stopping completely. That didn't leave Number 3327 a lot of time to make preparations.

He hated not having time to make preparations.

Epilogue

Before the Earth stops spinning, an awful lot of garbage is going to settle to the surface. The Delphi Council is dedicated to cleaning up the mess.

— Ellen Conners

129

Dennis Quartermain sat behind the great oak desk in the President's office in Houston, Texas. He ran his fingers over the wood, admiring its texture. Leaning back in the plush chair, he put his feet up on the desk and laughed. Yes! This seat felt very good! He liked it already! But the curtains would have to go. They were too … homey. The windows in the office of the President of the United States called for curtains that were extravagant.

Except for a blotter, a pen and pencil set, and a photograph of Wells' wife and daughter that rested in a simple frame, the desk was pristine. The President had cleaned up all of the papers that had been piled atop it since the last time Quartermain visited the office. There was also one other item on the desk, positioned neatly beside the photograph. It was an old baseball, sitting on a wooden holder. Quartermain lifted it from its stand, feeling the weight of it. He tossed it once, twice, catching it easily. He smiled. Then he noticed that the ball was autographed. Turning it slightly, Quartermain read the signature.

"Ace Decker."

He threw the ball into the trash basket beside the desk with a sudden fury. It made a loud, resounding clang. With the Decker memorabilia out of sight, Quartermain's mood brightened considerably and he smiled.

A knock at the door startled him. Quartermain quickly got out of the chair, moved out from behind the desk, and called, "Come in."

General Clay Powell entered the room, wearing a grim expression. Quartermain forced the smirk off his own lips. He knew what the General was going to say, and the thought made him feel powerful, omnipotent.

"I've just received the news, Dennis," Powell said

quietly. "It's not good. There's been an incident at Twentynine Palms."

Time to put on a show, Quartermain thought. "What happened? Is it the President?"

Powell nodded. "He was shot, Dennis. Point-blank range, in the head. There was nothing anyone could do."

"What are you saying, Clay?" Quartermain feigned.

"John Wells has been assassinated," Powell said, his voice cracking as though he were about to cry. "You're the President now, Dennis. The ball's in your court."

Quartermain dropped into the chair behind the desk, looking as shocked as he could. Actually, he had spoken to Lance Odell only a few minutes prior to this meeting and had been filled in on all the wonderful details.

"If there is anything I can do ..." Powell started to say, but Quartermain waved him off.

"Right now I'd just like some time alone, Clay," Quartermain said, choking back a fake sob.

"Of course," Powell replied, taking his leave.

When he was gone, Quartermain picked up the telephone. "This is Dennis Quartermain," he said when the secretary answered on the other end. "I need to make two phone calls. First, get me Ellen Conners over at the Delphi Council headquarters. Then, I want you to find a way to put me in touch with Quin Sebastian. Yes, I know he's in the field. But Wells would have left a way to reach him. Now do it."

Then he sat back to wait for his calls to come through.

130

Quin Sebastian sat in the mess hall of the relocation center in Frankfort, Kentucky. He had spoken to a lot of the people who had traveled up from New York, making notes all over the maps he had with him. He had a good idea of where he was going to start looking for Douglas Kent, once he made his way through the Zone of Silence and into Manhattan.

Sebastian had also gathered information about the invaders from both official and unofficial sources. The idea of dinosaurs and intelligent lizard men didn't frighten him. To the contrary, it fascinated him.

He finished his coffee and was preparing to get a second cup when an officer approached him. The relocation center was under military command, and officers frequently wandered around the facility. This was the first time one of them came over to talk to him.

"Quin Sebastian?" the lieutenant asked.

"Why?" Quin asked back.

"The farmer wants to talk to the field, sir," the lieutenant said seriously, giving him the code that meant President John Wells wanted to speak to him.

"Where?" Quin asked.

"This way," the lieutenant answered, motioning for Quin to follow him.

He did.

The phone wasn't one of the sleek, modern types. It was an old rotary model, molded in basic black. But it looked like it worked and it was in a relatively private location. When the lieutenant excused himself, Quin lifted the phone to his mouth.

"Yes," was all he said.

"Sebastian? This is Dennis Quartermain," the voice on the other end of the line said.

Quin was prepared to hang up the phone when Quartermain said, "Wells is dead. He's been assassinated. Want to talk now?"

"Go ahead," Quin replied, keeping his voice neutral.

"Your mission, whatever it is, is over," Quartermain

said hurriedly. "As President, I'm calling you back to the farm. I have another mission for you to perform."

"I was working for Wells ..." Quin started, but Quartermain cut him short.

"Wells is dead, and I'm going to give you an opportunity to bring in his killer. Is that enough incentive?"

Quin was quiet for a moment, letting Quartermain brew in the silence. Then he spoke. "I'll be back."

"Good. I'll give you more details when you get to Houston. But you might be interested in knowing who your target is."

There was silence on both ends. When it became evident that Quin wasn't going to ask, Quartermain cleared his throat.

"Your target is Andrew Decker."

131

Colonel McCall was in his office when the Delphi Council arrived at Twentynine Palms. Ellen Conners, the director of the agency herself, barged into his room without so much as a knock or a by-your-leave. With her were half-a-dozen dark-glasses types with heavy weaponry at their sides.

"What the hell ...?" McCall said, rising out of his seat.

"Sit down, Colonel," the woman said. She tossed a bunch of official documents at him. "Those state that the Delphi Council has permission to investigate the assassination of President John Wells in the most expedient fashion it deems fit. I have two dozen agents going over the base with a fine-tooth comb even as we speak."

"By whose authority are you sweeping through my facility?" McCall asked, enraged by her attitude and her lack of protocol.

"By Executive Order, Colonel," she said with a cold smile. "Where is Congressman Andrew Decker?"

"Decker?" McCall asked, puzzled. "He's on his way to the battle zone around the Sequoia National Forest. He's serving as an advisor to the troops. Why?"

"Because evidence that my people have turned up suggests that it was Decker who killed the President."

"What!" McCall shouted, leaping to his feet. "That's patently ridiculous! I was there, damn it! I saw the whole thing!"

"And what did you see, Colonel?"

The way she asked that question made McCall's blood run cold. He had heard of the Delphi Council, but he had no idea what kind of power games they were capable of. He also had no idea why they were handling the investigation of Wells' assassination and not some older, more reputable agency. He swallowed hard.

"Yes," Conners said, her eyes boring into him like hot daggers, "I think we need to have a long talk, Colonel."

"A very long talk."

132

Thratchen raced from room to room, frantically searching every inch of Illmound Keep that he could get into. The illusion of normalcy returned, and the walls were no longer dripping vile fluids — at least to casual observers. Thratchen went along with the sensory games, allowing the house to be as real as it wished. He had other concerns. He rifled through kitchens and pantries. He overturned bookshelves in libraries, tore open mattresses in bedrooms. In the Gaunt Man's tower, he even ripped up parts of the floor. He ran from uppermost floor to lowest basement, and then he did it again.

And again.

But the Darkness Device was nowhere to be found. It had disappeared. Thratchen, so close to his goal, wailed in utter rage, his voice rocking the very foundation of the manor house. Then, wild-eyed, he raced into the lower levels.

In the center of the Gaunt Man's vast workshop, a Maelstrom hung in the air. It was an amazing sight, all destruction and creation in a single instant. In the midst of the storm, Thratchen saw the Gaunt Man.

As he watched, the Gaunt Man was ripped apart by the waves of destructive force, coming apart in a blue-red burst of energy. Then, as Thratchen observed, the Gaunt Man pulled himself back together. It was a truly amazing display of personal power.

Thratchen applauded.

"Well done, High Lord," he complimented. "Well done."

The Gaunt Man seemed to glare out of the storm, but Thratchen wasn't really certain.

"They were resourceful, weren't they?" Thratchen asked. "The stormers I mean. You really should have worried about them a little more. There's something about this world that makes them bolder, more daring. If I might be blunt, that was your undoing."

Yes, Thratchen decided, the Gaunt Man was definitely glaring at him now.

"How long do you think this Maelstrom will last?" Thratchen continued. "I guess until either the eternity shard runs out of energy — or you do. Could take quite a while, I would imagine."

Thratchen walked across the room. Lying on the stone floor was the Gaunt Man's walking cane, complete with its Carredon-shaped head and the little eternity shard clutched in its mouth. He picked up the cane.

"In the meantime, I will run your realm and cosm for you," Thratchen said. "After all, it's the least I can do. But I need you to tell me something."

He moved as close to the Maelstrom as he dared.

"Where is Heketon? Where is your Darkness Device?"

The Gaunt Man didn't answer. Thratchen wasn't even sure if he could. But he seemed to be smiling at the techno-demon, laughing at him.

"I will find it myself!" Thratchen screamed angrily. "I do not need your help! I shall become the Torg despite whatever hardships you have placed in my way!"

Then he left the Gaunt Man to his endless cycle of destruction and creation.

Here ends
The Dark Realm,
Book Two of The Possibility Wars.

The story of Tolwyn, Bryce and
the Storm Knights continues in
The Nightmare Dream,
Book Three of The Possibility Wars.

Novels

Don't miss the
continuing saga
of The
Possibility Wars™!

BOOK ONE OF THE POSSIBILITY WARS

TORG

Storm Knights

Created by Greg Gorden and Bill Slavicsek

*Book One
of The
Possibility Wars*

BOOK THREE OF THE POSSIBILITY WARS

TORG™

The Nightmare Dream™

Created by Greg Gorden and Bill Slavicsek

*Book Three
of The
Possibility Wars*

Games and Sourcebooks

Don't just read The Possibility Wars, experience them!

... explore the realms ...
Sourcebooks

... *discover the possibilities.*
Adventures